The Inheritor

Gil Hardwick

Published by Crusader eBooks, Perth, Western Australia

Typesetting, Layout and Cover Design by Gil Hardwick

This edition printed and bound by CreateSpace,
https://www.createspace.com/

National Library of Australia Cataloguing-in-Publication entry:

Author: Hardwick, Gil.

Title: The inheritor / Gil Hardwick.

ISBN-10: 0-9872987-0-4, ISBN-13: 978-0-9872987-0-6 (paperback)

Subjects: Hardwick, Gil--Fiction. Cattle trade--New South Wales--Fiction.
Aboriginal Australians--Fiction.

Dewey Number: A823.4

CHAPTERS

CHAPTER ONE

There was a big shiny beetle, glistening iridescent in the sunlight filtering down through the tree tops. It looked like it was trundling along by itself, occasionally sideways, then half-tipped over, then back straight again, lurching and swaying like a bloke staggering out of the pub. Ned watched it curiously, and when it disappeared under a dry gum leaf he got down on his hands and knees to watch where it went. Gently he moved the leaf away with his fingertip. It was still there, but upside down now, and as he dipped his head closer he saw that it was being moved along by a dozen or so tiny ants. It was so big, and they were so tiny, he smiled to himself and leaned down closer to watch them at eye-level.

They seemed to be going in a direction, working slowly up and over whatever was in their way, and after a bit he started moving leaves and twigs aside to let them go. He made a tiny road, but they soon branched off in a new direction, back into the leaf litter to resume their struggle up and over major obstacles five and six times their size. Ned sat back a bit then, looking around until he spied a small swarm of the same ants that looked like it was coming together on a little road of its own. Along it traveled various drunken bundles like his own shiny beetle, so he settled back fascinated to watch the passing parade.

Eventually he heard his name called so he started up thinking it was his mother. It was odd because there was no sound, just the chirping and rustling of the bush, as if someone was thinking his name not saying it. A shadow fell across the path and he looked up, momentarily blinded by the sunlight through a gap in the tree canopy high above.

"What you think you're doin'?" a voice surprisingly close made him startle.

He looked around. There was a boy standing there and he glanced at him a moment, but his was the wrong voice, not the one thinking his name. He looked around to see another older boy leaning against a tree staring at him, a twig he seemed to be idly chewing sticking out of the

1

corner of his mouth. Ned shaded his eyes with his hand, and still on his knees stared back up at him matching his gaze.

"I said, what you think you're doin'," the first boy said, more loudly this time, but Ned held his gaze on the other sensing that was where any danger lay.

"Shut up, Pete! Fuckin' dead shit y'are sometimes," the other said suddenly. He hadn't taken his eyes off Ned, neither of them shifting, until eventually he said, "That's me stupid brother," then with a slight shrug added, "What's yer name, anyway?"

Ned continued his gaze a little longer and then said quietly, "You know my name."

"Do I now?" The glare came back more intensely now. "Yeah, I do. Collins isn't it. Edward bloody Collins, the bloody poofta. I know who yer Da is too, and yer Ma."

"Bloody our cousin, y'are, didn't know that did ya. Smart arse," Pete said suddenly from right beside him.

Without warning the other quickly leaned off his tree and stepped in close, giving his brother a resounding whack to his right ear with a sharp left-hand jab. The boy went straight down, then after a moment half got up shaking his head looking as if he was going to retaliate, when a third boy appeared from nowhere to come between them holding them apart.

"Shit, Sam! Cranky bastard! You didn't have to do that."

The bigger boy Sam pushed him away but the other had him by his shirt and hung on. Pete got to his feet then, grabbed Sam's arm and took a swing at his head, but lost his balance and the three of them went down rolling furiously around in the leaf litter.

After a moment Ned got up and brushed himself off. The ants and the bright glossy beetle were nowhere to be seen. Even the busy ant road with its traffic had disappeared under the mêlée. He went over to his bike and picking it up off the ground hopped on, and with only a brief backward glance rode quietly away.

CHAPTER TWO

That night at dinner Ned sat chewing his food, thoughtfully over and over, until he noticed his mother closely observing him. As he looked up at her she raised an eyebrow in askance, so he swallowed what he had in his mouth and cleared his throat.

"Mum, who are those boys?"

"Which boys, Ned, who are you talking about?"

"I don't know. They were down in the bush today, where I was riding my bike. Well, I was going to go for a swim but I saw this really pretty beetle. It was dead, ants killed it, and they were carrying it back to their nest . . . . "

"Ned. What about the boys?"

"Oh yeah, they were pretty rough. One was a bit evil. He had this way about him, you know, Mum, you know what I mean. He whacked his brother so hard, nearly knocked him out. Sam, he is. That's his name, Sam. His brother is Pete. Pete said I was their cousin, but Sam told him to shut up. That's when he hit him."

He sat quietly at his plate, frowning and thinking about it, then abruptly looked up to see his mother sitting there drawn and pale, staring distantly up at the wall behind him. Presently she stirred, slowly at first, and turning to him leaned over to pat his hand.

"Ned, be a pet and go over to Uncle Sandy's for me, will you. See if he is all right. Come back straight away and tell me how he is."

Just then, outside in the half-dark there came a sound of glass breaking, and stones hitting then rattling clattering off a rooftop. As he stepped out onto the front porch a scatter of shadows flickered among the trees along the road. Instead of running out among them he made his way past the back of the house, past the chook yard following the track out through the orchard and across next door's back lawn, under the clothes line, then gently through the broken splintered picket fence and what remained of old vegetable garden.

Stepping through rustling corn stalks over his head he made his way across to the overgrown path then headed back down toward the house. Nothing stirred, that he could see, so slowly he made his way around to the front and stood there, looking back up to inspect the damage. One window pane had a hole in it, as far as he could see, and there were a few stray rocks on the path with more scattered over unkempt lawn, but nothing else.

"Sandy!" he called softly.

There was no answer so he called again, louder, "Sandy, it's me, Ned."

After a moment he heard a faint clatter, then a thump.

"Neddy, my boy, come in, come in, there's a good lad," a voice slurred from inside.

Ned quickly stepped up onto the verandah and across to the tattered insect screen standing slightly ajar, which he opened and went through, the solid front door itself wide back on its old rusty hinges letting anyone in anyway, and as he did so peered into the dark of the front room.

His eyes only needed small adjustment from the moonlight outside to the inner gloom, and as he looked around he saw the old man half lying on the couch, half struggling to rise in greeting, an empty bottle on the floor next to a coffee table, and a glass knocked over spilling its contents onto a half-eaten dinner. The smell of stale grog was on him, and the boy stood there a moment taking it in.

Sandy sank back on the couch, his hand to his head, chuckling quietly. Ned grinned in spite of himself, then without thinking further he turned and started back out onto the verandah.

"Mum asked me to check on you. She has to go to work at the hospital. I'll fetch my things over." he said over his shoulder, then paused. "Silly old bugger, go to bed, all right? I'll be back in a minute."

Ned ran back home along the street, through his own front gate and up the path, but instead of going up onto the porch he went straight around to his sleepout on the back verandah. There he rolled his pajamas up with his pillow and eiderdown, and pulling the belt from his trousers tied them into a quick swag.

On the way out he poked his head quickly through the kitchen door.

"He is awfully drunk, mum. He can't stand up. Maybe I'd better stay with him. I can sleep there tonight, can I?"

She sat quietly a while longer, as if listening for something else, then seeing he had his things anyway she nodded her assent.

"Call me at the hospital if anything happens, Ned, there's a good boy."

Back at Sandy's house he checked to see the old man safe in bed, more or less. He tidied the front room as much as he could in the half dark before changing out of his clothes and settled himself with his eiderdown and pillow on the lounge.

The night passed uneventfully, and when he woke the sun was up. He sat and stretched to ease his cramped back and legs, gazing around to orient himself and think what to do with Sandy. With a sigh he got up off the lounge and poked his head through into the bedroom to see the old fellow sprawled there on top of the bed, snoring and mumbling in his sleep but otherwise dead to the world.

Nothing to do but leave him to sleep it off, he went through to the bathroom and made himself busy lighting the chip heater, and as the water ran warm he shed his pajamas and stepped under the shower. He was soon clean. He combed his hair and went out into the front room to dress in the his clothes.

In the kitchen he found some bread, a bit stale but good for toast, plenty of eggs and bacon in the fridge, and some lamb chops. Turning to the sink he took a cloth and wiped down the bench top, then went back into the front room where he cleared the table, then shrugged, deciding to get all the washing up out of the way and start again with a clean bench. When he had finished he went out into the orchard and picked some oranges from the overgrown grove and brought them in, checking the chook yard for more eggs while he was there.

Back inside he went in and stirred Sandy awake.

"Come and get yourself cleaned up, and I'll put on some breakfast," he said softly. "Go and have a shower too, you stink. The chip heater is going, no excuse," he added, standing over him to make sure he did as he was told.

The old man gave him a sly, rueful grin, and groaned as he got up off the bed and shuffled off into the bathroom.

As Ned got the fire going in the kitchen stove he heard the shower running, and the old man muttering to himself. He grinned, shaking his head, then as the stove top heated up nicely he took a pan and filled it with chops and bacon. As it was cooking he toasted the dry bread at the fire with a wire fork, spreading it with plenty of butter from the fridge. While the meat cooked he squeezed the oranges into a pair of glass tumblers, then spilled the chops and bacon into a tray and cracked half a dozen eggs into the hot pan to fry.

There was hot water in the kettle by then, so he made a pot of strong black tea with plenty of sugar the way Sandy liked it, and that done he called for him to hurry up his breakfast was ready.

Cleaned up the old bloke looked good; passing handsome in fact. As he come into the room and sat at the breakfast table Ned watched, and wondered that when he was young he must have cut a dashing figure. Care and attention were good for him, he decided, then tea poured and the aroma of bacon and eggs and fresh toast no longer resistible, he switched off his thoughts and soon made short work of breakfast. With the last piece of toast he wiped up the runny golden yolk and meat gravy from his plate, washing it down with the fresh orange juice, then as he finished looked up to see that Sandy had made quite as good a job of the meal as he.

"Who are those boys, Uncle Sandy? And anyway what did you do to upset them like that?" he asked suddenly.

Sandy looked up slowly, directly returning his gaze and not answering.

Ned waited.

The other stopped to scoop up the last few morsels from his plate and sat thoughtfully awhile, sipping his tea and swilling the brew in his mouth before swallowing.

He then placed his knife and fork tidily on the plate in front of him and said quietly, "Ma Clancy's lot, they are. She is your mother's great aunty Enid. Bad lot they are, all of them."

"You know what I mean. What else is going in, you're not telling me? You and Mum?"

The other leaned back in his chair, watching him closely, then grinned and nodded.

"You're a bright boy, young Ned. You don't miss much, do ye."

"Well someone needs to keep an eye on you."

Sandy leaned back thoughtfully. "She will use it against me, Ned."

"What? Use what?"

"How old are you now, boy?"

He hesitated, disoriented suddenly, than said, "Eleven, actually. I'm nearly twelve, close enough . . . it's alright, I still have to go to school but that's only a few more years . . . and Mum and Dad are OK . . . what are you taking about . . . ?"

The other looked up, then gazed at him a moment. "Nothing," he said, dismissing the thought, "You're a good kid, Ned. Don't worry about it."

"I'm not worried," Ned replied. "I can handle those boys. They are so stupid, you wouldn't believe it. Anyway it's you who needs looking after, not me."

He stood at that and cleared the table, then carried the breakfast dishes into the kitchen and began cleaning up.

Sandy followed him, and taking up a towel waited to dry the plates as they were being washed.

"Are you sure you're ready for it, Ned? Up to it, are ye?" he asked.

The boy turned on him. "Everyone has had enough, Sandy!" he said. "All this trouble all the time. If it isn't one thing it's something else. Now this. It's not worth it."

"Is that so? What would you know, laddie?"

Ned paused for a moment, deciding whether to put the hot kettle back down on the stove or to carry it across to the sink. Since he had already taken it up and had the weight of it he shrugged, then rather than putting it down again, without saying anything further he went about his task. Soap and hot water in the sink he adjusted the cold tap until the temperature was comfortable, then turning it off he began washing the dishes, and more and more of them. The kitchen was a mess. The moment he had one part clean another appeared to him as bad as the last, so he buried himself in the task and worked off his confusion without saying anything.

Most of the work done eventually he stopped, and said finally, "Sandy, you see, you're not here all the time you're somewhere else. You go somewhere . . . I don't know how to say it in words . . . through that space that sort of opens and closes . . . That Sam, he's like that too, like Mum. Me too sometimes, a lot of the time really."

The old man was watching him, eyes glittering even there in the bright morning sunlight streaming through the window.

"You see it yourself, do ye?" he wanted to know.

Ned paused, and looked at him. "Mother showed me," he said. "You're her cousin too aren't you, or something like that. She knows, and she showed me."

Sandy looked away, then back at him intently. "Why would she do that?" he asked.

The boy glanced at him only briefly. "She said she wanted to protect me," he said seriously. "She said it was better for me to know things young and grow up with them than stumble onto it later and get into trouble." Then he shivered slightly and went back to cleaning the kitchen.

Taking his cue the old man nodded quietly to himself and went about his own business of drying the dishes. That done he went back to the front room where they had had their breakfast, and taking a broom swept the whole floor clean, out the door onto the front porch where he scooped up the mess onto a shovel and tipped it over the rose garden. Having done that he stood out there on the porch awhile, thoughtfully, before coming back inside.

"It comes back down to kin," he said finally, but receiving no answer looked around. Ned by this time was in the bathroom cleaning his teeth, and Sandy had to follow him in and repeat himself.

"What?" the boy asked over his shoulder, then stood to gaze at him, there in the doorway.

"The Sight," Sandy said simply. "The Curse as they say, or the Gift more like it. You have it too, young Ned, isn't that right?"

The boy froze, shivering despite the warm day as the old man stood watching him.

"You have it through your mother, don't you lad," he said finally. "Yes, she is kin of mine," he continued. "It ran all the way through the clans in the old days, you know."

"Why, Sandy?" Ned asked finally.

"It's our inheritance. It's the way we are, that's all."

Instead of replying Ned simply turned to stare wide-eyed. The old man gazed steadily back for a moment, plumbing his depths, then nodded as if in recognition.

"It is not a bad thing in itself," he continued. "In the old times it kept us safe, but that was back when people had faith. What happened was they destroyed our faith, and when people no longer believed in anything the Gift became a curse."

The boy glanced away, thoughtful for a moment, then asked, "How can that be?"

"Well, it's simple enough. These days people need to wait until something happens before they believe it, when it is too late. Then they get themselves into a panic."

He looked as if he were going to say more, then stopped abruptly and dismissed it with a wave of his hand.

"That's enough for one day, young fella," he said gruffly, then turned and went, leaving him there alone suddenly to finish his teeth.

CHAPTER THREE

It was not until a few weeks later that Ned saw Sandy again. He was standing there on the front lawn just on dusk one evening calling to his father. Following a brief exchange he only half heard, his father's soft tread along the passage toward the back of the house had him alert, and by the light knock on his door he was on his feet. He knew it was for him the old man had come.

"Mr McKenzie wants to know if you are ready for a shot, Ned," Arthur said lightly. "There are ducks in his rice crop."

Ned was already pulling on his boots. "Yes I know."

He ducked under his father's arm and through the doorway. Making his way down the passage he stepped out onto the front porch, smiling shyly as he did so. Then without a word and without looking aside he went down the path and climbed into the truck. After a moment he looked back out the window, and thinking about it he opened the door again, stepped down, and went back up the path to where his father stood.

"Thanks Dad," he said. Turning again he caught Sandy's eye this time and stepped down off the porch toward him. The men chuckled, shaking their heads. As he drew alongside the old man reached out to ruffle his hair, then together they went down the path onto the road. Both seated, Sandy started the truck and they pulled out and trundled off along the street, then turned right and out of town.

The big old truck eventually turned off the main road onto a side track, and Sandy had to lean over and switch on the headlights to see in the dark there under the trees, though it was barely dusk outside. After a while he slowed to a crawl over the bumpy track. Soon Ned saw someone step out of the bush in front of them, and wave them to a stop.

There was a stooped old man on the track, one of the local tribe he thought. He'd seen him occasionally in town. Sandy stopped the truck as he drew alongside and the two spoke briefly. The other disappeared abruptly back into the undergrowth as Sandy changed down into first gear and edged the truck slowly forward along the rough track, until they came to a gate which had been left open for them. They went through and pulled over to stop on a grassy patch.

A small group of people were approaching through the gloom as they stepped down, and Sandy stepped forward to greet them. As Ned came around the front of the truck he turned, introducing them all one by one. There were two other men, and three boys one his age with another slightly younger and the third much older, about 15 or 16. They were all smiling so he smiled back; shy but observant, alert to know what Sandy had in store for the evening.

Eventually he learned over and said softly, "They didn't bring any guns."

"They can take turns," Sandy said. "That's what they usually do."

"Can they shoot?" Ned wanted to know.

"That old man back there on the track, he will be here in a minute, that's Peter Foley. His grandson Dan Foley is the club champion."

The boy's eyes went wide in recognition. "Dan Foley! I know Dan Foley, I shoot with him. I was the junior runner-up last year, did you know that?"

"Yes, we know," the other replied. "We thought you might enjoy coming out for a shot with us sometime."

Ned stood back a moment, thinking. "It's a bit dark now," he said.

They were all watching him.

"What do you reckon?" one of the older boys wanted to know.

"Well, if we were here a bit earlier we could have set some traps. You can get a lot of ducks in a cage like that. Then maybe have a shot tomorrow. We could have gone out early and cleared the traps, then had a shot after that, after breakfast."

They all glanced at each other, nodding, then back at him.

"That's just about what we would do," Sandy smiled, then turned and stepped back toward the truck. The others followed, climbing quickly up onto the back where they settled themselves among the old man's crates and tools. Ned stood momentarily confused, watching them.

"You comin', boss?" he heard from behind as old Peter suddenly strode past following the others onto the back of the truck, so he went around to the passenger side and climbed into his seat just as Sandy started the engine and moved off.

Presently they came up to a rambling homestead comprising a cluster of houses, sheds and workshops, and beyond them a big old main house. The truck stopped short to let the others off, then went on a little further to park in front of the big house. There was a light inside.

"There is some tucker there, in those two boxes," Sandy indicated to him as they got down from the truck and made their way to the back. "Bring them in if you like and I'll get the rest of the gear."

While Sandy sorted through his belongings Ned took one of the cartons and carried it up the steps and into the house. Not expecting anyone he went straight through to the kitchen and put the carton on the table, then looked up startled to see an old lady standing there at the stove smiling at him.

"You must be Ned," she said kindly, breaking the moment.

He struggled to find his tongue, but while doing so Sandy came in and saved him.

"I see you two have met," he said matter of fact.

"Sorry, Ned," he went on, I should have said something. "This is my wife Ellie. You call her Auntie Ellie."

After a pause Ned finally opened his mouth to speak. "I didn't know you were married," he said.

"Nearly 50 years."

"Really?" He glanced back and forth between the two, "How come you don't have any kids?"

The old lady glanced away, but Sandy just shrugged. "Things don't always work out the way you want, is all." He stopped, weighing his words, then after a moment continued, "There are big families here on the station, and we always had children here in the house to look after."

He nodded, reflecting, quietly to himself, then looked up and said, "Help me with the rest of the gear, lad. It will all come clear in good time."

When they had brought all the things in Sandy took him down the corridor and showed him a big old-fashioned bedroom with its own fireplace for cold nights, and said that was his room now, whenever he came to stay.

Ned looked around at the place, taking it all in. "I thought we were just coming out for a shot, Sandy, just this evening," he said, "but it was a bit too dark, that's all."

The other stood, head inclined, gazing steadily at him. He then looked down at his feet, and back again. "You didn't wait to hear your father out, lad," he said, then, "All right, listen a minute will you, and I'll let you know what's happening. You're still a boy and not properly listening yet, but you have a right to know."

Before he spoke further the old man stepped over to the fireplace and leaned against the mantle piece. He thought for a moment, then looked back at Ned directly. The boy sat on the bed, hands in his lap waiting.

"The simple fact is we lost our eldest son Hamish in the Great War. Every family in the district lost sons, we were not alone. I am not saying we are. We had two boys ourselves, but Ellie was very sick after our second boy Angus was born, and became barren. Then Angus was killed in an accident; he came off his horse, and we lost our remaining heir. You are the next in line, through your mother."

Ned looked at him quizzically, shaking his head.

"You mean all of it? This whole place?"

Sandy chuckled. "Oh no, there is a lot more. There is the house in town, and there are another three stations up north where we run horses and cattle."

"Don't worry over it, lad," he continued after a pause, studying his face intently as he spoke. "The family had it all arranged. Angus had a life policy, and there are investments to cover probate . . . if we are ever to get through this Depression."

He paused again, looking away into the distance then back again. "What I am saying to you, young fella, is if you are to succeed it is not money that's going to be worrying you."

The old man stopped abruptly, "Enough for now! No good comes of talking on an empty stomach. You must be famished. Let's get some food into you, and we will talk some more later."

Together they went back down the passage into the kitchen. Ellie had just then turned away from the table back to the stove, where she gave the gravy a last stir with a spoon before draining the pan into a small boater and placing it onto the table.

The two sat, and taking their serviettes spread them on their laps.

She paused at that, inspecting them both intently, then more or less satisfied wiped her hands on her apron and took her own place at the table.

"Ned," she said, passing across a platter of sprouts and carrots, "Some mint sauce for you as well, which will do nicely with the gravy."

Sandy reached over and took the platter and spooned the vegetables onto the boy's plate, then spooning gravy over them looked to him, nodding and inclining his head. "We didn't sell all our lambs last market. This shoulder is prime hogget. They don't know what they are missing."

Ned watched fascinated as the other dribbled fragrant mint vinegar onto the slices of meat on his plate. "What's hogget?" he wanted to know.

The old man set down his knife and fork, and looking at him brought his hand up to his lower lip and pulled it down. With his finger on his lower front teeth he said, "Two tooth. Just like you, boy, coming of age. In a sheep, after about eighteen months the two middle teeth get pushed out, and the adult teeth come through. After that the meat is still tender as lamb, but full of flavour."

He cuffed him gently, and taking up his knife and fork he took a big slice of the meat, and piling it high with vegetables he put it all in his mouth at once and sat back chewing contentedly.

After a while he continued. "Ned, boy," he said, looking down at his plate then back at him, "seriously, and I have to say this to you, none of this is about inheritance or money, it is about the land."

He watched his face, "Are you up to it?"

"Yes," Ned said simply, looking down at his own plate then up again steadily returning his gaze. He shrugged then, quietly, inclining his head thoughtfully, and quietly ate his dinner. When he finished he folded his serviette neatly then stood and pushing in his chair went around to Ellie and hugged her from the side.

"It's all right, I'll be good," he said, then glancing only sideways at Sandy went to his room.

There he took stock, looking around him at the old room, knowing it was not really his yet, then stripping off his shirt and boots he took a towel and went back down the passage to the bathroom. After running himself a bath he stripped and stepped into the warm water, then lay back and closed his eyes trying to sooth the sudden rush of events.

Gradually he began to soap himself, and taking a hand washer hanging over the water spout washed himself all over until the stray thoughts running back and forth through his mind settled, then sighing he stood and dried himself off with the towel.

Instead of pulling on his underpants and trousers he simply wrapped the towel around his waist and his clothes in hand went back down the passage to his room. There was an older boy about fourteen or fifteen sitting on his bed, and as he entered he looked up, expectantly, as if waiting for him.

Ned stood there a moment staring at him, then annoyed dropped his towel and reached past him for the clean pajamas Ellie had left for him. The boy continued to watch him closely as he pulled up the bottoms, then put on the top and began to do up all the buttons.

"You're Angus, aren't you," he said finally.

The other nodded.

Ned scrutinised him. "You are supposed to be dead."

Angus looked down, toying with his fingers, distracted momentarily.

Finally he looked up and said, "That old man out there, Peter Foley, he won't let me go yet. He is a magic man, and there is some unfinished business."

Ned looked away in his turn, then shook his head. Abruptly shoving the other aside, he pulled back the sheets and clambered into bed.

"I want to go to sleep now," he said, then added, "Turn off the light."

"This is still my room," Angus replied softly. "You are going to have to put up with it just like I do."

"All right then." Ned said wearily. "Have it your own way. But go to sleep now will you. I'm tired and I have to think about it some more, all this."

Angus chuckled. "I don't sleep. Like I said, you're going to have to get used to the way things are." He paused a moment, watching Ned's face. "You can have my bed, I don't care, and my old pajamas. It doesn't matter. You are taking my place anyway, in your world."

Ned sat up suddenly, and taking the feather pillow threw it at Angus but it went straight through him and hit the wall, knocking an old picture frame askew while the other just stood there grinning at him.

"And another thing," Angus was starting to tease now, "You are going to have to grow up, and I don't. I can stay being a kid."

"Oh yeah! Smart Alec! You think you're clever, because you're dead, but you're just chicken shit. You're a gutless wonder."

"Yeah? You think so! I'll lick you any time you want."

"No you can't. You're a ghost."

Then a thought struck him. "Angus," he said suddenly, "Do you think Old Peter can make you more solid?"

The other pulled up abruptly. "Why do you want to know that?"

"Because then I could give you a good hiding. You're not that much bigger than me. You're just a short-arse."

"Well he can't. And even if he could you'd have a job on your hands, Sonny Jim."

"Yeah, right." Ned said finally. "Doesn't matter. I'll think of something. If you annoy me."

Before Angus could answer old Sandy's voice came to them from the other side of the house.

"If you boys don't settle down I'll come in and give you both a good larruping."

They stopped suddenly, still as statues.

"He knows, does he?" Ned wanted to know, murmuring softly now.

Angus nodded shyly. "He and Peter are something like tribal brothers," he said quietly. Peter is paying back a favour he owed him, for something else, a long time ago."

"Really?"

Angus just stood, looking intently at him, an odd far-off look in his eyes.

Ned prompted him. "So why is only you here? Where is your brother?"

"He is in Belgium. He got married, did you know that? They were both killed, not in the fighting, just an accident. Anyway, they both wanted to stay there."

He looked away, oddly again and smiling inwardly, adding dreamily, "We know where all the family are."

Then he looked back at Ned abruptly and said, "All right, go to sleep. I might just sit here awhile and read my book."

CHAPTER FOUR

It was slightly chilly outside when he woke, and he sat up in bed to wipe the window pane clear of mist so he could see out. There was dew on the ground and a light fog still over the creek down there at the bottom of the house paddock, and he took it all in.

He lay back in the bed, his head on the pillow a moment while he looked around the room. It was empty, as if it were just another day, so he got out of bed and stripped off his pajamas to dress quickly in his warm day clothes. Pulling on an extra jumper from the chest of drawers he strode straight out into the passage and through to the kitchen where breakfast hit him warm and homely as if his mother were there.

Auntie Ellie turned smiling as he came in, a pan off the stove spilling bacon and eggs onto his plate, with hot toast and a steaming teapot there on the table.

"Sandy will take you back in later, Ned," she said brightly. "About lunch I think. He went off early to check the water but he will be back soon. Here, sit with me, and we will have breakfast together."

The growing boy found the food irresistible so he ate heartily as she watched, eyes intent.

"You met Angus," she said eventually, nodding wisely, looking him up and down.

He glanced at her.

"Auntie, we are just kids," he said.

She nodded at that too, then reached over patting his hand.

"As we were once," she said, almost to herself, before looking up sharply.

The front door opened then slammed shut, and he knew from the footsteps up the passage it was Sandy. As the old man strode into the kitchen and sat down for his breakfast the boy said nothing, merely glancing at him briefly as he raised his head enough to put the food on his fork into his mouth, then back down again quickly to focus on cutting another portion of toast and bacon, and coating it with runny yellow yolk.

"Mum always said I shouldn't speak badly of other people," he said finally, "or swear or use bad words."

They both turned to look at him.

"But grownups shouldn't tell children fibs either."

He paused then, thoughtfully, looking down at his plate.

"Maybe you didn't lie to me," he said quietly, "but you didn't tell me the truth either, I don't know. Too many things I don't know, not yet anyway. But what I do know Uncle Sandy is you bullshit too much, and you drink too much, and hide things from people. You shouldn't do that. Its wrong."

He looked up at that, back and forth to them both, suddenly abashed.

He glanced down at his plate again, knife and fork still poised. "I don't mean I don't love you," he said softly, embarrassed, "only you didn't tell me about Angus. You waited until I ran into him. You only said what you wanted me to think, not what I need to know, and I don't think you have told me much about anything else either."

The two of them glanced at one another but he went on, his dander rising. He was letting his frustration run, and flushed with his piping voice rising the tears ran down his cheeks.

"Maybe you got trouble with old Missus Clancy, but I cop it at school, and when I go home, always something. Then you come home drunk, Uncle Sandy, and I have to look after you as well. And I haven't got any brothers or sisters, nobody like that. I can't just be a kid like other kids either, because of this other bloody thing, whatever it is, something, I don't know what else. So I have a right to know, that's what I think."

They simply nodded, and without saying anything further Ellie turned back to the stove and started tidying up while Sandy simply took up his utensils and quietly ate his breakfast.

"Auntie," Ned added at length, "I didn't mean you."

"That's all right, son," she said softly. "Don't fret, there's a good lad. Tell me what you like for breakfast. And what are your favourites."

"Mum usually makes me porridge, is that all right?"

"A growing boy like you needs more than that, young fellow my lad," Sandy broke in, putting down his knife and taking up his cup of tea to wash down a mouthful of toast and runny egg yolk, his eye winking at him around the rim.

"Eat your breakfast, husband, and be off with you," Ellie broke in, "Let me speak with him."

At that Sandy obediently wiped his plate clean with the remainder of his toast, then draining his cup turned to leave.

"I'll leave a pony for you at the front gate, lad," he said, turning back briefly on the way out. "The boys are still having their breakfast. No rush."

Then from out along the front passage he called back, "We'll be down in the bottom paddock, you'll see us."

By the time Ned returned to finishing his breakfast Ellie had taken her seat across from him, ignoring Sandy and focused entirely on him, her eyes smiling.

"Now we can have our little chat," she said simply, then waited on him until he too had wiped his plate clean and set it aside.

He waited in turn while she poured him another cup of tea, watching her closely.

"This has got something to do with those Clancy boys," he said, not waiting for her to start.

She looked up, and leaned closer.

"Don't be angry with them, child," she replied patiently. "Their grandmother Enid is my sister, did you know that?"

"Really?"

"Yes. She is the eldest, and I am the youngest. There were eleven children in our family, the Malonies, from that line anyway. There were nine boys, and we two girls. She worries over me endlessly."

She looked up at that, and leaned back again giggling slightly, hand to mouth.

"She fully intended to marry Sandy and had it all arranged, but Sandy fell in love me instead. Then Hamish came along so Enid married Tom Clancy out of spite, he was a drover back in those days, after she was done finally helping mother raise the boys."

Ned looked aside, shocked at the idea, then back at her. "Old Missus Clancy was in love with Sandy?"

Ellie leaned forward again, and said quietly, thoughtfully, "She wanted the land. She thought she had a right because the family had so little, and so many children. It was hard on her, but it wasn't her fault. Father was alcoholic and Mother simply could not cope, so Enid took it all on herself, that was all. Times were so hard, Ned, and for a lot or people still not much better."

They both sat lost in their own thoughts, then Ned got up from his chair and picking up his plate and cup took them over to the sink.

"Now I know. I know who you are talking about. Is Paddie Malonie your brother too, and Frank, and old Seamus?" he asked. "That other boy is Seamus as well, isn't he. Young Seamus."

"Yes, Ned, mother married Sean Malonie. She was a Murphy. How did you know that?"

"I just know, that's all. Where are the rest of your brothers?"

She dismissed him at that with a wave of her hand, not unkindly.

"Oh, questions, questions, boy. Off with you now. The men are waiting." she said, then added quietly in afterthought, nodding to herself, "All things in good time."

He looked at her curiously, then leaned across and gave her a peck on the cheek.

"Off you go then," she smiled.

On the lawn just before the front verandah there was a pony hitched to the front fence as Sandy had promised. He opened the gate and mounted without further ado. The pony started at a walk until they were on the main track through the property then took off at a fast trot away from the houses. She seemed to know where she was going so he didn't argue, and before long he could see some of the others across the paddock, their own horses grazing nearby.

They were sorting through a pile of ducks as he rode up, and a group of boys were busy plucking them with feathers and soft down blowing and scattering in the soft morning light. Most of the down went into sacks for washing and stuffing pillows later, but right now it looked like a miniature snow storm had struck.

Ned surveyed the scene, bemused, until Sandy looked up at him in askance.

"You look organised. Anything you want me to do?" he wanted to know.

"We are pretty right, thanks, son. Go on down to the dam. Dan is there waiting for you, with Everard who you met yesterday. And I want you to meet Rollie Tanner as well, he'll be there. And old Peter will want another look at you as well, I expect."

"Righto then," Ned wheeled the pony to trot a way further down the slight slope of the paddock and through a belt of trees, coming out onto a flat where he saw the truck parked ahead, against a dam bank where another much smaller group of men were lounging around talking quietly among themselves.

He rode up, then slowed to a walk before halting the pony behind the truck. He slid easily off her back and looped the rein over the tailgate before walking over to introduce himself.

"Hello Dan," he said cheerfully, "remember me?"

"Yes I do," the other replied. "Ned, isn't it? How ya goin'?"

"Well, thanks."

He glanced at the others.

"Ned, this here Mr Tanner, 'e station manager," Dan said politely.

"Pleased to meet you, Mr Tanner," he said shyly, shaking hands.

The other simply met his gaze and nodded, and Dan turned to the older boy next to him. "And this my brother Everard Foley."

"How are you, Everard," Ned asked.

The other also nodded, glancing nervously down at his boots and up again, his eyes catching him directly.

Dan leaned in more closely and said quietly, "That old gran' father want to see you, all right?" He looked up, inclining his head toward the line of trees where he could see Peter sitting there on a log, with a small campfire burning next to him and on it a camp oven and a billy.

Ned dutifully went over and as he came close the old man watched him approach, then patted the log motioning him to sit.

"Cuppa tea?" he asked.

"Yes, thanks."

Ned waited while the old man poured him a cup from the billy and handed it to him, then passed him a paper bag of sugar with a spoon sticking out. He liberally helped himself to the sugar while Peter watched him, studying his movements and nodding to himself.

They both sat awhile as Ned sipped the hot tea.

Finally he said. "I met Angus last night. You know that don't you."

The old man chuckled. "Proper larrikin, that one. Plurry mischief."

Ned looked up sharply, but the old man simply grinned back.

"Ride like the plurry wind, that boy." He paused then, reflectively, then turned to Ned. "Rabbit 'ole got 'im. Plurry 'orse, young colt, put 'is foot in that puckim rabbit 'ole, broke 'is leg, eh. That boy flew right off, right over 'is head, bang head first into plurry tree stump." He shook his head sadly. "Buggered 'im up properly, that plurry stump. Pulled 'im up real quick."

Ned just stared.

"Don't tell 'im, eh? Don't tell 'im alright. Not yet anyway," the old man continued

He sat back at that, then leaned forward, seriously. "All too plurry quick. 'E don't know what 'appened, that boy, not properly. I take 'im straight away, 'way from there, before he could see what 'appened."

"Yes, he does," Ned looked at him thoughtfully.

Peter returned his glance, then looked away, and back at him again.

After a few minutes Peter said, "I tell you something, eh? That boy, 'e know 'e dead, but 'e don't know 'ow he died. You don't tell 'im, eh? Make 'im sorry, bugger everything up."

He paused a moment, then continued. "That Angus, 'e good lookin' boy, nice boy. Everybody like 'im. That stump buggered 'im up head, properly. Smashed 'im up. No good, that business. You don't talk about it, eh?"

"He's still not grownup yet," Ned replied obstinately. "He is only young, not even married. Why are you keeping him here like this?"

Peter stood and started walking off, then turned back a moment.

"Better 'ave a shot, eh? Dan, 'e plurry good shot. And you good shot too, eh. No worries, boss."

Ned took a breath, wanting to argue, but as he did so the thud of hooves came to his ear and he turned to see the other men riding up, apparently having left the younger boys to carry the night's catch back to their families.

He sighed at that, then followed Peter who slowed to match his shorter stride so they could approach the truck together. Ned sensed the gesture, and looked up at the old man's face.

"No worries, boss, eh?" Peter said softly, reassuringly.

"I'm all right. It's just sad, that's all."

The other glanced down, a sad look in his eyes too, then as quickly looked up again and waved to Sandy as he came in on horseback. The slightest exchange between the two sent a message across that everything was in order, and the other nodded briefly before turning his attention to the three others still waiting there at the dam.

CHAPTER FIVE

Peter took Ned by the arm and led him behind the truck, just out of sight of the others, and leaned against the cabin door.

"Wait here, boss," he said. "Sandy want to talk that Mr. Tanner first, alright? No worries."

"What does he do? Rollie Tanner. On the station I mean." Ned wanted to know.

Peter looked down at him again.

"'E's all right. Plurry good farmer, that Mr Tanner. Help us a lot."

"So what's the matter?"

"Oh well, that fella, 'e good man, good farmer, work for us long time. Good family, good wife, good kids. But 'e farmer, not businessman, alright. 'E know nothing 'bout business, can't see nothing, like that. We keep our business separate, alright."

He stood back at that, and opening the door took out a gun case which he gave to Ned, then picked up three more shotguns leaning back against the seat.

"I can take them," Ned said to him. "You bring the cartridges."

Staggering only slightly under the weight he stepped around the front of the truck to where Dan stood. The other hurried toward him and took the spare guns.

"Here, just lean them against the truck," he said, breaking each weapon in turn to ensure the breech was clear, then standing them in a neat row along the front bumper.

"Are the boys coming over?" Ned asked sheepishly, standing alongside his hero like that.

"They got some jobs to do, boss," Dan said quietly.

Ned stood back and looked up at him, cocking his head.

"I'm not your boss," he started. "Anyway, it's not hot today. The ducks will last a few hours, or someone else can gut them, if that's what needs to be done. They can have a shot, like us, that's all right."

"Don't upset the routine, Ned," Sandy called across, not too loud, but brisk and gentle.

Ned looked up. They were all looking at him, eyes bright.

Peter leaned over as gently. "No worries, Ned. You'll be right, fine young fella like you."

All of a sudden he realised the compliment they were paying him and turned away, slightly embarrassed.

"Well, let's have a shot then," he rallied, looking around him at the gear along the side of the truck. "There are only four guns, and six of us."

"Five," Dan said. "Granddad got some other jobs. I share with Everard, all right."

With that he picked up a gun and moved off, his brother with him. Rollie picked up the next, while Sandy took the case and opened it.

"Come here, Ned," he called him over. "Did you ever see such a beautiful piece?"

Ned gazed down at the polished wooden stock and shiny blue-steel barrels, nestled there in green felt.

"This is a hand-made Greener," Sandy continued. "It was brought out to Australia by my grandfather, who was Alexander himself. Same name as my own. I was named after him, and he left it to me in his will. Did you know that?"

He picked up the piece and assembled it, then handed it to him.

"I'll take that other single barrel. You'll be right, lad."

Ned stood speechless, eyes wide in wonder as he inspected the exquisite scroll-work and engraving, and the polished walnut stock and half-pistol grip.

Sandy bent down toward him.

"Show me how it fits, Ned. Bring it up ready to fire."

He leaned forward slightly bringing the stock up into his shoulder, and aimed the weapon out away toward the tree line. Its weight and balance brought the sight effortlessly right onto his eye, and he gasped in astonishment.

Sandy looked him over with a practiced eye, and stood back, nodding wisely.

"That gun was hand made in England for my grandfather, and it fit him perfectly. It did not fit Dad, and I was never quite right with it either. Once we got through this depression I was going to have it refit, after Angus died, at any rate."

Ned put the gun down and looked at him quizzically.

Sandy continued, sadly now. "It fit Angus perfectly, as if it were made for him."

"What about me? How much will it need to be adjusted to fit me."

"Well, there's the thing of it, lad. You might have been his twin. The fit is perfect, but for your size and age. You could feel it yourself when you brought it up. It might have been meant for you finally, when it's all said and done."

He paused briefly, nodding again. "It's yours now; you look after it, eh."

At that the old man turned away and picked up the remaining gun leaning there against the front of the truck, then bent down reaching into the ammunition box Dan had left there on the ground and took some cartridges.

"Six rounds each, Ned, no more. Make good use of them," he said, and he strode away after the others.

Ned carefully laid the gun on the seat, then bent down and closed the case and placed it as carefully back in the truck. He then took his allotted six cartridges and stuffed them into his trouser pocket, and picked up the gun to hurry after Sandy.

He said nothing further, still slightly overwhelmed but oddly relaxed finally accepting the inevitability of things. Their comfort with him and ready acceptance of his place among them warmed him, and his mind turned to the task at hand.

As they strode along Ned's eye took in his surroundings, then he looked up.

"Where those blokes are going, down that way, looks like it might be swampy. Is there a creek running into it, Sandy?"

"Over the other side, son," he waved his arm. "Come with me. I'll show you a good spot and you sit there while I head off further down. If we are lucky those blokes will send a few quackers our way."

They strode on in silence, then through a line of trees they came quickly onto a small creek, the water glistening through the undergrowth in the morning sun. Ned could see a spot to wait, and no time wasting turned to Sandy indicating his preference with a quick glance. The other nodded then walked on barely missing a beat, soon disappearing among the trees.

Ned took up his position, alone now, allowing the silence to absorb him sufficiently for the small sounds of the bush to penetrate his consciousness. He relaxed at that, breathing steadily while his mind reached out to focus on the one tiny twitter of a little bird, then on to the soft rustling of some small creature along the ground. A sudden thump and a crash over to his left made him turn his head slightly in that direction. It was a kangaroo, startled by Sandy coming onto it unseen, a bit too close for comfort.

A minute or two later he heard a series of quacks away back to his right, but had to stop himself from laughing and giving away his position.

"*That was Everard,*" he chuckled to himself, inwardly to stop any sound going out in case someone heard. "*Can't get the sound right yet.*"

"*It was pretty close, though,*" Sandy's own thoughts came to him, and he started. "*The ducks wouldn't know the difference.*"

Then, "*That boy properly clever, old man, 'e can 'ear right, no worries,*" Old Peter's thoughts chuckled merrily.

It was at that point Ned suddenly understood what was happening, and after that kept his counsel. The quiet of the bush did not just allow the small sounds, but keeping in touch, once you knew how to listen. He settled at that, and waited.

After a while he broke the gun and placed two cartridges from his pocket quietly one each into either barrel, then as quietly clicked the piece shut. The sound was barely audible; both Sandy and Peter listening in he could sense but no longer allowing their thoughts to intrude.

The fun was about to start, so he came alert and presently the clear whistling flight of ducks came to him at speed. The moment they appeared he let off the first barrel, but missed and got the lead duck with the second.

"*Damn!*" he thought, then quickly ejected the spent cases and reloaded. The bird had hit the water and was still, floating there upside down, so he noted its position to pick up later.

Within the next half hour, with shots echoing back and forth along the watercourse he brought down four more birds for himself. Happy with the effort he picked up the empty cases from the ground and put them in his pocket. Then he leaned the gun carefully against a tree and stripped off his clothes to wade into the creek and retrieve the birds. Only one was still splashing and trying to get away. He reached for it and cracked its neck. The five ducks in hand he waded back across and up the bank to where he left his clothes.

"We need to get you a dog, lad," Sandy said grinning broadly, standing there watching him.

"How did you go, Sandy?" He wanted eagerly to know.

"Three. Not as good as you, by the look of it."

Ned left his catch in a small pile on the ground, then took his shirt to dry himself before climbing back into his clothes. Quickly he finished dressing, then bent down to pick up the birds and taking up the gun the two moved off quietly back along the creek line toward the swamp. In short order they could see the others waiting for them up on the paddock, and as they came up to them they were all smiling happily.

"How many?" he called to them.

Everard held up three ducks. "Dan got five, and Mr Tanner got four." He grinned.

Quickly they moved off, back toward the truck with Sandy in the lead. Presently he pulled up thoughtfully for Ned to come alongside, glancing down at him.

"How was that, young fella, did you enjoy yourself?" he wanted to know.

Ned looked, taken aback up suddenly.

"You need to ask me that? You already know."

Sandy winked at him. "I thought you might want to say something."

"Of course I did. I don't know what to say. Don't embarrass me like that."

The other shrugged, turning to walk on without anything further.

When they reached the truck they packed up their gear and the men climbed into the back leaving Ned to sit in the front with Sandy. He was sitting still, silently, and the old man glanced across at him.

"There now lad, I didn't mean to upset your feelings."

He looked down, embarrassed. He shoved at him across the seat, and the old man chuckled.

"Anyway, I have to play footie this afternoon," Ned replied finally.

"Yes, you do. Sorry, Ned, I had forgotten about that. What time does your game start?"

"Not until two. We are on the second oval."

"No worries, we'll get you there all right," then added, "if we drag the chain your mother will have your togs sorted, won't she?"

"Yes, that's all right, mum and dad will be there. I can shower after the game."

They drove on at that, stopping in front of the main house to let the boys off. Ellie was there with a lunch basket which she passed up into the cabin, and after a brief exchange with Rollie Tanner Sandy started off again back down the track toward the front gate.

They drove back into town without saying a word, Ned lost in his own thoughts while Sandy only occasionally glanced across at him. Close to town they pulled off the road onto a side track, and instead of heading through the main street took the stock route more directly around to the sale yards, then past there to the football oval where a junior game was in progress.

Sandy drove slowly through the small crowd and parked the truck close to the main pavilion.

Ned sat still for a moment.

"Thanks, Sandy, for everything," he said quickly. Take the gun and keep it out there for me, will you. Is that all right?"

"As you wish. We'll see you again then, shall we?"

"Yes. You bet."

Sandy sat quietly for a moment longer, then said quietly, "Something important you need to know, lad."

"What is it?" Ned wanted to know.

Sandy glanced across. "Seriously now, I want your word on it."

"Yes, all right."

"I have to ask you not to draw attention to the children we have with us. Government welfare people are onto us about it, and want to take them away into their native hostel."

"What? Really? That's terrible!"

"Well, that's the way of the world, son. They are fine with us, Ellie runs a little school for them but I want you to not even think about them, if that's all right with you."

"I won't. You know me. There is Mum waiting for me anyway, I have to go now."

"All right, there's a good lad. I'll be in touch during the week."

"Come and have dinner with us. Don't stay by yourself, all right. Don't get drunk any more. Mum's a good cook," he grinned shyly then opened the door and climbed down from the cabin.

Without another word Sandy reversed the truck away from the building, then did a wide u-turn and drove away out the gate.

CHAPTER SIX

It was only a few minutes into the third quarter that Ned noticed Seamus Malonie coming up on him from the wing. The ball was in the air so he ignored him and instead ran up to take the mark, failing to see Sam Clancy and his brother Pete coming up onto him behind, running down from their forward line. He did not expect either of them to be so far out of position, and was simply not thinking about it. Later during the inquiry they swore they had run over to help their cousin who they thought was under threat from Ned Collins and his mates, but it was Ned out there by himself.

The ball had been carried off the centre line by a cross-wind and ended up in the half-back flank, but he went high and took it neatly on his chest for a clear mark. It was on his way down that he suddenly lost his legs, and instead of landing cleanly in his feet found himself badly over onto his left shoulder. An audible 'crack' brought a stab of real pain in his right leg, then he felt them pummeling at him. Last thing he knew was the ball there tucked under his sore shoulder and he was waving his right arm trying to fend them off, then everything went black.

He woke on the stretcher carrying him off the field. On the way into the change rooms he saw Sam's face leering down at him, his top lip curled in an ugly snarl. After that things became confused. The pain was immense, wave upon wave of it pulsating as he tried to speak through bloody swollen lips, but no words came. Briefly he saw his mother's face leaning over him and he felt a slight sharp jab in his arm, then everything went black again.

There was mail in the letterbox three weeks later, the day after arriving home from hospital, when late-morning he hobbled down the front path on his crutches to see what the postman's whistle had brought with it. He stopped to sort through the various envelopes and then, nothing interesting, hobbled back up the front path and went inside.

"Some mail for you, mum," he called down the passage as he made his way to the kitchen looking for something to eat. He was hungry. It was almost lunchtime, so putting the mail on the table he went into the pantry for bread and cheese, and a fresh tomato from the basket. Back at the bench near the sink he took down a bread board and started making himself a sandwich.

At the stove he set the kettle on to boil for tea, and as he did so he heard footsteps on the verandah and turned to see Sandy and his mother come inside. He stood watching them enter, surprised to see them, then finished making his sandwich and placing it on a plate on the table he drew out two chairs for them to sit.

"You sit, Ned," his mother said, "Have your lunch."

"There is a letter for you, mum, and some for dad."

Neither of them looked at Sandy who simply took his seat.

"How are you doing, lad?" he wanted to know, his face serious.

"All right," he said, glancing up at the old man there across the table. "I'll mend."

He looked down at his sandwich then took a bite and glanced up again. As he finished chewing he swallowed the morsel and cocked his head thoughtfully.

"Sandy, why won't you let Aunty Enid's daughter and her bloke move into your house?"

They both turned to look at him.

"Where did you get that from, son?" his mother wanted to know, but Sandy ignored her and instead gazed directly at him, steadily, a hurt in his look that caught at him.

"I would have thought better of you, boy."

Ned returned his gaze, as directly.

"I want to know, Sandy, that's all. I want to know what's happening. I didn't know you'd be here; you don't tell me anything unless I ask you, then when I do you sort of push me away as if it doesn't matter. They are picking on me serious now, not just you."

The two looked at each other.

36

"She wants possession of the place, you know that," the old man turned and said finally, adding quietly, "They are doing all right where they are, the pair of them."

Then he stopped at that, gazing curiously at the boy. "What would you have in mind, lad, yourself?" he asked.

Ned thought for a moment, biting on his sandwich and sitting back, taking in the mouthful. "It's unoccupied, that's all. It seems to me a shame, and a waste, if there are people who need a place to live, and can use the land; plant gardens and keep themselves, and pay rent."

They both looked at one another again.

"Do you know someone else like that, perhaps?" his mother turned and asked.

He sat back.

"Dan wants to get married," he said. "Dan Foley. His girl is real pretty. She is nice too. Her mother was in hospital and they were always there visiting."

They both looked away then back at him, both together.

His mother turned and went across to the sink where she started washing some dishes, distracted, briefly looking back at him momentarily before returning to her task. After a while she took up a towel and started drying the things, stacking them carefully on the sideboard.

"You need to understand something, lad," Sandy interrupted. "You are young and full of beans, I can see that, but there is a lot of learning ahead of you."

Ned looked at him quizzically.

Sandy sat back in his seat and sighed briefly, gazing out the window. He pursed his lips, glancing back at the boy sitting across from him, then he leaned forward both hands flat on the table to speak.

"These people are not citizens, Ned," he said simply. "They have no rights in law."

His mother glanced up at the words before returning to the dishes in the sink.

Without waiting Sandy continued, "The reason we still have Dan with us is because we can show that he is gainfully employed. The reason he is able to shoot at the gun club is it's a private club and we have a motion on the books to that effect. But he is not allowed to own land, and living in a house in town will only cause trouble."

Ned sat quietly, watching, for the first time noticed the small lines of worry play on the old man's face despite his steady gaze, that he had thought added character to an old bush larrikin but now revealed a burden of responsibility, and a natural affection he had yet to explore. He tucked the realisation away in the back of his growing awareness, then looked up at him again.

Then he said boldly, "But we can't leave it empty either, Uncle Sandy, with people having nowhere. That's just as bad."

"What do you have in mind? You've been thinking about it, haven't you?"

"Yes," he replied. "I have. Well, anyway, stock agents know people don't they, like Dad? He knows a lot of people, people looking for land, and for somewhere to agist their stock? He always has people coming in looking for farms, and houses. Why don't we ask him? If he finds someone for us we can let your block next door and you can stay here with us, when you're in town."

He went on, warming to his idea, "Mr Patterson won't mind. He'll be happy. Maybe someone can take the house and he can knock down the fence and get the back garden sorted out. He can grow his veges there . . ."

He stopped at that, embarrassed, realising suddenly that they had both stopped what they were doing and listened intently.

"Go on," Sandy said quietly.

Ned shrugged, still slightly embarrassed and a little confused.

"Why not?" He wanted to know.

"No reason at all, Ned. It's a good idea," his mother said from the sink. "Sandy, I will make up your old room and that will be the end of it."

"What room?"

The old man sat back, chuckling to himself.

"I grew up in this house, lad. You didn't know that, did you?"

Ned sat back at that. "Really? Is that right, mum?"

She turned and wiped her hands on her apron, then stepping across to the stove gathered up the pans and took them back across to the sink.

"This side of town was the family's first property in the district, Ned. Sandy's old house there now was the original homestead, and when his parents married his grandfather built this house for them. Mr Patterson's garden came later, after we subdivided just after the war, as the soldiers were coming home."

Sandy interrupted. "Basically I am with you, lad. You have a good mind. But about that block, well, perhaps we might leave it to your father. I'll drop by and see him in the morning."

They looked at each other, Ned weighing things in his mind.

"Provided it's all right with you, young fellow?"

"Yes," he said finally. "That will do the job all right."

He stood and went across to the sink and put his plate into the soapy water, the last morsel of sandwich in his hand. He put it in his mouth and leaned against the bench to finish it, chewing thoughtfully, then swallowed finally before trying to speak.

After a moment longer he added, "Might be better if we went over and cleaned the place up a bit."

His mother looked sharply at him. "That is quite enough for now, child." she exclaimed, "We can do that on the weekend. Right now you have some school work to catch up. If I see your head up in the next hour your father will give you a good larruping when he gets home, plaster or no plaster."

Sandy sat, eyebrows raised and lips pursed, gazing steadily at him.

"Your mother and I have some things to discuss," he said, then seeing him pause at that he nodded slightly, adding, "All in good time, lad."

Ned wiped his hands on a tea towel, shrugged, and taking his crutches obediently went out into the passage and down the back to his room. He sat and read the book his teacher had asked him to borrow from the town library ready for the composition he had to write in class, and stayed engrossed all afternoon until his father suddenly poked his head through the door reminding him to do his chores. He looked up, not realising that it was getting dark, and putting down his book took up the crutches again.

He hobbled down into the back yard to look in on the chooks, and noticed that his father had simply thrown the scraps over the fence without checking for eggs. Holding up his woolen jumper against his chest he went patiently from nest to nest, taking the eggs one by one until there were no more, then skipped out holding onto the fence for support and closed the gate behind him.

CHAPTER SEVEN

Back in the house he went straight into the kitchen where Sandy and his parents were at the table; the men with a glass of beer each and his mother looking up as he came in.

"You didn't get the eggs, Dad," he said, stopping at the bench next to the stove, and leaning against it for balance carefully took each precious egg from his jumper and placed it gently into the basket.

When he was done he went to the sink to wash his hands, then drying them turned to stand next to his mother.

"Would you like a cup of tea, son," she turned to ask him, her hand on his hip.

He looked at the men, standing aside there to leave room in the small kitchen.

"He can have a small beer with us, Jude," his father said, nodding his way.

She looked at him. "Just one Arthur, no more," she said, and stood and went over to the stove.

Sandy passed him a small glass, leaning over to half-fill it with beer. Ned took it up and had one sip, testing the stuff with his tongue.

They both watched him closely, then turned to one another to continue their conversation.

After listening awhile Ned looked up and stared at his father. "Dad, what do you know about all this business? You never tell me anything either."

The other glanced back at him. "I am your accountant."

"What does that mean?"

Well, I keep your books, son. I keep the accounts for the whole family estate, both sides. And a lot of other families. I do your banking, and keep your ledger."

Ned looked at him. "Are you our lawyer too?" he wanted to know.

They both sat back and laughed, then Sandy leaned forward and said, "Learn your ropes first, young lad," then returned to talking softly to his father.

At that his mother placed a large bowl of green peas in front of him and said, "Here, do these for me please, Ned. When they are done you can cut some pumpkin and peel spuds for me, then you can help me with dinner."

She motioned to the men to clear the table. "Arthur, take Sandy into the parlour, will you, there's a dear. The fireplace is set. I'll bring you another beer in a moment."

The two men dutifully got up and left, glasses in hand, engrossed in their discussion.

She listened as they settled themselves in the other room, then turned to her son.

"This is all happening far to quickly. You are not ready yet," she said, glancing his way, then paused watching him closely.

He nodded and looked up at her then sat back in his chair, clasping his hands behind his head.

He was thinking, eyes distant, and about to say something when she interrupted, "I thought as much. You are not going to let it rest, are you Ned. All right then. That's it. I am sending you off to boarding school, away from all this until you are old enough."

At that he looked up sharply, questioning, his eyebrows furrowed.

"We are going to get some pups, Mum. Seriously." He put his hands down on the table and went to get up, but knowing her son she held up her hand, inclining her head in askance.

"I had a think about it; nothing to do with Sandy's old house, something else," he stopped at that, looking at her, then said, "Sit down, Mum. Let me talk to you a minute."

She could see his eyes were bright so she did as he asked.

"Well," he said after a pause, "I thought what I should be is a vet. That's what I want to do. Or maybe I can do livestock husbandry if I don't get through school. But my marks are good, and if I go for the better job it all fits together anyway. We were going to get some pure-bred retrievers, and get started in breeding dogs. We can make good money introducing new dog breeds into the district."

She gazed at him intently.

"What I mean is," he went on, "getting some pups is a good start for me. It is a good way to start."

"What else, son?" she sat back, seriously now.

"Mum, really, things are a mess. Sandy is a mess, when he shouldn't be. He drinks too much. He misses Hamish and Angus something terrible. I know Ellie does. They see them in me. And so do the Clancys and the rest of them."

He paused at that, reflecting on what he was saying, then looked back at her earnestly.

"But that's them," he went on. "What I want to say is if I am going to inherit everything it all has to change for the better."

At that his mother held up her hand. "I hear what you say, Ned. I agree with you, and when the time comes I will support you. But first you will attend to your growing up."

She looked away thoughtfully, then back again. "Ned, let me talk to your father and I will get back to you. His old school has a farm, and if you are agreeable we can drive across during the next holiday and show you around."

"Really, can we do that?"

"Well yes, of course. They have some good teachers there, trained at university. It is more important that you talk to them, not us. They can point you in the right direction."

He sat back a moment, thinking through her words, then nodded and started again shelling the peas.

She stood at that and went across to the stove where she opened the oven door and took out the baking dish. Placing it on the stove top she took up a spoon and began basting the roast shoulder with gravy.

"Mum?" Ned asked.

"Yes, son?"

"You know about Angus, don't you?"

She tensed a moment, then nodded to herself, quietly.

"Yes, of course," she replied. "Don't say anything to your father, Ned, not ever. He doesn't understand these things, and they upset him."

She sighed at that, sadly, then shrugged.

"A place for everything, and everything in its place," she went on, almost to herself, then put down the spoon and returned the pan to the oven. Wiping her hands with her apron she went over to the pantry and selected a nice butternut pumpkin and some potatoes which she placed on the bench, then turned to Ned.

"Here, do the potatoes for me, and the whole pumpkin. Let me finish the peas, you are too slow and I need them done."

"When you have finished leave them and I will put them in with the shoulder. There is a bottle of beer in the ice box; you can take that with you and I will call you all when dinner is ready."

He looked up at her, nodding as quietly himself, then did as she said. Leaving the vegetables cut into neat portions on the board he wiped his hands, and taking the bottle of beer deftly released the seal and hobbled out into the parlour on one crutch where he leaned it against a chair and sat down thoughtfully.

They looked over at him, and without ado his father took the bottle and filled Sandy's glass then his own.

"Mum wants me to go to boarding school for a while," he said. "It's all right. I was thinking about becoming a vet when I finish school, that's all."

He met Sandy's eye first, briefly, and the old man simply inclined his head slightly toward his father before taking up his glass and taking a draught.

"Dad," he continued, "I thought maybe I could get into university, if I go away to school, and maybe learn better than I am doing here."

His father looked at him, his eye steady. "What are you thinking about, son?"

"I don't know. Maybe just a vet. I don't know really."

The two men glanced at one another, then back at him. Sandy sat back at that slightly, distracted momentarily, while his father leaned forward cocking his head in askance.

"Do you think you can run a busy veterinary practice?" He wanted to know. "There is another war coming, Ned, and we have our own business to attend to."

"I don't know. I wasn't thinking about that, starting another business I mean. I just thought that sort of knowledge would be good. It would be handy, you know."

He paused at that, embarrassed. "Well, what I mean is, the stock aren't looking real good, and we are losing too many with one thing or another. And everything else on top of it. Dad, I don't know. I just think sometimes things can be a lot better than they are, that maybe I can help, and that's a good way to help."

He paused, glancing back and forth between the two as they gazed steadily back at him.

"Maybe there will be a war, how would I know," he said finally. "I don't even know what a war is."

He stood at that, frustrated and upset, and went to leave. His father caught his hand and held him back a moment before drawing him onto his knee. He wrapped his arm around him as he had done when he was little, but said nothing.

Sandy took the cue and left, leaving the two of them there quiet for a moment.

After a while his father said softly, "Don't fret, Ned. It's not for you to be worrying too much, at your age. What is your mother talking to you about."

He squirmed slightly onto his side so as to look his father in the face.

"Nothing. She just said when the holidays come we can drive over and look around the school farm, and talk to the teachers. She said they can point me in the right direction, that's all."

The other nodded thoughtfully at that.

"All right, that is what we shall do then," he said after a pause. "Anything else?"

"Sorry I was rude before."

"That's all right son, don't fret."

Ned sat up and hand on his shoulder gazed directly into his father's face, who reached up with his hand and tousled his hair, smiling softly.

"Dad," he persisted, "why aren't you home more often than you are. I miss you a lot when you are away, when there is just me and mum here. And Uncle Sandy."

His father simply leaned back, inclining his head. He then pulled his son close and held him a while, saying nothing.

Eventually he said quietly, "You know I love you, son. I am trying to make it up to you. A lot of this is for you quite as much as the family. Sometimes I think there might be a better way of doing things, but the world is the way it is and there is no good worrying over it."

Then he said after a moment longer, "Just sit here with me Ned, until Mum calls us for dinner. We don't have to say anything to each other. When you start at Grammar you will meet a lot of new people who will help you in life. We will worry about things then if need be, all right."

Ned simply nodded against his chest, then as he lay there against his father slowly began to pick and fiddle with the buttons on his shirt. So engrossed he became that he did not hear his mother call from the kitchen, until the other stirred and picking him up bodily strode out into the passage and through into the kitchen where dinner waited, and sat him down in his chair at the table. After a brief grace they ate their meal, then as he finished Ned excused himself to go read his book, leaving the adults there to keep their own company.

Eventually he got up from his desk and went for a bath, broken leg up awkwardly to avoid getting the plaster wet, and as he brushed his teeth and went back to his room he heard his father's tread behind him along the passage. He followed him in and sat on the bed while Ned dressed in his pajamas. Without saying anything he simply began pulling the blankets back, motioning his Dad to stand while he did so. As he got into bed the other leaned over and tucked him in, then without another word went out again switching the light off on his way.

The soft murmur of their voices from the kitchen soon had him sound asleep.

CHAPTER EIGHT

Next Friday Sandy was there to pick him up from school, but rather than stopping off at home he pointed out the small case on the seat with his change of clothes, and the moment he was settled drove straight out onto the main road.

Ned turned to him eventually and smiled. "So how was your week?"

"So so," the other shrugged. "Just business."

A little later he turned and said, "You might be interested to know, young Ned, that your neighbour Mr Patterson has made us an offer on the old house. He was in at the agents' yesterday and saw our notice for a tenant, so straight away he made an offer for the whole place; walk-in walk-out."

Ned nodded, then his brow furrowed and Sandy glanced across at him.

"What's up, lad?"

"He's not going to demolish the old place, is he?"

"He may well do in time, it's up to him. It will have to go eventually. For the moment I understand he wants to move into the bigger house and extend his gardens, then let the smaller house."

"Do you think it is a good idea? Yourself, I mean."

Sandy pursed his lips thoughtfully.

"It's not a problem. We moved everything out that we wanted a long time ago, first into Dad's house, then after grandma died out to Wyandera. After that we let our own house to your parents. There is nothing in that old place much use to us any more."

"But that's not what you wanted, is it?" Ned challenged, glancing across.

"Son, my opinion is that Tom Patterson is a very smart fellow. He has always made a good go of things and we hold him in some regard. He knows the worth of the land and made no quibble over it. He gave me a good price right off, a very fair offer, so we shook hands and that was it."

Then he turned to him and said, with some finality, "Ned, young lad, I will tell you something, a lesson in life. Never trust a man who won't look you fair in the eye and give you a good firm handshake. That is the way we have always done business in these parts, and God Forbid things stay that way."

Ned thought over that for a moment, then said himself, "Well, all right, that's good enough for me too."

They drove on awhile deep in their own thoughts, then he turned to Sandy again.

"How is Angus?" he asked suddenly. "Do you see him?"

The other frowned slightly. "I don't see him, son, no. I have no wish to see him," he said softly, gazing out the window into the distance.

"What you need to learn yourself is the business is queer," he went on. "It is a fey thing. We each of us have a fellow-walker as we say, and everything is connected. Angus himself was kept here for all our benefit in the long run. He is not the one to be with you directly, though you will find all that out for yourself eventually. Let it be, lad, and say nothing of it to anyone. Everything will unfold as it should, have no doubt of it."

Ned stared at him, mouth slightly agape, working his jaw and studying his face intently as if to start arguing. He went to say something before Sandy stopped him abruptly.

"Speak no more of it, lad! Things will turn out. Leave it be."

Then the old man relaxed slightly, and turned to look at him before continuing.

"When my time comes I will stand before my Maker and give a full accounting of myself, that's it. I will do so to no man in the meantime, and let no man come between me and that day. I apologise to nobody. You're a fine young man and I have taken a great liking to you, I'll say that, but let that be the end of this discussion and raise the matter no more. I'll have no more of it, do you hear me?"

"All right," Ned said simply, then relaxed and looked over at him. "I didn't mean it, Sandy. I didn't mean what you thought. I am happy if you teach me things, but I've said that. Maybe you should listen too."

Sandy looked at him, and leaned over suddenly to shoved at him from across the seat, without saying a word.

They drove on, a new respect between them.

CHAPTER NINE

They arrived on Mount Tambla late in the afternoon after a long and dusty drive; as the old car made its slow grinding way uphill off the vast inland plain, stopping occasionally to allow the engine to cool. Only once did Arthur get out, as if he were still driving a buggy and pair, to refill the radiator from the spare water he carried in the boot. Unheeding of the new-fangled technology he finally eased the car up the last rise and simply let it make its own way over the top of the mountain into the town itself.

As they puttered along he pointed out the good farmland of the district, talking about its potential. As they passed neat fences and well laid-out paddocks, and beyond them the rambling buildings of his old school, he nodded absently to himself, and became lost in his own thoughts.

Ned sat back quietly taking it all in, wondering about this new life he was about to start, and new friends to make hopefully; glad to be away from his hooligan cousins and their mischief finally. They drove on past the school into the town proper and pulled up in front of a still elegant, rambling old two storey hotel situated grandly there on the main street.

Arthur parked the car just clear of the verge in front, slightly off the kerb so as to leave room for horses and avoid the watering trough and hitching rail there, and as they got out and stretched their legs a large portly man arrived smartly from the hotel, tipping his hat as he stepped up smiling.

"Hello, Art," he said convivially, and shook hands.

"How are you Judith?" he repeated, leaning over to peck her lightly on the cheek. "It is very nice to see you again. I trust you had a safe journey?"

"Good afternoon to you, Stan," she replied. "Yes, lovely, thank you."

As they went to get their luggage from the boot Arthur turned to Ned.

"Ned, I would like you to meet Mr Donovan. You will be seeing a great deal more of him." Then turning again to the other he said, "Stan, this is my son Edward. He will be joining the school."

The hotelier eyed him up and down. "There's a strapping lad. Very pleased to make your acquaintance, young fellow."

Ned simply smiled, looking up and taking him in without expression.

As they entered the hotel foyer he noticed people stopping to wave and call greetings while his father waved back in kind, and stepping in closer asked him softly, "Dad, how come everyone knows you?"

His father grinned. "I grew up here, Ned. Mr Donovan and I were in the same class at school. When we left school he went into the hotel business, and I went into the bank. His family built this place back in the gold rush days, did you know that?"

He put the luggage down, then taking his arm turned back to the door and stepping out onto the street pointed to another building across the road.

"See that old building there, Ned? It used to be a bank. I started off there as a clerk and finally rose to become manager, before we moved into the new building right next door there. That was before I met your mother," he smiled.

Ned listened, fascinated.

"Tomorrow we will open an account for you, in case you need a bit of pocket money. If there is anything else you need, call Mr Donovan."

He stopped then, kneeling down to talk to him face to face.

"I know son, boarding school can be a lonely place for a boy not used to being away from home. Any time you need to get away all you have to do is apply for weekend leave, and the Donovans will look after you. I will leave instructions with the school, all right?"

Ned simply nodded but said nothing, the whole experience new and interesting.

It was not until they were back inside the hotel and climbing the stairs up to their room that he said finally, "Dad, don't worry about me. I'll be all right. I will. Once I make some new friends, I'll be all right."

"Of course you will, son. I have no doubt of that. Just keep your options open, will you?"

He looked down and smiled, and the other nodded and smiled back.

Their rooms turned out to be a family suite. Ned had a bed in his own room while his parents occupied the main family room. They were hot and dusty after the long drive and it was getting late, so father and son shared a quick shower then dressed and waited patiently while their mother took her bath.

Finally they were all ready and made their way back downstairs to the dining room where Mr Donovan himself waited to show them to their table. Ned looked around him in awe. He thought it was all far too grand, with the sparkling chandeliers and starched white linen, and everyone dressed for dinner, with crisp waitresses bustling to and fro serving food and drinks. As one of the girls took his order and he sat waiting for his meal, he continued staring about him. When his drink was served he nodded politely and said thank you, absently, his mind not quite there in the moment.

Eventually he leaned over to his parents and said quietly, "This is not for me. I mean, it's nice, but all these people running around . . ." He stopped suddenly, embarrassed.

They both looked at him steadily, then as he continued sitting there saying nothing further, his father finally said, "It's all right, son. Say what's on your mind."

"I don't mean to be rude, Dad. I'm sorry."

"No, don't be sorry. Speak up."

"Well, I only mean that I don't really like people waiting on me like that. I would rather be my own person, and do things for myself."

His mother leaned back at that suddenly, her hand to her mouth and a twinkle in her eye.

Then she leaned toward her husband, hand on his knee, and whispered conspiratorially, "There, you see Arthur, there is no escape."

His father leaned across, beaming.

"Ned, don't you ever change!" he chuckled, then more seriously he cocked his head and continued softly, "Only one thing. People have to make a living for themselves, and there is nothing wrong with providing a service. Never look down on them for it, that's all."

"No, I won't Dad. I'll never do that."

Then his mother leaned closer for her own part, her eyes still a-twinkle, "So long as they do it well, Ned. Don't ever let them get away with half measures."

At that a waitress appeared at his side with his meal, so he sat back and taking up his napkin lost himself momentarily in the delicious aroma coming up off his plate. He looked up at his mother, smiling at her now with his new realisation, and nodded acquiescence.

His father continued looking at him as he ate. "If you want to make some extra money, Ned, Mr Donovan will give you a job here during the holidays, or weekends perhaps. It won't hurt you to learn something of the hotel and catering business."

He frowned slightly, but his father held up his hand and continued, "You are a good cook, son. You love cooking, let him teach you a few tricks. It is something you will never regret."

Ned thought about that, then cocked his head and nodded.

"Not holidays, Dad. I want to be home with you when I can, and Sandy and Auntie Ellie."

He was going to say something further but glanced away, thinking of Angus suddenly. The waitress was there now with their remaining order so he put his thoughts away in the back of his mind and directed his attention instead to dinner. By the time they had finished he realized how tired he was after such a long day, so he went straight up to bed while his parents adjourned to the lounge and sat awhile listening to the big radio on the mantelpiece before turning in for the night.

Next morning they were up early enough for breakfast then went outside for a stroll along the street, looking through all the shops and stopping occasionally while mother went in and bought various things; a new hat and some skirts and pullovers, and balls of wool and bolts of new cloth she would be able to make up when she got home. By mid-morning she had them both loaded up with bags and cartons, and smiling sweetly led the way back to the car.

"Well, we had better get you off to school, Ned," she said eventually. "I am sure you are quite looking forward to meeting your new friends."

"Eleven o'clock we have to be there, mum. We can have a cup of tea first if you want."

"The school dining room will be open for parents," his father said. "We can have tea there, and I can catch up with some of my old friends while your mother takes you across to enroll."

That said they all agreed, and getting into the car drove off out of town until they came to the big gates of the school and made their way up the long tree-lined driveway. As they drew close Ned could see the fine old buildings were showing signs of age and disrepair, like everything else in keeping with the hard times. Even then there were quite a few cars parked, and people milling around lugging suitcases and fussing over boys of all shapes and sizes.

The morning went swimmingly enough; after they had finished their morning tea and headed across to the main office they sat awhile until his name was called, then they filled out forms and nodded and smiled and bumped into people, and nodded and smiled all over again while boys trying to stay clear of parents eyed one another. Finally they were done.

Back in the dining room they caught up with Arthur, who nodded as they came in then turned to extricate himself from his own crowd. Together they went back out to the car and drove away from the main buildings past wide sporting fields looking across extensive farm paddocks and orchards, then through a narrow belt of trees to another set of buildings.

"Here we are then."

They got out and like everyone else started to unpack the car boot and lug cartons and cases across the quadrangle and upstairs. Inside their allocated building were two floors of dormitories; three on each storey with each containing sixty beds, and another smaller dormitory of thirty beds at the northern end of the top floor, above the house master's flat. They made their way through the crowd until they found his place, with 'Edward Arthur Collins, 1934' etched neatly onto a brass plate at the foot of the bed, and another likewise on the door of an adjacent wardrobe.

Arthur stood there, hands in his pockets, a flood of memories coming back suddenly. He took out his right hand and motioned to his son.

"Your turn now," he said absently.

They both turned to look at him, but he quickly came back to attention. He looked at them slightly more focused, then embarrassed in his own way said, "You have to change into your uniform, son. Your day clothes come home with us."

Ned looked up and placed his suitcase on the bed, then opened it and took out his new summer uniform. He stripped down to his underpants and socks, then took his time dressing while they watched. Finally he opened the wardrobe door and looked at himself in the mirror. Something amiss he cocked his head and turned aside, and taking his Billy Bunter cap from the suitcase put it jauntily in his head, then turned to them and smiled.

Then he gave his mother a quick hug, but turning to his father he said simply, "Go now, all right. Don't worry about me."

At that he turned away and began organising his things, taking his underwear and socks and handkerchiefs out of the suitcase and arranging them neatly in the wardrobe shelves, then the rest of his small things, and finally his shirts and trousers and suit, and hung them from the hanger rail. By the time he had done that they were already down the aisle and at the door where they turned to look back at him. He waved, dismissing them, and promptly turned his attention to the boy on the next bed.

"What's your name?" he asked, but when the other just stood looking at him he jumped up and reading the engraving at the end of his bed cocked his head in recognition.

"Michael Stanley Donovan, is it?" he wanted to know. "From the hotel? That lot?"

"Your family are hooligans, Collins, though on your mother's side. Your father is a good man, I must admit," the other flashed back at him.

Ned froze.

"So, you insult my mother do you? We've only just met."

The other stood, staring at him, but Ned eyed him closely then relaxed and smiled.

"All right then, just joking. If you remind me I'll make something of it. Why don't you just tell me your name. I mean, what do you like to be called, by your friends?"

The other nodded. "Michael will do for now," he said quietly, then more confidently, "Ned Collins, eh? So father has you in his sights now, does he?"

"I don't know what you mean."

"You'll be staying with us."

"Yes, and I'll be sleeping next to you by the look of things."

Then he looked back at the boy, fair in the eye, and asked, "Are you good for anything aside from all that, Mr Donovan?"

"What are you saying now, Collins?"

"Ned to you." Then, "Can you shoot, or kiss girls, or play footie? I mean, what else are you good for aside from your family's grand hotel, with all your servants and being waited on day after day."

The other grinned, then shrugged and looked away, slightly embarrassed.

"Quid pro quo," he murmured finally.

Ned turned at that, skipping backward along the dormitory aisle until the other boy rounded his bed, then disappeared down the stairs. He waited at the bottom until he heard steps coming down, and trying to be clever stepped out to bump the oncoming body aside, but made his move to soon and got skittled himself in the rush. Donovan it turned out was three back from the front, and grabbing his cap on the way past, the moment he was outside threw it up onto the roof of the building.

Ned came outside and looked up at what he had done, then staring at him there in the midst of the pack turned his gaze, and looked down and turning aside walked away.

"*All right*," he thought to himself, "*that's the way it's going to be.*"

Years later he found cause to think, that was a defining moment of his life, although later that day when Michael approached him he pushed him away.

CHAPTER TEN

There was nothing much to do that afternoon so he went on a long walk across the oval and around the farm, arriving back early enough for a shower before dinner. Back beside his bed he undressed and wrapped his towel around his waist, then taking up his bathroom kit went through to the showers. Donovan was there third shower from the other end so he stepped quickly under the first shower head at his end simply to be by himself. By time he soaped up other boys came rushing in and soon there was a packed crowd. Losing himself among them he rinsed and dried himself off and went back to his bed to dress and prepare for dinner.

Michael followed him out, and followed his moves.

"Sorry, Ned," he said plainly enough.

Ned turned on him.

"Prove it," he said flatly, still simmering. Then he looked him fair in the eye.

"If you are sorry, climb up and get my cap."

The other shook his head. "What's a stupid cap?" he wanted to know.

"The cap is nothing, it's what you did. If you want to be sorry undo what you did, that's all."

He stood glaring at him in frustration, and no small hurt, then not wanting to dwell on the matter walked away down the aisle. Instead of waiting there for what he had earlier thought might be a bit of fun at the bottom of the stairs, he went straight outside to make his way across to the dining room alone.

Just outside the building he was pulled up by a loud stern voice.

"Where is your cap, boy?"

He turned to see one of the house masters standing there stiffly in his mortar board and academic gown, glaring sharply down at him.

He looked up and pointed to the roof.

"It's on the roof."

"On the roof, sir."

"Yes, sir."

"Would you care to elaborate on how your cap happens to be on the roof?"

"No sir. I mean, it was my fault, sir."

"New boy are you? Your name?"

"Collins, sir."

The old teacher looked him up and down with a cold practiced eye.

"So you are the Collins boy, eh? I taught your father, did you know that?"

Ned smiled, "No sir, I didn't know." Then he cocked his head quizzically. "You must be Burgie," he said, then catching the sharp look quickly corrected himself. "I'm sorry, sir. Mr Burgess, I mean."

The other rocked briefly on his heels gazing at him, lips pursed, then suddenly, "Off you go then, Collins, and we'll speak no more of this, shall we?"

As he turned to leave the teacher added, "I will have the janitor retrieve your cap. You can pick it up from the purser's office during morning recess tomorrow."

The other boys had streamed out of the building by this time, glancing across and sniggering among themselves at his detention, but the moment he was released he ran to catch up with them and they opened ranks to bring him in, crowding around bumping and jostling at him.

"You're lucky," one said.

"Burgie is a real bastard," broke in another.

Their banter went on, so he slowed a little to break rank and walk by himself, glaring ahead at Michael who glanced back over his shoulder at him.

"You'll keep," he projected his thoughts into his glare, making the other turn away abruptly to walk on ahead of the crowd.

Reaching the dining room they were lined up in long queues by senior boy prefects, and Ned hung back a moment watching for what he was supposed to be doing next. One of the older boys came over to where he stood waiting.

"You are Collins, aren't you?"

"Yes, that's right. What's your name?"

"Donovan. I am Michael's brother, Patrick."

Ned started back at that, his eyes cautious, but the other grinned then leaned closer.

"I know he's a little shit. If he gives you any trouble just let me know and I'll deal with him."

He then stood back. "Where's your cap?"

"On the dormitory roof."

"Don't tell me."

"I won't. It doesn't matter. Burgie is getting it down for me. He said I can pick it up tomorrow morning."

Patrick looked away thoughtfully, then back at him. "All right. You are in Robertson House. Whenever you come to the dining room line up in that queue there." He turned and pointed, then thinking further a moment indicated for him to follow and led him over to a group of boys there in the queue.

"This is Ned Collins," he said. "His father and mine are old boys together."

They all looked him up and down.

"Michael is being a shit," he went on and they nodded. Then without another word he went back to his duties.

"All right, get in line with us Ned," one of them said once Patrick had left. "I am Percival. You can call me Trevor."

"Call him Scunge," another interrupted. "That is Scunge Percival, the one and only. Don't listen to him, for love or money."

Ned stood there looking from one to the other.

Percival turned to him with an air of authority now.

"You will meet everyone, don't worry. The only one you have to watch here is Ramsay. He's got odd balls and a complex about it."

"Christ, you're a dickhead. You're a real scungey bastard." Ramsay muttered, turning to Ned. "You can see where he gets his name."

Percival beamed broadly. "There, you see young Neddy my lad, we all understand each other perfectly well here."

Before he had a chance to reply the line started moving ahead so they all trooped in to the dining room. Halfway through the door Ramsay leaned over and said, "You are on my table. Ken Wilson is our head, he's good. Patrick is good too, but he's three tables down."

Ned stood looking at him, the first boy here to whom he had taken a genuine liking.

The other picked it up straight away, and smiled.

"I am Ian, anyway," he toyed with his crotch absently as he spoke. "Don't take any notice of stupid Percival."

Ned glanced down momentarily.

"Is it true," he grinned, slightly embarrassed.

"I had a hernia once that's all, when I was little. Those bastards won't let me forget it." Then he said, "You'll cop it too, Ned, everyone does. They'll find something."

"So why do you hang around with them?"

"No talking, you two," another prefect interrupted before he could answer, so they made their way quietly to their table and sat down.

"We have rats on Mondays," Ian leaned over and whispered. "Rat's tails, greasy mince, foul."

"No talking, Ramsay," Wilson said quietly from the table head, then looked at Ned.

"You're Collins, the new boy, are you?"

"Yes."

"I am Wilson. While you are on my table you will behave yourself, is that clear?"

"Yes, I'll be good," he smiled. "What's for dinner?"

The rest of the table turned to stare, a look of disgust on their collective face. As one they turned to Wilson who slowly lifted the lid from a big steaming pot on the table in front of him, then dipped the spoon in and with due reverence raised it aloft, letting the grey muck slop back into the pot with a soft sickening 'splot'.

Ned looked on curiously.

"Do we have to eat it straight like that?"

The collective stare rippled back to his place at the table, not quite looking at him but at some unimaginable horror just there beyond the edge of their vision.

"I mean, can we have it on bread and butter, with sauce?"

"Collins, this is serious," Wilson said abruptly, taken aback at the utterance of such heresy.

He simply gazed around him at the pale set faces, then back at Wilson.

"Vegetables? Do we get vegetables?"

One of the smaller boys retched audibly, while his friend next to him patted him ruefully on the back.

Wilson then raised the lids with great ceremony off two smaller pots, to reveal one of boiled cabbage, and another of boiled potatoes.

"Right, good," Ned said softly to himself, then set about taking two slices of bread and spreading them liberally with butter, and when he had done passed the plate along the table to Wilson.

He took it in one hand, and with the other began to ladle mince onto the bread. He looked up at Ned, eyes slightly aglaze.

"One more," Ned held up a finger, nodding and smiling.

Wilson went through the same ceremony with the potatoes and cabbage until Ned was happy, then passed the plate quickly back along the table like something tainted, glad to be rid of it.

The meal finally before him Ned then proceeded to add a dash of Worcestershire sauce, and another of tomato sauce, then salt and pepper and finally an extra dab of butter on the potatoes.

Finally satisfied, he began to eat.

Ian nudged him. "We have to say grace first," he whispered, "and anyway you have to wait for us."

Ned put down his knife and fork and sat hands in his lap waiting for Wilson to serve the rest of the table. Finally a polite cough was head from the end of the hall, and he looked up to see one of the duty masters standing head bowed.

"Lord, bless us this day, and make us truly thankful for what we are about to receive."

The entire room murmured a blurred and fractured 'amen', then broke into a babble of voices.

Ned ate with relish, chewing and savouring each mouthful until eventually he took another piece of bread and with it wiped the whole plate clean. He sat back, licking his lips, then without ado reached over and poured himself a cup of tea from the big pot in front of him.

"Ned, you want to buy mine?" Ian sitting next to him asked almost inaudibly. "Trade you an orange on Wednesday, and cake Saturday lunch."

Ned looked at him, noticing that he had not eaten one spoonful.

"If you leave it until it's cold, Ian, of course it will taste crook. Add some condiments like I did, then shut your eyes if you have to."

The other boys looked at him, still staring blankly.

Finally one of them piped up and said, "You must be a rat's tail yourself, Collins."

"No, a rat, only a starved rat could eat that muck and enjoy it," another said.

"Rat Collins."

The murmur swam back and forth across the dining room until a loud rap was heard from the duty master's table and all went quiet again.

"You've done it now," Ian said, then added consolingly, "at least it's not as bad as Odd Nuts."

CHAPTER ELEVEN

As the first few weeks went by Ned quickly settled into the routine. For the first time he took up swimming, there being no football training until after Easter, and to keep fit joined a few of the others before showers on long five-mile cross-country runs around the town's new airfield and back.

Apart from the compulsory English, Physics, Chemistry and Mathematics he took up three electives being Agriculture which was the reason for his being there; History because it was so interesting; and to keep his hands busy Woodwork instead of Art. After dinner each week night were two hours of preparation, when they were shut up in their classrooms reading and doing homework.

Cadet Service was also compulsory, with close order drill in full uniform twice a week. He was impressed to learn that the school had been the staff headquarters for Southern Command during the Great War, and was accorded favourable treatment by the army with a fully equipped quartermaster's store and a rifle for each cadet; the notion only palled by the looming prospect of another war. The senior boys were being prepared for leadership in that event, and he decided then and there that as time went by he too would follow their example. At least he would be ready, he thought.

During those first few weeks he and Michael settled into an uneasy truce. He decided eventually that it was not worth being sour on him, which sat well in his mind once he realised that he was still no real friend either. Not yet. It did not matter that much, which proved interesting some time later again, following the Easter break after Ian had managed to do a deal with a boy on his other side to swap beds so he and Ned slept next to each other, when Michael settled down quite a lot and the three simply began to hang around together.

It was during Easter that he and Ian became really close. Ian's two sisters were away with their own friends for the holiday, so his family invited him to stay on their own small farm in the mountains. A week of letter writing and telegrams had it all arranged, so when the Thursday arrived his parents were freed from the long journey from Weethangara and the two boys piled instead into the back of the other car.

Ian's father was quite elderly. He had been in the Royal Navy and retired with the rank of Commander, which he explained was one short of Captain, and had married late with the two older girls and a boy as the result. His mother was quite nice; somewhat delicate Ned thought, so used as he was to the stout, no nonsense women out in the station country, but with a clear sharp mind and kindly eyes.

He need not have worried as she turned out to be a fine horsewoman, and a keen judge of both horses and cattle. It was the first time he had seen anyone ride side-saddle, with long skirts and embroidered blouse complemented by a sun hat, and he watched fascinated as she saddled up for their long morning ride. The family kept a small herd of Black Angus which they showed every year, and another slightly larger flock of black-faced Suffolk sheep. Mixed in with them were shaggy, long-horned Highland Cattle kept as pets.

As they rode around the farm he listened for hours on end to her explaining to him their intensive, two-tier farming system with broad shelter belts of trees, and the lines of drainage her husband had installed throughout the property to harvest every bit of rain and direct it into the small storage dams dotted everywhere. It was a revelation to him after the vast extensive pastoral holdings to which he was so accustomed, and he eagerly soaked up every bit of knowledge she imparted to him.

After lunch each day he and Ian were free to wander. On Saturday they went fishing and caught some fine trout, which he was given the honour of cooking for dinner that evening; Ian having whispered to his father that he had this odd thing about food. The meal won him new respect when he fried the fresh fish lightly in butter, whole, with only a little salt and pepper and boiled potatoes with garden salad tossed in a small vinaigrette he thought up at the last moment.

"Where did you learn to cook like that?" they all wanted to know.

"I don't know. I just picked it up."

He cocked his head thoughtfully.

"All our family are good cooks," he explained. "There was a French great-grandmother once, Aunty Ellie told me, who never allowed anyone to eat tinned food, and that was it."

The elderly couple glanced at one another, Ian's mother indicating the vinaigrette and nodding.

"I think she was a Huguenot, or something like that," Ned continued. "That side of the family were very religious, you know, had firm ideas about a lot of things. Uncle Sandy told me to respect that, so I do."

"How fascinating! We never realised you had such an interesting family," she said.

"*You haven't seen half of it yet,*" he thought soberly, then out loud, "There were a lot of people here in the early days, a lot of Chinese and Afghans as well. Still some. After the gold rush there was a lot of money, so everything went all right for a fair time. People learned from one another a lot."

They listened intently as he continued, "I think the early family were brought out from Ireland as farmers, or maybe the West Country, then the McKenzies from Scotland. I don't know where Dad's side came from yet, the Collins family I mean. I think they might have been bankers, or book-keepers, something like that."

Then he looked up. "What about your family?" he wanted to know.

"The Ramsays go back the Normans, you know. They were scientists and physicians and quite well placed," Mr Ramsay said. "The distaff side are clan Graham."

Ned looked sideways at Ian, nudging him, then looked back again, smiling.

"James Graham, Marquis of Montrose. 'He either fears his fate too much, Or his deserts are small, That puts it not unto the touch, To win or lose it all.'"

He looked up at them. "He was drawn and quartered for his efforts. We studied him in History."

They all gazed at him, astonished, and at that he looked away somewhat embarrassed.

"I thought that was very brave of him," he said, almost apologetically, but Ian's mother leaned over and patted his hand, delighted.

"What do you plan to do on leaving school, Ned?" she asked.

"Veterinary Science," he said simply, then paused a moment seeking to explain further.

He learned forward to engage their attention. "We have several large holdings, but a fair way out. A lot of it is native country and we need more doctors as well, so I thought that was the best thing for me to do."

"Won't you have enough responsibility?"

"What do you mean? No, I don't think so. No, not really."

He sat back, confused.

Ian's father looked at him, apologising almost in his own turn.

"There is going to be another war, lad."

"Dad said that too. Do you think there will be? When, do you think?"

The old man sat back a moment, then nodding quietly to himself picked up his pipe and slowly packed it with tobacco. He lit it then with a fresh match off his boot, and taking a deep draught eyed him through the fragrant curling smoke.

"By the time you matriculate," he said stiffly. "A little later if you are lucky."

Ned sat back in his seat and thought for a moment.

"Later will work out all right," he replied finally, looking him square in the eye.

"There's a good lad."

There was a pause, then Ian breaking the mood nudged him away.

"Crib, or Euchre or Monopoly?"

"Yeah, cribbage." He looked over again. "Sorry, please excuse us."

The two boys carried their dinner plates over to the sink then quickly took their leave.

The next day was Easter Sunday, and following an early breakfast they drove into town to attend the morning service. After a light lunch the parents decided there was work to be done. Taking some crates they directed the two boys to the apple orchard and set them to the task of bringing in the whole crop. The job turned out to be fun except that by noon the next day between them they had eaten an entire crate and spent the afternoon taking turns on the toilet, much to the old couple's amusement.

That night in the bath Ian showed him his scar from the operation to close the hernia he had done when he was eight, on the right side of his scrotum, and talked to him about it. They chuckled nervously realising they would both soon be young men, with the prospect of war very much on the horizon it seemed.

It was nowhere such a long drive back next day to Mount Tambla from the farm up in the Wellesley Range as it was from Weethangara, and the car made it by morning tea. Ian sat in the front with his father, talking seriously with him all the way, while Mrs Ramsay and Ned sat in the back earnestly discussing cattle and sheep, and soil, and pasture grasses, and the problems they were having out in the station country.

She was especially interested in the welfare of their natives, she went on to explain, but he looked aside at her questioning until eventually she went back to discussing some of the finer points of pasture improvement, and worm control in sheep, and the dreaded anthrax, and difficulties they faced importing finer bloodlines in their cattle.

That was how Ian and he became such close friends.

Back at school Ned began to worry about how he was ever going to introduce him to Angus, but once he moved into the next bed and the thing with Michael took shape he more or less put it aside, and slipping back into the school routine found too many other things to do.

Football training on the main oval started on schedule, and by the eighth week of term the inter-school competition was under way. He found himself in the back pocket where he played such a good defensive role the coach soon moved him up through the centre line into the forward flank As the season progressed he settled well into that job, several times coming close to scoring a goal with his long straight kick from the side line, but in any case within easy passing distance to his centre-forward and from there get the ball through the goal post. It was his first real experience at team coordination, and he reveled in it.

CHAPTER TWELVE

It was not until they had a bye one weekend that there came a chance to take leave and stay with the Donovans. It was a long walk into town so the car was there to pick them up straight after class. All they had to do was walk back over to their dormitory to get their things and they were away. Nobody said anything during the short trip into town, and when the car pulled into the back of the hotel they all simply tumbled out and went inside.

Michael headed straight off to his own room without saying anything, leaving Patrick to show courtesy to their guests, but when Mr Donovan saw him go, as the others watched grinning he called him back and gave him a sharp lecture on manners. At that the older boy went off instead with his father leaving the three classmates standing there awkwardly.

Ian and Ned as one turned to gaze at Michael, who eventually looked back at them and said, unconvincingly, "You want to see my chemistry set? After I show you to your rooms, I mean."

"Right, that would be tops," Ian said, and picking up his bag turned and went.

Ned nodded likewise and followed Ian. After a few steps he turned back, beckoning Michael to come, then walked with him hand on his shoulder until they caught Ian and the three of them ascended the back stairs together where they reentered the building by the second storey balcony. Michael showed them a short way along the back corridor to their room, staying with them while they unpacked and changed out of their school uniforms before leading them back two doors to his own room.

Inside was the maddest jumble of books and toys and model ships and airplanes they had ever seen. There was nowhere to move, apart from a bare patch on the floor next to the bed and a pile of dirty clothes that looked as if it had been there forever, simply growing bigger year by year. The two stood there, mouths agape, dumbfounded by the chaos before them, while Michael stood there in the midst of it grinning shyly.

Finally Ned could stand it no longer.

"At least you could take your clothes down to the laundry, you grubby bugger. A big place like this, with all those servants waiting on you, right?"

"Doesn't matter," Michael shrugged. "Wait till I show you my chemistry set."

"It does matter, Michael." Ned persisted. "You have all these servants running around, they can do it. It's not like it's a chore for you."

Michael stared at him blankly.

"If you don't have it cleaned up we'll tell everyone."

He went pale at that.

"I agree." Ian butted in. "You're a grub, Donovan."

Michael shook his head. "But you haven't seen my latest experiment. I want to show how I can grow real crystals. It's amazing, you'll see."

Ned cocked his head, still glaring at him. "Where is it?" he demanded to know.

"Well, I just have to get another packet of salts. Everything is in the back shed."

He paused at that, then said plaintively, "They won't give me anywhere to work, or any decent equipment; nothing."

Ned was going to say something but Ian interrupted, nudging him aside to look Michael fair in the face.

"What are you talking about, Donovan? What do you think you are doing?"

Michael looked up, startled, then glared back angrily, resentfully.

"What are you talking about, Ramsay? I am going to be a chemist, and make medicine. To help sick people. Look at yourself. What's on your mind, just another war?"

Ned broke them up, then paused, thinking a moment.

"All right," he said finally, then stood back letting him have his way.

Michael went over to a set of shelves, and rummaging around took up a crumpled yellow envelope then went straight out the door. They turned and followed him back along the corridor and further along the back balcony, then down the outside stairs and across the yard to an old shed where he carefully unlocked the door and let them in.

Inside, along one of the windows, was a roughly fitted shelf on which sat a row of glass jars. In the jars were arrays of crystals of all shapes and sizes. The late afternoon light slanting through the window lit them up in flashing sparks of colour.

Michael stood there beaming proudly, his eyes alight.

"There, you see," he said breathlessly as the two stood there mouth agape.

Ian went over to the window, and went along from jar to jar gazing in wonder, then back again. Then he turned abruptly on his heel.

"All right, Donovan, you're in . . . on one condition."

"What's that?" Michael wanted to know.

"Clean your room up. At least get your laundry done."

Ned glanced back and forth at them both, then nodded finally.

"I agree, Michael. And no more bullshit, all right."

At that he glanced down at the packet in Michael's hand, and after a long pause asked him, "So, what's your next trick?"

"This makes red crystals," the other replied. "It is called Red Prussiate of Potash."

"Potassium Ferricyanide," Ian broke in, and Michael turned to him smiling now.

"How did you know that?" he wanted to know.

Ian gazed intently back at him, declining the question. "We can start the new solution in the morning," he said finally. "Rat is supposed to be helping in the kitchen so that will give you and me something to do."

74

"He has to clean up his room first, at least get the laundry out," Ned interrupted.

"But there's a new picture tonight, at the theatre," Michael turned on him, "by Charles Chauvel the new film director, and it's got Errol Flynn in it."

They looked at each other. "All right, deal," Ian uttered shrewdly. "That's the new film about the Bounty. It was made in Sydney. Burgie is going to love us!"

"All right by me," it was Ned's turn. "Clean the room up first, then showers and early dinner. What time does it start, Michael?"

"Seven thirty." He looked glumly at them. "Do we really have to clean my room?"

"Yes!"

They turned on him, and grabbing both his arms shoved him outside. Standing close so as not to let him get away while he locked the shed door behind him, they marched him straight back across the yard and up the stairs.

"Come on, Grub, you'll feel a lot better afterward," is all they said on the way up, then Ian stood guard while Ned went off to find the housekeeper for laundry bags and a broom.

He finally found her having a cup of tea in the kitchen. When she heard his request she shook her head in amazement, then chuckling to herself took him off through the pantry to the laundry where she found the things he wanted. As he went back upstairs he heard the rest of the women chuckle among themselves. All next day they gazed after him smiling fondly.

The job was not so difficult as it first appeared, mainly consisting of Ned and Ian in turn shoving everything they could get their hands on into the laundry bags while Michael scrambled anxiously after them retrieving his various treasures. An hour later they were more or less done, and leaving him there on his bed to commiserate lugged the three big calico bags full of washing out onto the back balcony, ready to go down with the next morning's bed linen.

It was still only about five thirty, so they went and dragged Michael outside and back down the stairs again, and out onto the back lane where they made their way to the street. They turned downhill and taking a full half-hour sauntered idly along one side then crossed over and came back up the other. Ian had been at the school since he was five years old, and for Michael of course it was home, so the venture was nowhere near so interesting for them as it was for Ned who had grown up away out in the back country and made them follow him through one shop after another while he explored this whole new world.

Finally Ian looked up at the clock on the town hall at the top of the street and gave him a nudge, and together they turned back to the hotel and this time went straight through the front door and up the main stairs. It was a little confusing to find their way from the front of the building but Michael quickly had them down the right corridor. He waited while they undressed, then showed them the way to the bathroom before returning to his own room to do likewise.

There was only one bath but it did have a shower head with plenty of hot water so they each took turns while their newly pubescent deep and meaningful discussions on the state of the world continued unabated, and as they finished drying themselves stood waiting for one another. Returning to their rooms they dressed quickly back into their day clothes, then made their way together down to the dining room where they were shown to their table.

After dinner they went straight out onto the street again and made their way over to the theatre, not wanting to be too far back in the queue. As it was there was quite a line. It took them a good twenty minutes to purchase their tickets, and some sweets and an ice cream cone each at the kiosk, but eventually they were inside. Ned sat and enjoyed the film except that Ian kept interrupting with his quiet criticism of the ships and rigging, analysing every minor detail until finally people around them also started becoming restless and kept turning to him to shoosh.

Michael thought is was boring, too romantic by half, and wanted to go home but they made him sit and he did, mumbling to himself all the way through. By the time it was over they each had their homework clear in their minds, and walked quietly together back to the hotel where they went up to their rooms and straight to bed.

Next morning in the kitchen Ned was given an apron and loaf after loaf of bread to slice and put through the toaster. He had never seen one of these new-fangled electric element toasters before, but the idea seemed sound and it made a lot of toast very quickly, so he picked it up soon enough and by the end of breakfast felt he had achieved something. The real work began when the dirty dishes started coming in from the dining room, though as he worked at washing them up he noticed Mrs Donovan out the corner of his eye watching him, and talking quietly with her chef.

He came over and spoke quietly in his ear, "Mrs Donovan does not want you here doing the dishes. The girls can do that."

Ned looked up at him in relief, then dried his hands on the towel and turned to follow him across the huge expanse of kitchen where he was handed over to the lady of the house. He followed her then, along the back passage to the linen room where he was outfitted with a smartly pressed page's uniform. He left his day clothes there for Mrs Abbott the laundress to attend to, then followed Mrs Donovan obediently back along the passage and through the kitchen into the dining room where he was handed over to Patrick.

She looked down at him.

"Patrick will teach you the business, Ned," she said to him, then glancing across at a table where one of the waitresses appeared to be engaged in conversation, graciously bustled off to attend to the matter.

Ned looked up at Patrick, then down at his crisp starched uniform and shrugged.

"That used to be mine," the other grinned, then glanced down appraisingly. "It fits you pretty well, just right."

"So," Ned wanted to know, "what do you want me to do?"

"All right, you stand here at the till. As our guests finish their meal the girls will give them a tray with a docket, like this."

He showed him a little silver tray, and an invoice from a stack of small papers on a spike next to the till.

"When they bring the money over, ring it up and give them the receipt. See, it will print out here. Then you put the docket on the spike." He paused a moment. "If they leave some money in the tray it is a tip. That means they are happy with the service, and you put that in the jar here, under the counter."

"We divide it up later," he added, smiling. "That's our bonus, all of us. We get the extra in our pay at the end of the week."

Ned nodded thoughtfully, then watched attentively as Patrick showed him how to work the till. As each girl brought the money over he ran it through. Each time he made a mistake he was made to do it again until he got it right. It would be much quicker to do it in my head, he thought at first, but resigned himself to operating the machine and as the morning wore on found he was working quickly and accurately.

Eventually Patrick left him to it, and only during a lull in trade did he come over to help him clear the till and leave a small float there to provide change. There were still patrons coming in for a late breakfast and morning tea, then finally they were clear and the girls began to change the starched white linen and reset the tables for lunch.

In the small office Mrs Donovan entered the receipts into a big ledger, and sat him down next to her to explain how the trail of paperwork kept the whole business in good order with three separate accounts for the house, kitchen and dining room, and two more for the public and lounge bars at the front of the building where Mr Donovan himself held sway.

Ned was astonished at the size of the business and how many people worked there. He knew it was a grand building but had no idea how busy it was even late at night, and in the wee small hours of the morning. It made him think about Michael living here in the midst of it all, with no interest in the place whatsoever, and it gave him pause.

Early on Monday morning Mr Donovan drove them all back to school just in time for breakfast.

By the end of term Ned realised that the three of them had begun to cement their new friendship in ways he had not expected. They had both opened up to him, and shared their secrets with him, and for some time he worried over how he was going to return the compliment. He wanted to invite them home for the holiday; that was his real interest, and in the end simply let the matter of Angus slip. Whatever he decided things were going to happen anyway, so he shrugged resignedly and for the last few weeks set his mind to his schoolwork and football training.

CHAPTER THIRTEEN

Sandy was right in one respect at least; things do have a way of resolving themselves without Ned having to worry about it. One afternoon in the last week of term he was late returning from a cross-country run. All the other boys had finished their showers and were dressing for dinner when he came in. Quickly he stripped and wrapping a towel around himself ran down the dormitory to the ablution block, and hurried to turn on a shower and get himself clean.

Not expecting anyone else to be there he was startled as a figure moved out suddenly from behind one of the toilet cubicles.

"Don't worry, it's only me." It was Angus, dressed this time in riding britches.

Ned stared at him, disbelieving, "You are not Angus. He is a lot older. No, you are too young. You are younger than me." Then finally, "What are you doing here anyway?"

"I can be as young as I want," Angus replied simply. "Peter sent me. He is not well and wants to see you. He is going to die soon. He needs to tidy a few things up before he goes."

He thought about that a moment.

"That's fair enough," he said finally, then glanced thoughtfully at the other boy. "I will be home in a couple of days. I am bringing some friends with me."

"Yes, we know."

"Collins!" A loud voice came from the doorway. It was Burgie. Angus disappeared in the steam vapour as suddenly as he came.

"I am sorry I was late back from my run, Sir," Ned called back.

"Hurry up then. Who is the other boy with you?"

"There is nobody else, only me, Sir."

"I saw you with someone, boy, and heard you talking. I brook no lies in my house."

"Excuse me, Sir, I was just talking to myself. I am running late, that's all."

The house master came all the way in and glanced about him, but saw no one apart from Ned standing there under the shower, then shook his head in astonishment and walked out again muttering.

"Hurry up and catch the other boys then, Collins," he called back over his shoulder as he disappeared himself into his quarters.

Ned did so, and quickly turning off the shower dried hurriedly and ran back to his bed and dressed. Opening his locker door he combed his hair, then satisfying himself that he looked reasonably tidy ran out and down the stairs then along the path toward the dining room, and caught up with the others just as they entered the building.

Michael and Ian held a place for him in the queue, and he was panting as he joined them.

"You look as if you have seen a ghost." Ian stared closely at him.

Ned started. "What made you say that?"

"What is going on?" Michael wanted to know.

"I am late, that's all. I went around that bald hill to make up another couple of miles. It took a bit longer than I thought."

"That too," Ian interrupted, "but what else?"

He sighed, glancing from one to the other. The line had started to move into the dining room by then so he said simply, "I'll tell you later all right, after dinner, I promise."

As promised, he did, though hesitating at first and they had to prod him to start. There was half an hour of free time before prep and while some of the boys went to the library or played snooker and darts in the games room, the three went for a long walk around the big playing field.

Finally, well away from the buildings and clear of any others he asked almost absently, "What made you ask me if I had seen a ghost?"

They both looked at him.

"Well, it just came out, didn't it." Michael said.

"And you reacted like it was true." Ian added.

He thought about that. They had got to know him pretty well, that was certain. After a while longer he stopped, and turned to both of them.

"I have this cousin, you see, actually my second cousin through my mother. I should say I had this cousin, because he was killed in a riding accident, but I can't rightly say that, because he isn't really dead. He is the ghost, all right, and he comes to see me sometimes. He was waiting for me in the showers when I got back. Burgie saw him too, or thought he did. That's what happened."

They said nothing at that, so neither did he and they started back. It was not until they were close to their classroom again that he started to finish what he had been trying to say.

"His name is Angus. His brother Hamish died in Belgium during the Great War, so it was up to him to inherit the family properties. Then when he died I was the next in line, that was all. I really don't know much else yet, all right. You have to promise not to say anything to anyone about it, either of you, it's serious all right. Promise."

They both nodded sombrely.

"Cross your heart and spit and a curse on your family and hope to die!" he said fiercely, suddenly scared himself, starting to lose his sense of what was real and close.

The others stopped, nodding.

"It's all right, Rat. Don't get upset." Ian said quietly, then added, "You shouldn't have said that, just now. We are your friends. You should know better than that by now."

"Yes, Rat, that's right," Michael said. "We never made you promise anything like that, neither of us."

"So you believe me then?"

"Christ Almighty, Rat Bloody Collins, sometimes you're a real dead shit, you know that!" Ian groaned, and smacking his head with his hand turned and walked away with Michael on his heel.

At that a fourth voice spoke from behind Ned.

"Don't I have any say in this?" Angus said, somewhat too loudly. "I mean, after all it was my fault nobody else's."

The two froze, then turned slowly to look back. Michael went as white as a sheet and his hand dropped to his crotch to stop wetting himself, then fell flat on his back in a dead faint. Ian simply stared, the colour drained from his face as well.

"I am Angus," Angus introduced himself, "really."

Ian didn't move, but stood there mouth agape.

Ned intervened. "Angus, this is my friend Ian," he said. "That's Michael."

Angus cocked his head at them, then turned to speak, "Ned, I am really sorry about all this. I shouldn't have let Striker have his head like I did . . ."

"Rat," Ian interrupted. "His friends call him Rat."

"What?"

"He eats rats, that's why."

"Ah, shut up, Ian," Ned glared at him, then turned to Angus.

As he looked at him he noticed something odd about the way he held his head, as if he had a permanently stiff neck, then glanced away thinking about what old Peter had told him about the accident. He bit his lip, then to distract himself bent down seeing instead to Michael. He wiped his brow and shook him awake, then pulled him up off the ground to sit with his head between his knees a moment longer while he had recovered.

"It's all right, Michael," he said softly, then helped him to his feet. Ian bent down to help, and as they stood him up as one the three turned to face Angus again.

He was shifting from one foot to the other, gesticulating in some embarrassment.

"I am sorry, Ned, I really am. We bought this new colt, a real thoroughbred. It was such a thrill for me to take him out for a ride, that was all."

"It's all right. Stop talking about it." Ned interrupted, his temper still short for comfort.

"Everyone is upset," he added. "You have put me in it now, and I don't know what's happening any more. And anyway, you have to stop appearing and disappearing suddenly like that. We'll have to work something out, all right."

He stopped at that and took a deep sigh, then turned to his two schoolmates standing there completely bewildered.

"I guess you won't want to come over for the holidays now, eh?" he asked sheepishly.

They turned to glance at one another, then back at him.

Ian cocked his head, frowning. "What would make you say something stupid like that, Collins?"

"I just thought . . ."

"No you didn't think, did you," Ian interrupted. "You are not thinking at all. We are your friends, right? What is the use of friends unless you're in strife?"

"Yes, Rat," Michael put in his threepence worth, by now somewhat recovered. "What sort of friend are you? You didn't carry on when we told you our secret stuff, so why would we?"

He nodded briefly, then the three turned to Angus again.

"Deal?" Ian wanted to know.

"Righto, deal," Angus replied, smiling now, then turned back to Ned somewhat more seriously.

"But I have to go now, Ned, really. Peter needs to talk to you. When you get home Dad will be at your place, and he will bring you out in the truck maybe after the footie game on Saturday. Is that all right with you?"

"Yes, no problem," Ned said absently, then turned to look him in the eye. "I'll be there. We'll be there, I mean. See you then all right."

At that Angus turned and waved, then smiling shyly instead of simply disappearing slowly faded as he walked away, giving them a chance to see him off. Once he had gone the three stood there a moment, then without another word made their way into their classroom for prep. There were still two more exams to sit, Physics tomorrow afternoon, Wednesday, and Chemistry the last on Thursday morning before they left for the term holiday.

By Thursday afternoon after it was all over Ned thought he had done well enough. As he packed his things to leave he knew his marks would show through, and decided then that everything was going to be all right. Folding the last of his shirts and trousers and socks and underpants into his bag he simply did up the clasps and taking up the bag walked out and started down the stairs.

His parents were halfway up and lost in thought he bumped straight into them. It was a good thing they saw him coming otherwise he would have tripped on the load he carried, but instead he looked up at them, then shyly leaving his things there on the landing he led them back upstairs. Ian and Michael were making their own way along the aisle through scattered parents and half-packed luggage so they waited for them there at the top of the stairs, and as they met up turned again and made their way back down together.

Smiling and jostling, as shyly they clambered into the back seat of the car, and Arthur dutifully took the wheel and had them out on the road home in good time. The long journey went quickly enough, once they had cleared the inland slopes and made their way out onto the seemingly endless plains through town after town, until nearly dark they finally arrived in the back roads of Weethangara and pulled off onto their street. Sandy's old truck was parked in front of the house and as they pulled into the driveway he came out onto the front verandah to greet them.

Ned nodded to him and smiled as they lugged their bags inside, then led his friends all the way down the passage to the back porch where they had the spare sleepout opposite his. Leaving their things on beds they went straight back inside and into the kitchen, where his mother had started at the stove knowing they would all be hungry. She put her spoon down and wiped her hands on her apron as they entered, then reached out and gave him a big hug and held him close. Still holding her hand when Sandy came into the kitchen with Arthur he introduced Ian and Michael, then without further ado they sat down for dinner.

Of course they were hungry, and not another word was spoken until they had made their way through a roast forequarter with all the vegetables and gravy, followed by a steamed pudding covered with a rich yellow egg custard. It was not until tea was served that they found their voices again and the small talk started, about school and how the exams went, and football, and since they all knew the Donovans allowed Ian to tell of his family, and his mother's plans for their small farm.

Eventually the talk died down, and Ned sat quietly for a moment eying Sandy until he caught the old man's attention.

"What is it, lad?" he asked softly.

"We had a visitor the other day."

"Did you now?"

"Yes. He is very worried about Peter Foley, said he wanted to see me."

Sandy looked around the table at the grave faces, all staring at Ned, the mood cold suddenly. He coughed politely then stood to excuse himself from the table, then motioned the boy to follow. Hand on his shoulder he led him out and down the passage to the front verandah. It was chilly outside with the first of the evening dew, since the sun was now well down and it was dark. There was enough light from the lamp in the front room at that end near the driveway, so they sat there opposite one another to continue the conversation.

After a long pause Ned took his cue and continued.

"He is really sorry about what happened, Sandy, and all the trouble he caused. But right now he is worrying about Peter. Is he sick or something?"

"He is dying," the other said simply, then cocked his head thoughtfully. "There is nothing wrong with him apart from old age, like myself. I guess you could say he decided it was time to go, and he wants to tidy his things."

Ned nodded. That seemed to him eminently sensible, and he sat back thinking that was probably the way he would like to go too, when the time came, but as he began slipping away into that space Sandy interrupted him and brought him quickly back to the present.

He blinked, and stared suddenly frightened. Then he coughed to clear his throat.

"He met Grub and Oddie, did you know that? Michael and Ian I mean."

Then he chuckled, "Michael nearly wet himself when Angus appeared, then fainted, flat strap on his back on the ground. Good thing it wasn't on the concrete or he would have cracked his skull."

"Do you think that is a good idea, young fella?"

Ned looked up at him. "Ah, it's all right. We just had to explain a few things to him about his coming and going, that was all. So he won't scare people like that. Anyway, he is just a boy like us. I think he is a bit lonely, really, and just wants someone to hang around with."

"He can go riding any time he wants to go out."

He thought about that for a moment, then shook his head.

"It's not the same. No, it's all right, don't worry. He will be all right with us."

Sandy continued to gaze intently at him, until finally he retorted, "I don't want to talk about it any more, all right."

The other nodded, wisely now, new respect in his tired old eyes.

"You are a good lad, Ned, that you are. We are on the right track, you and I, so I'll say no more." He pulled his coat around him suddenly. "Ah, it's chilly out here. There is a nice fire inside, and your friends won't get to know us any better our being out here and they inside, will they."

Sandy rose from his chair at that, and as Ned stood he placed his arm affectionately across his shoulders, and together they went back inside.

CHAPTER FOURTEEN

Years later Ned would often think that the next two days were the very best of his life. Sandy was every bit as good as his word, realising that he badly missed his parents after ten weeks away and wanted to be close to them, and went out of his way to keep Ian and Michael amused.

On Saturday he played football with the local team, his home club, and scored three goals from his new position on the forward flank. He was growing quickly now, and lanky like his father but much faster on his feet and extremely fit, so they all cheered every time he took a mark. After the game they waited while he showered, and then the three of them piled into the truck for the trip out to Wyandera, with Arthur and Judy following behind in the car.

When they arrived Everard was at the gate waiting for them, and as they went through Ned caught a glimpse of Peter standing back away from him in the bush, half out of sight. They drove on along the track past the various houses and pulled up again in front of the main house, while Arthur went past and parked the car in the big shed at the other end of the house rather than leave it out in the dew all night.

Auntie Ellie was waiting for them on the front verandah as one by one they trooped past and Ned introduced her to his friends. In the kitchen was another surprise waiting and Ned put down his overnight bag to stare, then smiled in recognition.

"Uncle Don! And Auntie Mollie! Gee, I haven't seen you in years."

Then he stopped as suddenly, and stood there gaping at the two girls sitting there smiling as brightly back at him.

Ian nudged him from behind, then whispered far too loudly, "You didn't tell us you had cousins, Rat."

"Shut up Ian," he said, then turned back apologising. "Um, sorry, these are my cousins Catherine and Elizabeth McKenzie." He grinned then and shoving Ian aside took Michael by the elbow and dragged him forward. "This is my friend Michael Donovan, boy genius and very hard to get along with. And this bad mannered creature behind me is Ian Ramsay. You don't want to know him at all."

Ian cuffed him on the ear and they all fell about laughing, then Ned remembering himself went around to shake Uncle Don's hand before leaning over to give his aunt a peck on the cheek.

By the time he looked up at the others again there was a sharp tension in the room. Ian's and Catherine's eyes had locked together while Elizabeth's face flushed a bright crimson. Ned forgot himself for a moment in wonder, then quickly recovering went back around the table and seizing Ian by the shoulder pushed him bodily out into the passage, bumping right into Sandy coming up from the front door with Ellie and his parents. The old man's eyebrows went up, then when Ned glared at him shrugged and went past into the kitchen. Brooking no nonsense Ned continued shoving Ian further along the passage until they got to their room, which was Angus's old room, and once inside turned on him.

"Stay away from my cousin!" he ordered.

"Too late!" Ian chortled happily. "It's too late, I'm smitten, and it's all your fault."

"Why is it my fault? What are you talking about?"

"Having such ravishing creatures for cousins. And of course such dashingly handsome best friends," he added, chuckling loudly now.

"That's not my fault. Heck, I haven't seen them since Elizabeth was a baby. How would I have known? I didn't even know they were going to be here."

It was all too much, and with Michael standing there grinning from ear to ear he backed off, then shaking his head he stormed out and went back to the kitchen. It was crowded by then. All he could do was glance at Elizabeth and shrug before being taken over by the rest of the family.

Michael more or less followed him with Ian tagging along last, but by that time Auntie Mollie had wisely she thought drawn her daughter close and was keeping a stern eye on things. In the suddenness of events she forgot that the chair on the other side was empty, so not to be outdone Catherine simply motioned Ian to sit there beside her, which he did, and safely ensconced that was the end of the matter; for the time being at least.

Sandy and Arthur looked on bemused, then the old man grinned and shook his head and without saying anything turned to the ice box and retrieved a bottle of cold beer. At the bench took an opener from the top drawer and did the honours.

"Does your Dad let you have a beer, Mr Ramsay?" he wanted to know.

Ian looked up at him and nodded. "Just a small glass, thank you." he said, holding up one hand to indicate with his fingers. Catherine had her hand on his knee under the table, and he was trying not to squirm.

"Mr Donovan?" Sandy continued.

"No thank you, I don't like it. Ginger beer is all right, or cordial."

He took down two small glasses and poured them, handing one to Ian and the other to Ned without asking. Ned took the glass and the old man reached up and ruffled his hair in affection as he did so, then turned his attention to the other men. Taking another bottle from the ice box and opener in hand, he led them out into his study at the front for a bit of peace and quiet.

"Catherine, you can help me with dinner," Ellie said once the men had gone. "Edward, you take your friends to your room please and unpack your things. I will give you a call when we are ready."

Nobody moved for a moment.

"Now, Catherine," Ellie said sharply, then turned to the boys. "And you. Off you go."

As they left she was heard to say, "We will have some manners in this house young lady. There is plenty of time for kanoodling once you come of age, but until then you will respect the good name of this family."

Catherine started to argue but Ellie pulled her up short, while out in the passage Ned simply glared at Ian, then nodded. "Just remember that yourself Mr Errol Bloody Flynn."

Ian stared at him a moment, stunned. "Rat, sorry. I forgot myself." Then he blurted, "but you have to admit she is a real sort, isn't she. I am going to marry her, and that's the end of that."

"Well, yes, all right," Ned sighed, then shrugged again and looked at him seriously. "I'm going to be your best man, is that what you're saying?"

"Ah, cut it out you two," Michael stepped in, his mood waning as well now. "I am going to have a shower and get cleaned up. You finish your beer."

Ned looked at him. "Down the end there, on your right," he pointed, then took Ian by the arm and led him back up the passage to the front parlour where the men were sitting talking softly.

"Sit down, boys," Arthur said when they came in, then, "Please excuse us, Ian, we have quite a lot of family business to discuss. I hope you don't mind."

He simply shrugged, then Ned broke in. "Well, it looks pretty much like he is going to marry Catherine, so I guess that makes him family already."

The men snorted as Don sat shrewdly taking the measure of him, then after a moment simply nodded and without a word took up the second bottle and refilled everyone's glass.

"Don runs one of our bigger stations further up north, Ian, right up there in southwest Queensland. A place called Eurongera," Arthur explained. "We run a lot stock up there when the rain is good, then bring the rest back down as stores when it gets too dry and finish them off either here or down in the Western Districts. Occasionally we run them up in the high country if need be."

Ian's ears pricked up at that, and noticing the sharp change in his expression and the obvious interest he showed the men relaxed and went on with their business.

"Ian would make a good agent, Dad, he can work with you," Ned said suddenly. "He is real sharp figuring things out."

The men looked up, reappraising the boy, then nodded quietly and went quietly back to their conversation. After a short while the two boys drained their small beer and excused themselves.

Michael was back from his shower by then so Ian disrobed and wrapping a towel around himself went off to take his turn. By the time he had finished and returned to their room to dress for dinner Angus was sitting there in his favourite chair near the fireplace, which seemed quite a lot bigger on him now, and he looked up as Ian came in. They all waited while he pulled on his underpants and trousers, then put on his shirt and tucked it in.

His hair was still disheveled, but as he sat on his bed to put on his shoes and socks Ned interrupted him.

"Ian, we need to ask you a real big favour, all right."

"What favour?"

"Well, it's just that you are not to say anything about Angus to Catherine or Elizabeth, all right. Not ever. Or Uncle Don or Auntie Mollie either. They don't know anything about what happened, only that Hamish and Angus were killed and I have to take their place. That's it."

Ian looked up, seriously for a moment, then after thinking about it further said. "I promise, Ned, don't worry. You don't have to press me on things like that."

"You weren't even supposed to know, or Michael, but that was his choice, not mine."

Angus sitting there nodded briefly, then with a faint smile faded away again as he too had promised he would.

CHAPTER FIFTEEN

Dinner that night was very special. Ned sat quietly all the way through thinking about how wonderful life can be, everyone was so happy. Again, he was to think later, it was almost as if there was a spell on the place; a glamour on them bringing everything into order, so enchanted was their evening together.

He went to bed content and dropped off straight to sleep, tired nonetheless after such a full day. I was not until the wee hours of the morning that he became restless; shadows and voices intruding on his sleep and bringing with them wild dreams that made him toss and turn.

As the hours wore on there grew louder a backdrop of keening and wailing that pierced him to the core, and the voices became louder and louder again until suddenly Angus appeared and took him by the hand. That calmed him, and he was led outside or so it seemed, in his dream at least, and across the open ground past the houses back up the track near the front gate, and into the bush there along the fence where Peter always appeared whenever the truck arrived.

Everard was there, and led them into a cleared camp where Sandy and Peter stood waiting to greet them. Peter's eyes caught him, staring at him, drilling through him, until Sandy put up his hand and it stopped suddenly. Angus was standing just a little behind him but he felt him smiling, and he saw Everard smiling.

"Ned, lad," Sandy said almost from a distance, "we have to go now. What can be done has been done. It is up to you now. Don't be worried, these boys are all with you, and your friends are good . . ."

He did not hear the rest of it. Everything began to fade away suddenly and the keening and wailing returned. He was back in his bed, and tossing and turning again when he heard dimly his father's voice, then his hand on his shoulder shaking him gently awake. He opened his eyes and slowly brought his face into focus.

"Dad?"

"Ned, come with me will you."

"What happened?"

Arthur looked down at his hands, then back again.

"Son, your Uncle Sandy has passed away. He died in his sleep."

He nodded and glanced away, then sat up and getting out of bed put on his bathrobe against the cold, and his slippers. Outside the chill keening went on and on, for real now and he looked up and cocked his head realising what had taken place.

"Peter has gone too." he said.

"That's true, he has. How did you know that?"

"I didn't. It must be, I mean, for the women to be wailing like that. Sandy said he was going to die soon."

It was still dark outside, barely dawn with only the first light appearing, and it was deathly cold. Their breath clouded about them along the passage and they rubbed their hands together until they reached the kitchen where Don had the fire going in the stove, and they crowded around it.

"You all right, son?" he wanted to know.

Ned simply nodded. "How is Auntie Ellie?"

The men glanced across at one another. "The women are with her."

"Is everyone else all right?"

"Yes. Ned, it was expected."

He nodded, distracted, quietly to himself, then turned to go. He stopped at the door and nodded again briefly, then made his way back down the passage to his room and went back to bed. A few hours later he woke again to see Michael and Ian sitting there watching him. He got up and pulled on his robe, then bent for his slippers. Standing and doing up his robe he glanced aside briefly then looked up at them, and motioned them out ahead of him. Glancing back Angus was sitting there at the fireplace just out of the corner of his eye, and he cocked his head and nodded and followed his friends down to the kitchen for breakfast.

There was a bustle and arranging things in the study, but he ate the meal prepared for him then went back up and changed into his day clothes. Coming out again he stopped to see what was happening, and saw everyone crowded around a big old coffin in the front room. He went in to see Sandy laid out there cold, with no complexion left, and thought that didn't look quite right.

There was something missing. The loud wailing outside disrupted his thoughts, then he went back over to the coffin and looked Sandy right in the face. He stepped back.

"He doesn't want to be stuck in here, inside here," he said abruptly, then glanced quickly up at Ellie and away again, embarrassed.

She looked at him.

"Yes, he would never have wanted that," she said quietly, almost to herself.

She stood and looked around the room, then calmly out loud, "How quickly we forget those days, how soon they are gone. Those boys grew up together, he and Peter; they were brothers, like family, in those times, when all this was still station country, out away from everything."

At that she stood and went out onto the front verandah, and went to sit there on one of the chairs, pulling it away from the wall out next to the railing, then taking off her bonnet began to wail out loud, her shrill keening slowly echoing from the camp down below, past the old houses, more and more until the air was full of it.

The rest of them carried Sandy's coffin out onto the verandah next to her, not wanting to take it any further, then watched as the camp brought Peter's tired old body on long sheets of stringy bark out onto the open ground between the houses.

Dan and Everard were there, watching them, and on cue Ned stepped down and looking back up at Arthur cocked his head, smiling, and they took up Sandy's coffin again and carried it down and out across the yard to set it down beside Peter.

The two families sat across from one another as the dawn came and all through the morning, exchanging stories and crying even more, about a lot of things, then straight after noon without any signal suddenly the men went across the yard and right there where the track came up from the front gate set about digging two graves side by side. They buried them there and went home; apart from prayers without another word to each other.

Only later toward evening, as it was starting to get dark, there was a polite knock at the door and Catherine went to answer it. She came all the way back along the passage to the kitchen to announce that there were two gentlemen to see Ned. It was Daniel and Everard, so he went back inside to get his warm coat than came back out to sit with them on the verandah.

They sat there, then after a while Dan looked up and said, "Everything cutting loose now, boss. What's goin' on?"

He glanced past him at Everard, then sat back thoughtfully for a while.

"Nothing," he said finally. "I don't know past that, not really. If I knew I would tell you, all right. Everyone says there is going to be another war. I don't know really. Maybe Auntie Enid Clancy will cause us trouble. Maybe Sam and those boys will be up to something. I don't know."

Everard nodded and said quietly to his brother, "Everybody sad now. Crying too much. Come home now, all right."

Then he looked at Ned, his eyes glinting in the dark. "No worry, boss. We like you, all right."

He stood and left, disappearing into the night, then Dan stood to follow. He looked back past the bottom step nodding as he went and Ned nodded back, then he too disappeared.

CHAPTER SIXTEEN

Early next morning Arthur and Don drove into town to consult with their family doctor. They had started to worry about whether they should have buried Sandy without a death certificate, although Arthur had long served as Justice of the Peace and his statement made against their medical records would be sufficient he felt to justify natural causes due to old age. But the paperwork had to be completed and they went off in the car to do that.

After moping around the house all morning Ned finally went off to find Everard. The camp was still keening and the sound haunted him. He knew it would go on for weeks.

Steeling himself he walked quietly along the track past the houses until other voices began to echo back and forth. The other boy stepped out of the bush then and greeted him with a shy smile, and motioned him for to follow. He recognised the path now as the one along which they had led him in his dream. Quickly they came into another cleared camp with a couple of humpies there ordinarily out of sight behind the houses. Daniel was there too with some of the old men and women, and they all stood when he came in and politely shook hands before sitting again. They waited silently watching him, until he spoke finally.

"I just wanted Dan and Everard to show us around the place. Mum and Auntie Mollie are looking after Ellie. Dad and Uncle Don had to go and see the doctor, that's all."

He looked away then back again, and shrugged.

"It's no good for us kids to be sitting around," he said quietly. "Everyone is crying, and this was supposed to be our holiday. So I thought maybe we should get out of the house."

"Who that other boy?" Dan wanted to know. "That old father worrying about him, eh?"

Ned looked around, confused. "They are my friends, from school."

They looked at him.

He shook his head, thinking. "Who, Michael, or Ian?" he wanted to know.

They spoke quietly among themselves, then Dan turned to him and said, fairly directly, "That one, Ian. How you know 'im?"

He cocked his head at that, then smiling raised his hand and wagged his finger at them, and shook his head.

"He'll tell you if he wants to. That's his business. He's good, he's my friend, all right."

Dan turned back to the elders and they spoke quietly again, then he turned to Ned once more.

"He close-up you like brother, eh? That right?"

"Yes. Maybe. But that's his business too. Let's wait and see."

Everard spoke up at that, taking on his older brother, and the camp went silent.

"That grandfather worry too much, close up finish." He tapped his head, then stood and looked around him, and taking Ned by the elbow led him away again back toward the main house.

"What is the matter with Daniel?"

"People scared now, that's all," Everard said quietly. "That father big magic man from old times, keep everybody safe. 'E gone now, and that Uncle. Both finish."

Ned looked at him more closely.

"But he taught you, didn't he?"

"Maybe. Little bit." The other shook his head, worried, then shrugged almost to himself. "Not much fun, that business."

They walked on a little further, then Ned shrugged as well. "We won't talk about it then, all right, just wait until things come and see what happens. Show me the place."

Everard nodded, then stepped off the track and made his way along a wide path to a smaller building, and stepped up onto the porch and went inside. There was a blackboard on the east wall with wide windows to the north allowing the sun to stream in on warm days, and three neat rows of desks with slates and chalk. At the back of the room were neat shelves stacked with books.

"That old Auntie teach kids here; call 'er granny, properly. School 'ouse, this one."

Just then they heard footsteps on the porch, and Michael and Ian came in with the two girls in tow.

"We saw you down the track." Ian said.

"And we need to ask you something," Catherine interrupted.

"Ask me what?"

"Can we stay? Elizabeth and I? Please say yes."

"Mother thinks it is a good idea. Ellie needs someone to be with her," Elizabeth piped in.

He stood back at that, astonished, shaking his head.

They all stared at him.

"Does than mean no?" Michael was the first to speak, while the girls looked on dumbfounded.

"What? No. I mean, why are you asking me?"

Ian's eye's drilled into him, and it was his turn to shake his head. "It's your place now, Rat."

Ned stared back, then looked away embarrassed. He glanced at Everard who stared back at him as one with the others, then it hit him finally what this was all about. He turned and sat at one of the desks and stared at the neatly arranged slate and chalk there, then at the other desks and up at the blackboard.

"Can you teach?" he said suddenly, to nobody in particular, then turned to Catherine and asked her directly. "Catherine, can you teach? Kids, I mean."

"Yes, of course," she nodded, "I was going out to work as a governess. I've completed by Certificate, but now this has happened."

He looked at her and nodded. "What about these kids? Can you teach them too?"

"Yes," she nodded again.

"All right, I'll give you a job then. You can help Ellie run this school."

"And what about you, Elizabeth? What do you want to do."

"She has to go back to school . . ." Catherine started, but he held up his hand.

"I have to return to school," Elizabeth answered, then added, "I was thinking of spending my holidays here instead of going all the way home every time. It takes three whole days."

He sat back at that, glancing from one to the other until he fixed his gaze on Ian, which he held thoughtfully for what seemed an eternity, until finally he simply nodded then stood and went out the door. Out on the porch he paused a moment, then through the door indicated for Everard to follow and the two of them stepped down and made their way further along the track toward the houses.

Passing by the old stables, he turned and went inside. The place was dilapidated and untidy, and stank of stale old straw.

"Do you ride, Everard?"

"Like the wind, boss."

He thought about that a moment, the words suddenly familiar, and smiled and nodded then walked out again. The rest of the morning they spent walking over the whole place, from one end of the homestead to the other and right around the boundary looking out over the station proper.

CHAPTER SEVENTEEN

Eventually they heard a loud Cooee! from the main house and a clanging from the big flat iron triangle hanging outside the kitchen door, so he took his leave of Everard and went across for lunch. As he entered by the back door it was good to see Ellie up and about, and busy at the stove.

He went over and put his arm around her and she squeezed his hand tightly, but elbowed him away gently indicating that she wanted him seated at the table with the others while she finished the gravy. Finally she took her place and they waited while she said grace, and their meal blessed they quietly ate.

Halfway through dessert Ned finally asked her how she was doing.

She looked up at him and nodded. "As well as can be expected," she smiled.

"Are you happy for Catherine and Elizabeth to stay? Elizabeth still has to go to school, but Cath can help you with the children's lessons."

He paused thoughtfully, watching her face.

"I'm sure Mum will be out every other day, with Dad still going away a lot, if she can learn to drive the car," he grinned.

"That is enough of your cheek, young man," his mother looked up and flashed at him. "I've had my driver's license since before you were born, don't worry about that."

At that everyone started to speak at once, until after a while they all settled again and Mollie got up and pushing her chair in took her plate across to the sink. She then began to clear the table of dirty dishes leaving them to finish their sweets.

"Rome wasn't built in a day," Ellie said simply. "We have another week or so, and when your father gets back from town with Uncle Arthur we can have our little chat then."

They continued eating quietly, until Catherine finished and she got up to pour their tea, drawing a smile from Ellie as her mother looked on a moment, then glanced away and went back to cleaning up the dishes. One by one they made their way to their rooms while Ned sat a while longer, talking quietly with Ellie and his mother and auntie. After a while he went down to his room and called Ian out, and they went out onto the back verandah.

Outside he turned to face him directly, then looked out over the landscape and back at him again.

"What?" Ian wanted to know.

"Um, you're my friend, all right. You are a good friend, I don't think anything else about you."

The other looked at him.

"I mean, I don't want you to take this the wrong way."

He paused, looking at his friend directly now, and when he said nothing relaxed a little then continued.

"What I mean is, my family have been out here a long time now. I am the fourth generation in this country, did you know that?"

Still no reply.

"Sandy's father went back once, after he made a lot of money in horses mainly, and cattle, on a fast clipper ship just to show off, but aside from that we have sort of adapted."

He turned to face him then.

"Your family have just come out. You have a better education, and move faster. You are clever, you know. But here things happen more slowly."

Ian reached over a clipped him in the ear at that, and started laughing. He pushed him away.

"What's so funny?"

"I thought you were going to tell my I can't go out with Catherine, or something like that."

"What? No. We are happy about that. Ellie likes you. That's not what I am talking about, nothing like that at all, except maybe you move too fast like I said."

"Ha! Haha! Like Errol Flynn. That's me, yes, Errol Flynn."

"No you're not!" Ned pushed him away starting to laugh himself. Then he jumped at him grabbing him around the neck and tossing him off the verandah onto the lawn, and they rolled around wrestling until Ned with his greater fitness had him pinned.

"Just do the right thing," he said panting, gasping for breath. "All right?"

Ian looked him fair square in the eye at that, tongue tied, then nodded.

"Odd Nuts."

His eyes narrowed at that, and in a sudden rage he tore his arm loose and whacked Ned on the side of the head, overbalancing him, and he took the advantage and held him down, fiercely now.

"I agreed, all right!"

Ned lay back, his eyes fixed on him, but made no move to defend himself. Ian pressed himself on him but he did nothing, even when he hit him again and again. He simply held his stare, then as the moment passed physically relaxed.

Eventually Ian relaxed as well.

"You didn't have to say that," he said finally.

Ned looked away, then back again, and nodded.

"We understand each other then?"

Ian let go and rolled over onto the lawn, and lay there for a moment his arm over his eyes, then sat up and wiped the tears away.

"Bloody Scunge Percival can be a real bastard, you know."

"But we aren't," Ned said after a moment. "We don't hurt people like that."

"Oh yeah? So what was that all about?"

"Just making sure; see how you'd react."

He turned to him then.

"Ian, sorry, this was only supposed to be a holiday, like at your place. We knew Peter was dying, but nobody thought Sandy would go with him."

"Cranky old bugger," he added a moment later.

They lay on their backs on the lawn for a while, then suddenly Ian said, "Does that mean I can marry Catherine?"

Ned rolled over and looked at him, then stood and turned to go.

"Maybe," he said almost to himself halfway up the back steps, then disappeared quickly inside.

Just inside the door he bumped into Michael on his way out, wanting to see what was going on, then Ian came rushing in hot on his heels and they collided, and went sprawling along the passage. He whacked his nose hard on Michael's forehead on the way down, and came up with blood spurting everywhere. Michael was groaning on the floor, his hand to his head, and with the blood everyone thought he had been injured and ran to help him.

Ned sat up holding his nose, then realising what had happened jumped up and pushed his way through to the bathroom where he rushed to the basin and let his nose go. He turned on the tap and rinsed his face, then looked in the mirror to check the damage.

"Ned?"

"It's all right, mother. Just an accident."

She came in to check on him anyway, then with one look made him sit on the edge of the bath with his head back. Taking a face cloth from the basin she rinsed it under the cold tap then wiped his face clean. It was a little while before the blood stopped. His nose was bent badly out of shape, and when Ellie came in she took one look at it then promptly taking his head in her arms pressed her thumb sharply against his nose and pushed everything back into place. She held his head back, then nodded with a practiced eye and went out again muttering to herself.

"I think you had better find something useful to do, Ned, before you get into any more strife," his mother said.

He shook his head in frustration. "I was just going to organize everyone to come and help clean the stables, Mum. It's all right, don't worry about it."

She glanced at him, one eyebrow raised, inclining her head in askance. He simply looked at her helplessly.

"You had better get on with it then."

He turned to the sink and started cleaning up but she dismissed him saying she would do it, just take the circus outside.

He went out at that, and brushing past the crowd in the passage went straight out the door.

"Come on," he turned and said, then stepped down off the verandah and started across the lawn toward the stables. Elizabeth ran to catch him, then caught his arm to pull him up and turned him around so she could see his swollen face. The others stared, one after the other as they caught up, but he shrugged and shook his head then turned on his heels again.

At the back shed he entered and took two shovels and a broom then carried them across to the stables. There was an old pitch fork there already so he leaned the other gear against the door, then went inside and started to pitch the mouldy old straw into neat piles. Ian took one of the shovels, and without a word began shifting the mess out the back door where he threw it onto an old compost heap, then Michael took up the other shovel and did likewise while Elizabeth started sweeping up behind them.

Catherine looked on curiously.

"What are you planning to do, Ned?" she asked finally.

"Uncle Don is bringing some of your stock horses down for us." He looked up. "I want to start a breeding program, stock horses and retrievers. I am going to get some Curly Retriever pups, but later when I leave school, not yet. Maybe I'll build a skeet range as well, later, but horses first. We have to get this place back up to scratch."

He stopped at that and went back to pitching straw. His face hurt and his voice was nasally from his nose being blocked up.

Ian was watching him.

"You are going to have two seriously black eyes, Rat. Do you know that?"

Michael glanced at him and said softly, "I wouldn't say much about it if I were you, Oddie."

Ned looked up at them both. "No, it's all right," he said. "It was my fault, I shouldn't have been mucking around like that."

"It was not your fault, Collins," Ian insisted, then stopped and looked around. "If we have to find someone to blame, ultimately it was all Catherine's fault."

"Me!? Why me?"

"Because you are just too beautiful for words, sweet love, and you stole my heart away is why."

She stood and glared at him, her eyes narrowing, then shook her finger at him. "You'll keep! You mark my words, Mr Clever Ramsay, sir!"

Then she turned sharply away and took the broom from Elizabeth who just stood there giggling, and without another word began to sweep up.

CHAPTER EIGHTEEN

It was late summer and hot outside. The teak paneling in the solicitor's office was rimed with a thin layer of dust and a blowfly butted itself loudly against the window trying to get out. Once he had got over the initial shock of learning the full extent of their landholdings, and the number of horses and cattle they ran in total, Ned's mind slipped away as the insect buzz mingled with their lawyer's drone reading out the details of Sandy's will. At length he heard his named called, and he came back from his reverie to see them all looking at him.

"Did you hear all that, Ned?" his father wanted to know.

He nodded absently and leaned forward to inspect a large sheaf of papers thrust in his direction, then absently took the offered pen and began signing, following the old man's finger as they came to page after page. Then it was Stan Donovan's turn, and when he was finished the lawyer himself bent to the task.

When it was all done finally Arthur turned again to ask, "Are you clear with everything, son?"

"Not really," he said.

They all nodded, looking at one another.

"Mr Donovan and Mr Faulkner are your trustees until you come of age. If you need to know anything all you have to do is ask either of them, all right?"

He thought about that for a moment. "Yes, that's all right," he replied, then stood to shake hands.

He was tall and gangly now, having grown rapidly and catching well up with his father during the more than thirty months since Sandy died, with a lot of filling out to do yet and muscle to put on once he left school and physically started to work.

In the meantime Enid Clancy had challenged the will on the grounds that her eldest son Hamish Alexander Clancy was in fact Sandy

McKenzie's not Tom Clancy's offspring, and that he was the rightful heir. But she was unable to provide proof, especially against her sister Ellie's wedding certificate and clear testimony on the date of her engagement. Enid's argument was that her Hamish had been born a mere seven months after Ellie and Sandy were engaged to be married, when his birth certificate showed in fact that it was closer to twelve months. The case was thrown out before it got to trial.

The loss brought the usual bitter tirade, and for some time after Ellie continued to receive long letters from her sister warning her that she would "rue the day" she turned her back on her "own flesh and blood", and let the land out of the family. She sighed to herself, and tied them all neatly with ribbon and left them in the bottom draw of her desk.

As they made their departure from the lawyer's office Ned turned and thanked Mr Faulkner for all the hard work he had done, then followed Arthur and Uncle Don out, with Stan Donovan taking his leave the moment they were on the street.

"Friday night, Ned, as usual?"

"Yes, I'll see you then. Thank you again, Mr Donovan." Then he turned to his father and uncle and wanted to know, "Where to now? Lunch?"

Arthur turned to Don, suggesting, "I think the ladies have a picnic organized, down on the river."

"Is that right? I thought only you and Uncle Don came over."

"No, we are all here, son. Ellie and Catherine are here too, and we picked up Elizabeth on the way through. We thought we might make a trip and be done with it. Don hasn't been this far south since he left the army, after the war."

"You should have told us, Dad. Why didn't you? Nobody said a thing."

"Why, son? Is there a problem? We thought it would be a nice surprise."

"No, I mean, Ian is going to be real upset if he finds out Catherine is here and he isn't allowed out to see her."

The two men glanced at one another, confounded.

"She will want to see him too, I bet. They write to each other twice a week."

"Is that so," Don glanced at him, frowning.

Arthur took control at that. "We had better get this sorted, Don," he said firmly, then led the way back to the car where they got in and drove out to the school again.

There they made their way to the headmaster's office and explained the situation; how the wires had been crossed, that Ian Ramsay was their guest for lunch, and after a quick telephone call to the farm up in the Wellesleys they were issued with a leave chit. Ned raced out along the main corridor to their classroom, precious paper in hand, and after a brief exchange with Burgie emerged friend in tow.

"What is going on?" Ian wanted to know.

"You'll never guess."

"What?"

"Catherine is here with Ellie, and Mum and Elizabeth, and everybody."

Ian stopped dead in his tracks, then glanced at him and away again, taken completely aback.

Not waiting for him to recover Ned grabbed his arm and dragged him physically out to the waiting car, where Arthur opened the door to let them in while Don nodded curtly, then reached over to shake hands. As the car moved off he gazed at him intently. They were right, this boy was one very handsome lad indeed; one flash of those eyes would make any girl swoon, then as he thought about it realised that perhaps they were all better off his being devoted to the one girl else they could all be in strife not too far down the track.

"What are your plans, son?" he asked.

"Well, my father wants me in the navy, Mr McKenzie. If there is a war coming that will be it, I suppose, then after that see what happens. Ned and I are thinking to enlist together."

Ned glanced at him and was about to say something but that moment they were pulling off the road into the riverside park. They could see Uncle Don's big old Chevrolet there under the shade of some trees. Ian was no longer listening anyway.

"Thanks, Ned," was all he said as they pulled up, before opening the door and getting straight out. Catherine likewise it seemed, once she caught sight of him, broke away from the women and with considerable dignity took his hand and walked away briskly along the riverside path with him.

Mollie glared at Don who only shrugged, then called out after the pair, "Ten minutes, young lady."

"Oh, sit down Mollie," Ellie broke in. "Leave them be."

Ned turned to her, but was stopped in his tracks by Elizabeth standing there watching him. He caught her eye and felt himself stir, but quickly glanced away red-faced and bent over to give Ellie a peck on the cheek, then stepped over to his mother and gave her a hug in greeting.

"Sit here with me, Ned," Judith said smiling. "Let me look at you."

He sat and was passed a plate of cold roast chicken with some buttered bread and fresh garden salad. It was Elizabeth again, so he made a space and she sat next to him then busied herself making up plates and passing them around.

"How did you go today, son?"

"I don't really understand all that legal stuff, Mum," he owned. "But it's all right, I got the gist of it. Mr Donovan and Mr Faulkner are the trustees. I guess we'll just have to see how it goes."

He looked at her. "I really only want to get the place up and running properly. If there is a war the country is going to need provisions. We can supply beef. I don't know what else yet."

"You look after yourself first, Ned," Ellie was listening intently. "Sandy never had the chance you have, rest his soul, and you should take it while you can."

"I was thinking about leaving next year, Ellie, once I have done my Intermediate."

"Don't you dare! No, I will not allow it. Absolutely not."

"Now, Ellie," Mollie said. "Let him speak."

"Fiddlesticks! That's enough! You hear me young man. I want your matriculation on my desk, and that will be the end of it. If there is a war you can go to University later, but you will finish your schooling."

The old lady looked around from face to face, her eyes set, rigid in her determination, and they all turned away quietly attending to their picnic. Ned felt Elizabeth's warm presence right next to him pouring him a cup of tea, and he looked down at her hands as he picked quietly at his food. Only once did he glance up at her, and straight away she caught his eye. He looked down again and continued eating. Just at that moment Ian and Catherine arrived back from their walk, trying without much success not to hold hands, and took their place on the big rug. Ellie and Elizabeth made themselves busy again piling food on fresh plates and passing them across, so nothing more was said.

Arthur waited until Ian and Catherine had finished and were sipping their tea, then said finally in his soft reassuring voice, "I do have something to add, and I would like you to listen as well if you don't mind, Mr Ramsay."

They all turned to watch his face.

"The simple fact of the matter is that my son Edward is now the owner and nominal head of a very large pastoral company, in a highly protected industry. No matter what happens the nation must secure its food supply."

Ned looked at him. "What does that mean?"

"What it means is, and Sandy anticipated this in the terms of his will, and while it may not be legally binding of course if the government declares a state of emergency, Ned, you will not be allowed to enlist for war service."

He then looked across at Ian. "Young man, and I know it is not my place to intrude upon your family affairs, but if you are to be joining us in whatever capacity you should be properly appraised of the situation. Am I understood? We would rather you did not enlist either."

Ian nodded, then glanced across. "I will have to talk it over my parents, Mr Collins, if that is all right with you, sir."

"Certainly, of course."

He glanced then at Catherine, then across at Ned and back to Arthur again. "I need to know what it is you will be expecting of me."

"How is your family situation?"

"My father is a brevet commander on half pay, sir. His service was honourable but he is elderly and I am his only son. I have two older sisters." His eyes flashed.

"Go on."

Ned winced. He knew Ian's pride, and what this was doing to him.

Ian cocked his head, then leaned back and said to nobody in particular, "We are on something of a queer street, to tell the truth. My parents can barely keep me at school."

He stopped at that, staring Arthur Collins in the eye, waiting for the next shot, but when it didn't come he turned his head away and look down.

"The school has to send them reminders," he said quietly, almost to himself.

After a pause Arthur nodded quietly.

"Bravely put. I respect your honesty and courage, young man, and your integrity. So, this is my suggestion; it might as well be out of the way," he paused again. "We are in a position now to offer you a bursary, dependent of course on your academic progress. Let's see how we go after that, shall we?"

Ian sat stunned, then slowly nodded to himself, but instead of saying anything rose and walked around to the other side of the car where he paced back and forth. Before long he came back to join the group and when he did Catherine rose and stood next to him, taking his hand.

"Thank you, sir," he said simply, eyes flashing this time at Ned.

"Off you go then," Ellie said brightly, "anyone under twenty five, and leave us in peace."

They looked at her in surprise, then Ned started to chuckle. He stood and leaned over to pat her on the shoulder.

"There is no doubt about you, Auntie Ellie," he smiled happily, and she patted his hand then gently pushed him away.

"Be off with you, lad, and don't be late back."

"We won't," then without thinking he turned and took Elizabeth's hand, and she got up to stand beside him causing everyone to stare, but Ellie simply nodded wisely and turned away to engage Arthur in some detail of business she had in mind.

They wandered off. There was a track leading along the edge of the water and they followed it some way beyond the edge of the park area into more wild and unkempt bush. They heard a sound of splashing and children laughing and went to have a look. It was some boys there in deep water on a bend of the river, and swinging out on a rope from a tall gum tree, so they cut across so as not to disturb them and eventually came to a quiet shady place.

Ned stopped suddenly, alert, and held up his hand. Peeking through the underbrush he saw a small animal sitting on a log out there on the water, eating a small crayfish, and he motioned to the others to look.

"A water rat, eating a yabby," he whispered, then, "and look, over there on the other bank." He pointed tapping his finger in the air to where a platypus had just come up out of the water and was waddling its way up the bank before disappearing down a hole. They waited, enchanted, while the rat finished its meal and busily cleaned its face and whiskers until with a faint 'plop' it disappeared into the water, and they came out of hiding to sit on the short grass along the bank.

It was warm, but nice here under the shade with dragon flies dashing about and small birds trilling and piping to one another.

"I wouldn't have minded a swim, Rat." Ian said finally. He had been thinking about the boys laughing and skinny-dipping around the other side of the bend, and loosened his shirt and tie against the heat.

"Why do you call him Rat, Ian?" Elizabeth glanced at him, wanting to know.

"Because he eats dead rats, and he eats their droppings for desert, and enjoys it, that's why."

Ned grinned, and leaned over and cuffed him on the top of his head.

"Boarding school food, he means."

"Really? Do you like that? I mean, that! Yuk!"

"Well, you make do with what you get." He shrugged. "It's not that bad, with sauce, and a bit of imagination."

He glanced up. "So what is PLC food like?"

They both grimaced.

"The less said about that the better," Catherine said coldly, then looked at him in turn, cocking her head. "So, while we are on the subject, why do you call him Oddie?"

He looked up sharply, half grinning, then stopped himself. "Do I do that?" he paused, stalling for time, then deftly combined the two jokes, "because he is odd, peculiar. He has no palate, and fails to appreciate fine cuisine, that's why."

She glared at him but he gazed back, expressionless, then grinned.

"But I will say this for him, he does have an eye for fine horseflesh."

"Shut up now, Collins, before I clock you good and proper," Ian said quietly, then stood to leave. "We had better be getting back, anyway."

"Oh, not yet," Elizabeth started.

Ned looked at his friend thoughtfully. "Yes, stay a little."

Catherine was up already so they both rose to follow, but instead of going straight back Ned led them away around the next bend in the river, showing them the small things of the bush that had always attracted his attention so. After a while the girls started to go on ahead, bored with it, and he hung back a moment with Ian.

"You are my best friend, Ian. I never met anyone like you. I want you to know that."

"It's all right, Ned."

"No, not quite. Not yet."

"What do you mean?"

"I'm sorry I didn't know your family were struggling like that." He looked closely at his face as he spoke. "That's why you have been acting tough all the time, and coming on the way you have, isn't it. It had nothing to do with your hernia at all, you just let everyone think that."

Ian simply returned his gaze, his eyes wide and glistening just a little. His lips moved slightly as if he were about to speak, but he clamped them shut.

"Percival knew, didn't he," Ned persisted, "that's how he was controlling you, and making you afraid. Until I came along. Isn't that right?"

The other nodded.

"All right, now we know. But it's not your fault, Ian. It's not my fault either me ending up with all this money and property. It's not like it even has anything to do with me," he shook his head in wonderment. "It's just not so easy, like people might think."

The other cocked his head at that, looking through him almost, then Ned caught his gaze and paused, thinking back.

"You remember that day I broke my nose? Do you remember what I was trying to say then, while you were whacking me outside on the lawn?"

He nodded again.

"Our people have been out here a very long time, since the old days. But without Dad Sandy would have been in real trouble. He was always a bit rough and ready; had his mind on other things all the time, but he was right in what he did. I don't know how to explain that any better, and I'm sorry about that sometimes. What I mean is, I am a bit too much like Sandy, I know, and Mum, and so is Elizabeth by the looks of things."

"She is your cousin, Ned."

He looked away at that, then back again, "Second cousin."

Then he looked away and shrugged. "Nobody is going to argue, maybe it is better that way, I haven't even thought about it yet. But I know my family and they will want to hang onto their land, come what may. It's just the way they are, that's all."

"Come along you two, we will be late back if we don't hurry," Catherine called from just ahead.

"Coming!" Ned replied, then turned back quickly to Ian. "Work with Dad, all right? And don't bottle things up on me like that, like you've been doing. Never again, you hear."

Ian simply nodded once more and they both quickened their pace. After a short walk they arrived back at the park together just as the adults were starting to pack up. Catherine quickly pulled Ian behind a tree and kissed him full on the lips, then as quickly pushed him away from her again and walked boldly across to where the cars were parked, somewhat less in the shade now that the sun had moved across.

Ned and Elizabeth watched her intently then gazed into each others eyes for a moment, both slightly foolish suddenly. He reached up and brushed her cheek tenderly with his thumb and she started, trembling just a little, her eyes bright and breathless like an wild filly he thought later, and she smiled shyly and turned quickly on her heel to follow her sister. Together the two girls climbed into the back seat of the big old Chevrolet and sat waiting.

The boys followed quietly, then as Arthur looked up to see them coming they began to hurry. Ned took the last basket from Ellie and handed it to Don who was busily packing the boot, then went around and opened the front side door for her, gently helping her into her seat. As he leaned over she took his face in her hands and gazed gently into his eyes, then in the same motion gave him a peck on the cheek. He squeezed her hand at that, then as he let her go glanced at the back seat to see Catherine staring out the window, tears streaming down her cheeks. Elizabeth simply sat there next to her smiling shyly, and he smiled back then turned to close the door.

Ian was already sitting in the back of Arthur's Ford with the door open waiting for him, not so unhappily it seemed, and Ned simply went over and got in the car.

CHAPTER NINETEEN

The next few years went by almost unnoticed as the boys became lost in the unrelenting routine of study, sport, cadets, weekend leave at Donovan's, and school holidays at either Weethangara or on the farm up in the Wellesley Range. Ned had Ian playing football as well by this time, and found him a good winger with his speed and ball handling ability on the ground. Even Michael he found a place in the seconds team playing his old position in the back pocket, determined to get him fit. In his fourth year at school he was made team captain in the district roundup, then vice-captain of the Mount Tambla combined schools team playing state-wide during the annual Country Week.

Apart from football, gradually he began to spend his free time out at the school farm focusing his attention on selective breeding and blood-stock improvement. Three years in a row he won first a red ribbon then two blue ribbons for his calves at the Mount Tambla agricultural society's annual show.

Prompted by his teachers to try out new ideas he became so enthusiastic that he finally persuaded the farm manager to replace the great Scottish Clydesdales they used for ploughing with the much older breed of French Percherons, which he considered quite as powerful but far more versatile and adaptable. They were more evenly tempered than the energetic Clydesdales or the huge, athletic English Shires which he also liked, and better suited to the school purpose.

During the whole time he saw nothing of Elizabeth; her mother having insisted finally that she come home during holidays so she would have some family at least way out there, whereas Catherine had settled well into her new life under Ellie's patient hand away from her doting mother, and apart from her teaching duties rode every day to become a highly competent horsewoman.

Don had brought down a pair of riding hacks for her on one of his droving trips, and a young thoroughbred for Everard which annoyed Ned somewhat because he had wanted him riding good quality stock horses, and at dinner one night he said so. Nobody said anything, except that next holiday he noticed the race horse gone and in its place three very acceptable Australians, one of which took to him straight away. He rode it then whenever he was back on the station, while Catherine for her part decided to try one of the others at a local camp draft one weekend, and won the event.

Don never said much, just did things. Ned looked at him quite differently from then on.

Ian decided not to matriculate after all, but on completing his Leaving Certificate left school and went to work in Arthur's office in Weethangara full time.

In that year with the war looming ever closer only three of the boys in Mount Tambla sat for University entry, being Edward Arthur Collins and Michael Donovan, and another boy whose father worked as foreman at the saw mill, who came across from the local high school wanting to train as a doctor.

There was nothing much left to do during those last weeks at school apart from their unrelenting study. While the Leaving and Intermediate Certificate students had long completed their schooling and had gone home immediately following graduation, there were still Fourth Year boys with work to complete, and the whole of the Junior and Prep Schools. Being the only two senior boys left Ned and Michael were granted a special place at the duty masters' table in the dining room, as an inspiration to the students, Burgie said.

On the last night at school, after the last exam, they were each formally presented with a handsome desk set in polished teak from Malaya, and after a number of badly told jokes about caps on roofs and other misadventures; he was no comedian, and with the honour of having taught fathers and sons from both families, Mr Burgess after 47 years of teaching announced his retirement.

There was only one thing left to do. When Arthur arrived next morning to pick him up they went to see the headmaster waiting for them in the purser's office. His secretary showed them through where they signed the papers making Ian's bursary award, now that it had been fulfilled, available to others. Their agreement was that should the school encounter a boy with his potential in like circumstances they were to advise his family that help may be available, then after too many fawning handshakes for Ned's liking they were out of there.

Heading down the front steps Arthur glanced across and stopped. Ned sensed his pause and stopped too, distracted for a moment.

"Ned, lad, you are my son and now you have finished school. How well do you trust me?"

He had never thought about that, and stood scratching his head.

"What? Why would you ask me that? You're the best. I could never have asked for a better Dad. I have never questioned you, or Mum, or Ellie, just missed you a lot sometimes. Sometimes a real lot." Then he stopped, looking down thinking of other things, and shook his head.

"Well, maybe that's the best part of it," Arthur said. "No problem. Ned, I just think you always took the weight of things far too early. I know you carry it well; I never could have at your age, but we are not ready to run yet and neither are you."

Ned thought about that. "Yes, all right, what are you thinking about?"

"Don will be down with some more horses next week, and a few days later all going well we have a big mob of cattle to take back up to Eurongera, then some stores have to be shifted across to Dadjari. I want you to go with him, and no reflection on Ian's ability in the office I want you to take him with you."

"We might as well do the whole job in one trip," he added as an afterthought.

Ned stopped him there, frustrated. "All right, good. So what's the problem?" Then he turned away gazing out over the school grounds. "It's Catherine, is it?"

"No, not really, be fair with her, son." Arthur shook his head. "She is a young woman madly in love, and she knows it, and behaves very well in fact." He paused there and Ned looked at him in askance.

"No, we have much bigger fish to fry," he went on. "Clancy and his boys are coming against us, for one thing. They haven't given up yet but we can deal with that if the time comes. There may be instability in government; that's another matter. Mr Stevens looks unsteady, and so does Mr Lyons in Canberra. There is no unity where there should be and it's becoming a worry. Right now when Europe and Asia are under such pressure we have no real idea either where England or America stand with their appeasement policies."

He shook his head. "First I need you both up in the back country to learn the business, that's all. Let's see what happens after that."

Ned nodded and they continued down the steps and across the quadrangle to the car. This new Ford Cabriolet Arthur had purchased was far more modern and stylish, quite unlike Uncle Don's big old 1930 6-cylinder Chevrolet. It had a flat head V8 instead and a dickie seat in the back, and you could let down the hood. He walked around admiring it, then got in and sat back on the seat and rubbed his hand thoughtfully up and down the new leather.

"Ned," Arthur took his place in the driver's seat and looked across at him with real affection, then sighed thoughtfully, "you know, there has never been anyone in our family so well qualified as you, or so well positioned."

He sat back, left hand on the steering wheel and his right hand up to his mouth, with his forefinger tapping absently on the side of his nose.

He chuckled to himself, and shook his head. "I married your mother, and after you were born found one Sandy McKenzie on my doorstep. In many ways I really don't know too much more about anything than that, but that's the way it is."

Ned listened carefully as he spoke, looking down at his hands then up again finally, his right thumb scratching absently at his left palm. "I don't know either, Dad. Let's just take that run up into Queensland, eh, me and Ian. It will be good. I agree with you, all right."

Nothing more said they drove over to the dormitory to pick up his bags, and placing them on the back seat drove off. The school grounds being well out of town they were quickly onto the main road and drove straight off. After a while Ned leaned over to watch the lights and gauges on the dashboard, noticing the way his father manipulated the pedals and changed gear.

"Dad," he said eventually, "seriously, can you teach me to drive this thing?"

Arthur looked over at him, then slowed and pulled up by the side of the road. He got out and went around to the passenger side and opened the door to get in, indicating for Ned to slide across and take the wheel. As he did so he leaned over abruptly and switched the engine off.

"Why did you do that?" Ned wanted to know.

"I don't want to end up in the table drain. Let me show you the pedals first, and then we'll see how we go."

They spent the next ten minutes or so while he got the feel of the controls, and Arthur tried to explain how the thing worked. After too many questions he finally shook his head, then got out and went to the front wheel where he opened the bonnet on that side and called to his son to come and have a look, and he would show him all the various parts and how they worked.

Ned was a keen student; his mind as sharp as a razor from months and months of study and a whole week of examinations, and soon he nodded and went back and sat behind the wheel. He started the engine easily enough, but from that point his first few attempts at driving off were acutely embarrassing as the big car suddenly hopped and lurched from one side of the road to the other. Finally he got the hang of it, and easing the clutch out slowly this time got the car rolling, then picked up speed and they were away.

It was funny when they arrived home because everyone was in town waiting for him. Ian and Catherine were out on the front porch and saw them turning off the main road with the hood down, and ran inside yelling for everyone to come out, quick. Just to show off Ned drove past all the way down to the end of the street then turned around and came all the way back again, tooting the horn and waving happily. As he pulled into the driveway Cath came running down off the porch and when he stopped went around the back and pulled open the dickie seat, and she climbed in beckoning to Ian to hurry and get in.

"Take us for a ride, Ned," she cried, and he looked across at Arthur grinning.

"All right, one lap. Just remember you don't have a license."

Everyone settled he reversed neatly out of the driveway and drove up the street and down again, repeating his manoeuvre, then came back and parked neatly in front of the house. The pair in the back were laughing gaily, and sat there while he took his bags and set them down on the lawn.

"All right, you two, out," Arthur said finally. "Ian, give me a hand with the bags."

Then he looked at Ned, "Now, Mr Clever Ned, see if you can park the car in the shed without scratching the paint."

Ned looked up, confused, but Cath simply grabbed his hand and pulled him bodily to the back of the house. Where the old chook yard had been there was a new shed to garage the car, with a new run between there and the back fence where the old vegetable patch used to be; the fence repaired now where he would cross Mr Patterson's back garden when he was little to look after Sandy, whenever he was in his cups.

He nodded and they walked back to the car together. Cath sat in the front passenger seat while he got in and started the car again. The first try he was a bit close on one side and he could not open the car door to get out, so he backed out again and got it right the second time. They stopped to pull the hood back over and shut the dickie seat on the way out, then closed the shed.

Standing close beside one another he placed the bar across and the moment he had done so she grabbed him and squeezed him tight, then lifted him bodily off the ground. He lifted her the same as soon as she let him down, smiling brightly.

"Cath."

"Welcome home, Ned," she pecked him on the cheek then turned hand in his to walk across to the house. Ian was at the top steps when they came up to the porch, and he let her go and ran up to give him a big hug and lifting him off his feet spun him around as well, then the three bustled noisily into the kitchen.

Ned stepped forward to greet his mother, but she held him away from her a moment gazing at him, then he bent down and kissed her as she fondly patted his cheek. Nodding quietly to herself she passed him on to Ellie who simply took his hand and squeezed it tight, her eyes glistening.

"I wouldn't have done it without you, Auntie Ellie," he said, but she pushed him away.

"Stuff and nonsense! You deserve every credit, Ned."

She then turned and added, "You children need a push in the right direction sometimes, that's all."

At that she caught sight of Cath standing there near the door and stopped short, shaking her head.

Cath caught her expression and her eyes narrowed. "When we get back, Ellie, all right. I told you already," she blurted out.

They all stared at her.

"Back from where, Cath?" Arthur wanted to know, then sent a warning glance across to Ian who simply shrugged and shook his head.

She caught that too and stood glaring angrily from one to the other.

"Oh, you are not telling me I am not going, Uncle Arthur, surely not."

"Going where, girl. Tell me what you think you know."

"Father is bringing horses down from Eurongera, then taking those stores back up. They are wanting them out at Dadjari and Chatham as well. I am going with him, for the run."

"That is not what we were thinking about, Cath," he said gently, but she flashed back at him, eyes ablaze.

"Well, you had better start thinking about it!"

They stood there, stunned, and she glared her defiance all round before turning abruptly on her heel and stormed out.

Ned shook his head and chuckled. "No doubt about her," he said, "that's Cath."

Then he looked up, seriously. "We had better take Dan and Everard with us as well, and one or two of the other boys." He paused. "Maybe some other people want to come too."

Arthur began to protest, "You have been back all of two minutes, son . . ." but Ellie held up her hand for silence suddenly, her face widening in recognition.

"That is exactly the way Peter Foley said it would happen," she declared, then looked out the window almost into the far distance. "Well I'll be blessed!"

She nodded quietly to herself then turned and bustled the men out the door, calling loudly, "Catherine, come back here and help Auntie Judith in the kitchen will you, there's a pet."

When Cath came back in Ellie promptly handed her an apron and set her to work chopping vegetables. Ned and Ian dawdled, bewildered at the sudden turn of events, but she dismissed them sharply.

"Off you go boys, I mean it. We'll call you the moment dinner is ready. I am sure you are starved," she smiled impishly after them, "but you are going to have to wait. Go on, scoot!"

CHAPTER TWENTY

Three days later they were out riding around the swamp when they heard shouting from back near the homestead, and turned their horses to see what was going on. Cath stood in her stirrups almost sniffing the air, eyes bright, then turned to the others and said loudly, "That will be Dad, with the horses," then with a whoop spurred her mount and took off at a gallop back toward the front gate.

The boys already had the stockyard gate open when they arrived as hooves thudded up the track and across the open ground in front of the main house. The first of the horses appeared through the trees then propped, ears up and eyes flashing, but Cath wheeled after them and took up a flanking lead, then not allowing them to lose momentum and become confused took them at full gallop straight along the fence and through the gate. Ian and Ned simply took up the rear as Don came through with his outriders, but the mob was in by then and all the boys had to do was shut the gate and secure it behind them.

"Hello Daddy," she called out to him, and he waved to her then turned and nodded to the two boys, then cantered over to the yards and dismounted.

As they came up he stood waiting for them. Ned leaned down from the saddle and shook his hand in greeting.

"How was the trip, Uncle Don?"

"Fair enough," he said, then stood back looking up at him. "Coming up, aren't you lad? How did you go with your exams?"

He grinned, "Yes, good. I think I did quite well in fact."

"That's the way. Ready to roll then, are we?"

He nodded.

"Who have you got coming?"

"Well, all of us. Except Mum and Dad, and Ellie of course."

"Righto," Don said, glancing across at his daughter still mounted and looking on quietly, then added, "Anyone else?"

"Daniel and Everard Foley for certain, probably Thomas and Bertram Nichols, maybe Jimbo." Then he paused, thoughtfully. "I have an idea some of the old people want to come too, if you can fit them in the wagon."

"How many?"

"Oh, four or five I guess, at most."

Don glanced away, thinking, then nodded. "We can take an extra wagon. That's all right."

Then he looked at Ned.

"I have to pay some of these boys off, son, if that's all right with you. But I'd like to keep Ah Poy and his missus." He nodded then, saying almost to himself. "You can't beat a good cook out there on the long paddock," then glanced up at Ned to make his point.

"Righto, then," Ned finished up, then turning his horse rode across to the house.

Ian went to follow but Don called after him.

"Ready for it, young fella?"

"Yes, sir," he said, but at that point Cath nudged him with her boot and he went silent.

"I want no nonsense from you, father," she declared.

"And you will get none, daughter." He looked up at her. "So long as you both remember something. I am the captain of this ship, and when I say jump you jump. You and Ian both, and Ned too, make no mistake."

Then he turned abruptly and walked across to join Ned in the house while they stayed and watched the men go about settling the horses down, making sure they had enough water, and bringing good hay across for them from the big stack there behind the shed.

Cath couldn't help herself. Dismounting, she let herself through the gate and with a practiced eye walked through the mob picking out one or two she liked in particular. She walked back over to the fence and took a pair of halters, then went back and cut them out.

"Go and get Ned," she called to Ian, and he wheeled his horse and cantered over to the house where rather than dismount he simply called to him.

After a moment Don and Ned both came out onto the front verandah, then seeing what was happening followed him back across. Immediately they realised what she was doing. Rather than chastise her Don simply climbed up onto the top rail and pointed out two or three others of the same type. Ned looked them over closely as they were each led out the gate, then went through himself and picked out another, and turning after thinking about it another again, and led them both out.

"What are you looking for?" Ian wanted to know.

"Conformation, mainly," Ned explained, then pointed with his finger. "Look, you can see the big smooth walk for yourself, and their big barrel chest and deep girth, and broad strong rump. They have good legs too. Look there at the bones and tendons and you can see what I mean. I like the fine head and neck as well myself, and bright eyes; the way they look straight at you with their ears pricked up like that, like big puppy dogs wanting to be taken out for a run."

"Like you, Ned. That's you, isn't it. A wild colt," the other replied. "You are like that when you play footie. I see it every time you run out onto the playing field. That's how you know, isn't it."

Ned turned on him. "I'll bloody snot you in a minute."

Ian veered away chuckling to himself and he backed off.

Cath was watching him, listening intently, then turned away smiling.

He looked after her smiling back, and watched in turn as she swapped saddles and gear from her riding horse onto one of the station brumbies she had selected. She murmured quietly as she approached and waited patiently while the animal settled at each move she made, and when she was done quickly mounted. It shied and bucked a little on receiving her weight but she settled it again, and taking a deep breath put it through its paces while the others looked on with interest.

One by one she repeated the process, and when she had finished culled one of her own choosing back into the yard, and one of Don's. But then Ned made her take them back, and climbing up onto the rail again picked out three more, then had her put them through the same paces.

"All right, those ten," he said finally, "we'll take them with us."

"We just brought them all this bloody way and you want to take them back again?" Don began to argue.

He looked at him oddly. "You walked them all the way down, Don," then cocked his head. "No, that's easy. This time we'll ride them back up and give them a run, then when we come back we'll bring them down again. One hundred and ten minutes of good solid work out of a hundred, is what we want."

He nodded to himself, face set, then turned and addressed them all.

"If we can't prove our stock we don't have a business, do we? But they are not to be knocked up. Anyone I see maltreating an animal or anyone under him will be dismissed on the spot, you hear?" He paused for effect. "But they have to earn their keep. Everyone has to earn their keep; that's what it's all about. We are a team, people and horses. That is the way it is going to be."

Don looked at him and after a moment shrugged, nodding agreement.

"Right then," he said, "you heard the man," then turned away and barked orders to his ringers. At that they set the selected mounts aside into their own string ready for the trip back.

Ned turned and looking directly up at her said, "Cath, you are our breaker. Once we get on the road you work with the ringers and learn everything they can teach you, all right? Don't worry about anything else."

She nodded, then wheeled her mount and straight away joined the men with the horses.

Next morning Arthur arrived with buyers in the new Cabriolet, and just for fun with Ian and Cath in the dickie seat Ned drove it all the way down to the far paddock and back again, then covered in dust and grinning from ear to ear settled down to watch the business of horse dealing with professionals. He sat on the fence, observing closely all morning as Arthur and Ian went deftly about their arguing the pitch and toss, but at the end he was nowhere near happy with the price they settled.

Over lunch he made his feelings known and they all sat patiently hearing him out while he extolled in detail the fine quality of their stock, and complained at their being so poorly valued. Ian began to interrupt, but Arthur stayed him and let Ned finish his piece.

When he did finish finally the older of the two nodded wisely. "Looks like you're in good hands, Arthur," he said with a chuckle. That made Ned bristle.

"This is Mr Jim Russell, Ned," Arthur interjected. "I am sorry you weren't introduced, but you took off in the car."

Ned looked up at that. Jim Russell was a legend in livestock circles, and he knew it.

"Sorry Mr Russell. Please excuse me, I didn't know."

"That's quite all right, son." Then he leaned closer, engaging his attention. "I knew your great grandfather Alexander McKenzie, and Hamish, then Sandy, did you know that? I've been doing business with your family for over 45 years, and our company another 40 years before that. You might say we grew up together."

Ned nodded, awed now into silence, then after a pause cocked his head.

"Can I ask you something, then?"

"Sure, go ahead."

"Why are the prices down so low? I don't mean specifically. Maybe we could have done better if we had left the best mounts in with the mob, except they are more valuable to us anyway. What I mean is, if we had left them in it would have been far too big a loss letting them go like that."

"Fair enough. But let me point something out to you."

Now it was his turn, and he sat back ears pricked listening intently.

"When we came in this morning," the buyer said, "first thing you did was take your dad's fancy new car out for a spin. There's your answer. This coming war is going to be mechanised, especially if the Americans come in. Then after it is over, who knows? The Germans and the Japanese are both building up their heavy industry, so either way it goes machinery is the way of the future."

"Do you think so?"

"I know so, lad. Thank God I won't be here. This is my last trip, you know, for old times sake, then my dear wife and I are retiring over onto the coast for a bit of fishing. We have a small shack down on the Bermagui River. That's where we will be if ever you want to look us up."

He stood at that and made to go, then Arthur excused himself as well and they trooped out to the waiting car. Ned followed doggedly on Jim's heels, but then the old man turned and looked him in the eye, and held out his hand in farewell.

"You'll do all right son. If anyone, it will be you, and others like you. Just keep your standards up, and let me tell you something keep breeding those fine horses of yours. After the war get out of these pastoral Shorthorns and put your money on establishing a good stud line; Black Angus perhaps, or Hereford, then breed back again to improve the overall type. Make those bastards out there come to you. Make them line up at the front gate."

Then he leaned in closer, confidentially, and said quietly to him alone, "You are a good lad, Ned, and I am pleased to have caught up with you finally. But mark my words. After the war it will be all about feeding industry, feeding the cities; that's not where you want to be. This way of life will change but you stick to the old ways. In good time things will iron themselves out."

CHAPTER TWENTY ONE

Over the next few days they paid off the extra hands Don had brought down with him. When Arthur and Ian went into town for supplies they came across an Afghan driver passing through with a team of camels and a big flatbed wagon which they promptly hired. They put him up at the local hotel for the night, in a quiet back room away from the rowdy stockmen cutting out their wages in the front bar, and sent his gear straight across to the blacksmith's and the saddler's for refitting. Next day they brought him out in the car.

There were moments when Ned shuddered at the mounting expense, although as Don slowly brought the droving plant together, bringing in extra cattle from the outlying stations and the thing tangibly took shape, he relaxed and settled into the routine.

Several more weeks went by and he began thinking they would never get away at this rate, when late one afternoon he looked up as the strangest sight he had ever seen make its awkward ungainly way up the track from the front gate. Small children ran screaming in terror, then came back out behind their mother's skirts to watch Achmed's complaining camels slowly pulling his wagon across in front of the house and stop there.

Don rode over on his horse to speak with him briefly and he set the camels going once more to follow him around the back of the houses where two of the old men came out. As he stepped down they shook his hand warmly. That done, Don turned and rode back over to the yards where they had all stopped to watch the camels.

"All right, we are away," he said. "Four o'clock start, is that clear?"

"Tomorrow morning? Four o'clock tomorrow morning?" Ian wanted to know.

Don glared at him, then shaking his head said loudly enough for everyone's ear, "No, next bloody stupid Christmas, if that's all right with you young fella!" Then he wheeled abruptly and rode over to the house where he dismounted and tied his horse, and walked briskly up the steps and inside.

They all turned to look at one another, grinning broadly, then one of the ringers called out to Cath and she went to join them, but halfway across stopped suddenly. Instead she rode over to the house and presently came back out again with her saddle bags packed, which she carefully tied behind her saddle. Mounting again she rode over to Ian, and leaned over and kissed him, then patting his cheek she said, smiling sweetly, "See you when we get there."

Then she rode over to Ned and did likewise before turning and cantering off after the ringers taking their strings of spare horses up onto the stock reserve at the five mile peg to hobble them overnight, where they would camp there with them.

Once they were out of sight the drive foreman rode over and politely touched his finger to his hat.

"Mr Collins, sir," he said.

"Andrew, yes, what is it?"

"I won't need you until about 3.30, if that's all right with you. Go and get yourself some sleep, we'll manage tonight."

He looked at Ian then back again, and nodded, and the other returned the courtesy and rode off.

"Come on mate," he said, then rode over to the house and untied Don's horse. Taking both horses over to the stables he dismounted and began to unsaddle them and brush them down. Ian did the same with his mount. When they had finished they filled the water trough and fed each horse a full biscuit of hay, then walked together to the house.

As they came in the door Arthur called Ian into the front office with Don, to go over their final accounts and the last of their purchase orders he had arranged with the various stores along the way. Ned made his way directly to the kitchen where he crossed straight over to the stove to gave Ellie a hug. She smiled, then sat him down and poured him a cup of tea, and taking the pot back to the stove came and sat next to him.

"All ready, Ned?"

He nodded and shrugged, sipping his tea absently, then turned to her and asked, "How many cattle have we moved up and down over the years, Ellie, do you know?"

She sat back to think, her eyes distant, moving back and forth across those years, then she leaned forward and said, "Sandy and I married in 1889. We lived in the old house in town then. That is where we met Mr Russell, whom you have met. Hamish brought him home for dinner one night, old Hamish I mean, just before he died. He held to the opinion that Jim was a very bright young man indeed, and wanted to introduce us."

He watched her face.

"After Hamish died, in 1897, Jim married my cousin Mary Forsythe and they went to live in Mount Tambla. He is an old boy as well, and that is where he met your father and got him a job in the bank."

"Ellie," he said, "you didn't answer my question."

She looked at him, shaking her head. "There is no counting them, Ned. How much water does a river carry, or an ocean? Ask yourself that. Perhaps one day Arthur will give us an answer, or your clever Ian once he finds his feet."

"We have other business to attend," she then said, somewhat mysteriously. She gazed deeply into his eyes, then nodding to herself added, "I am sure everything will turn out for the best."

"What do you mean by that?"

She leaned over and patted his hand, smiling inwardly, her old eyes bright and piercing, then she got up and went back over to the stove.

"Go and get cleaned up, there's a pet," she said, "I have a special dinner for you tonight. Your favourite, roast pork with apple sauce, and lemon meringue pie."

He sat back at that, and without a word she turned and smiled again.

"Scoot! Off you go," she said.

He sat there a moment longer but she only smiled again so he got up and went out down the passage to his room. As he undressed he turned to see Angus there, sitting in his big chair next to the fireplace watching him. He stripped and wrapped the towel around him, then looking back briefly went down to the bathroom to take his shower. When he finished and came back to his room Angus was still there.

"You are a mischief, do you know that?" he said, annoyed now, but the other smiled, like Ellie just had, and he looked at him thoughtfully a moment. He took his time dressing then stepped up to the mirror and combed his hair. Satisfied with the way he looked he turned and sat on the bed again.

"All right, what?"

"When you get up to Eurongera Dad might want to stop by and have a chat. He has something he wants to discuss with you some more."

Ned looked at him. "He died, I know, I saw him, and he went away."

"Up on Eurongera, with Peter," Angus replied, himself confused now. "That's where they are."

"Really? Is that right?"

"Yes, of course."

"Well, what is Peter doing?"

"I don't know, Ned," Angus replied. "I don't understand that blackfella side of things, not very well anyway."

He looked at him. "What do you think?"

Angus shrugged. "I said I don't know, Ned. Maybe ask Everard."

"Everard? What does Everard have to do with it?"

"He can ride, don't you know that? Ride like the wind, but he was Peter's apprentice as well."

"Yes, I know, but . . ." Then something hit him, and he turned to look at him again, at the slight crook in his neck.

"It was you and Everard, wasn't it? Having a race? When you came off. Isn't that right?"

"No, not Everard, he wasn't even born then," Angus looked at him, "and neither were you. No, Daniel. It was me and Daniel. He was my best mate, but he was thirteen then and I was fifteen; reckoned he could top me." He chuckled at that, almost at his own joke.

"So where does Everard come into it?"

"You know that already. Gee you're dumb sometimes. He is like you and me, and the rest of us. Everard is going to be the next businessman. He is going to be the next doctor, traditional law man, after Peter."

He sighed, and shrugged again. "Anyway, Dad wants to talk to you Ned, all right. I have to go now." Then he disappeared.

At that moment Ian hurried in from the bathroom with a towel around him and a bundle of dirty clothes in one hand, and his boots in the other. He was dripping wet, hair disheveled, and he threw everything down in a pile on the floor and began to dry himself briskly.

"What's wrong with you?" Ned watched him curiously.

"Your Uncle Don Illiterate Bloody McKenzie never even went to school, did you know that? He signs all his bloody chits with an X!"

"No, that's not right."

"Yes it is, Ned. It's true, Arthur just told me, not half an hour ago, and when I asked Don he just nodded."

"No, well, Dad's got it wrong too. Fact is, most of the time he doesn't sign at all. He keeps it all in his head. He does all his business on a handshake. The storekeepers up the track sign our chits with an X."

Ian stared at him, stunned, his mouth open and his jaw working, but no words came out.

Ned cocked his head, frowning. "You'll catch a fly if you keep that up."

The other slammed his mouth shut, glaring now.

"No, Ian, you'll manage. If we didn't know you could do the job you just wouldn't be coming. I could do it but I have too much else on my plate."

Then he sat back thinking a moment while Ian dressed in clean clothes for dinner.

"We have to learn from Don this trip, that's why Dad wants us to go; both of us. What you will need to do is keep track of all the invoices and receipts, that's all. Just sign for everything, and don't worry about it," he went on, then added, "I'll wager that when it comes to tallying up you'll be out and he'll be spot on. You don't know him very well yet, but he is a legend around the back country. Nobody has a memory like Don McKenzie of Eurongera Station, I learned that when I was little, learning to walk. Mum never stopped going on about him. Problem is it makes it hard now for Dad to keep track without having to go ask him every little thing. He goes crazy trying to get our tax done sometimes, and Sandy was even worse."

Then he waited a moment longer and continued. "Sorry Ian, no offense, I thought you knew. Everyone knows Uncle Don. I'll tell you something else. By the time we get back every station manager and drover, and every store keeper between here and the Kimberley will know you drove cattle north with Don McKenzie. When we get back you will be able to get work anywhere in Australia."

"Is that right?"

He was gaping again, but caught himself then looked away shaking his head.

"So long as you don't get the idea into your head that we'll be letting you go, Ian Bloody Odd Nuts Ramsay. You are family, all right," he paused. "Anyway, we better hurry. Ellie told me she has something special cooked up."

He waited for him while he sat and pulled on his socks and boots, then quickly combed his hair, and they both went down the passage together to the kitchen. The table was bare, but just at that moment Ellie came in with a big pan and placed it on the bench.

She cocked her head and smiled at them, her lined old face radiant with happiness. "My, my," she murmured softly, "look at you, such handsome young gentlemen."

Then she came over and reached up adjusting Ned's collar, then Ian's belt buckle so it sat just right, in the middle, in line with his fly and his shirt buttons. She stood back at that, more or less satisfied, then turned and went back to her stove where she took up a spoon to stir the gravy.

"We are in the dining room," she looked up at them briefly then went back to her task.

Ned nudged Ian aside, his curiosity pricked suddenly at her manner, and he went out the door and crossed the passageway into the formal dining room. He simply had not thought of it since the dining room was so rarely used, not since the old days, before he was born, but what he saw stopped him in his tracks and Ian coming behind bumped into him.

The table was set with white linen and silver service, with three big candlesticks alight in the middle making the whole room glow. Don and Arthur were standing at the mantle, the fireplace screened off over the summer months, and next to them was his mother, and Catherine in a fresh cotton frock that took their breath away.

At that moment Ellie came in with her sauce boat which she placed on its saucer just beyond the first candlestick, then nodded to Don who promptly pulled out a chair and had his daughter seated at his right hand at the head of the table, with Ian to his left. Arthur then had his wife Judith seated likewise, and accepting his place Ned took Ellie as his partner for the evening and sat her between Ian and himself, opposite Arthur.

Many, many years later Ned was to look back on that dinner, so brief and to the point, as another of the defining points in his life. It described to him in its tacit way who he was, and what was expected of him and those about him, as his family ventured forth on another of its projects. There were no long speeches. They were simply together at the dinner table and as they finished following a toast to their success they turned in early.

After dinner Cath changed back into her riding britches and Arthur drove her out to the ringer's camp in the car, but the boys were sound asleep by the time he returned and they didn't hear him come in.

CHAPTER TWENTY TWO

Next thing he knew was Don shaking him brusquely awake, then Ian. It was just past a quarter to three and they were both out of bed quickly though it was still dark outside, and pulling on their trousers made their way down to the kitchen by lantern. Ellie was at the stove negotiating a great sizzling pan of bacon and eggs, but when he saw her there he went over and gently bumped her aside.

"Here, let me do that."

"I can manage, Ned," she protested, but he would hear none of it.

"I am a real expert at this," he grinned. "I worked at Donovan's nearly every weekend for five years, you know. That's how I made my pocket money. We fed 50-60 people some days when we were busy. Sit down and have a cup of tea, Ian can do the toast. He has done plenty of that as well."

Don stood watching them work, then scratched his head. "Well, I'll be damned."

"Right," Ian said, "now it is our turn to show you something. And this is just the start, old timer."

Don leaned back and roared laughing at that. "You know, we might just start to get along you and me, young fella."

Ned threw in some extra chops, and piled all the eggs and bacon into a baking dish and set it on the table, then turned to help Ian butter the toast. Within minutes it was all done, and wiping their hands they set to the task of getting it all eaten. Ellie did protest loudly this time when they started cleaning up after themselves, and pushed them merrily out the door to get their things ready.

Outside it was still dark with just the faintest glow on the eastern horizon and they carried their luggage over to the first of the wagons, then went across to the stables to brush down and saddle their horses. By the time they came out again Don had the lead wagon away with its big load and light sulky tied to the back, followed by Ah Poy's cook wagon pulled by donkeys, then Achmed's camel wagon bearing the old men and women, and with them some extra women and children who had decided at the last minute that they wanted to come too.

Those slow vehicles formed into convoy and went on ahead first. Late in the afternoon they would select the night's camping place and prepare for the main mob to catch up, followed by the ringers with the spare horses.

"Mr Collins, good morning, sir!" A voice came quietly through the semi-darkness.

Ned looked around to see Andrew riding up, and when he came alongside leaned over to shake him by the hand.

"Ned to you, Mr MacFarlane."

"Right you are, then," he said, and was about to continue when Don's voice came across from the front verandah.

"Mr MacFarlane! You keep those two boys close under your wing, do you hear? And do not move out until I give you the say so, precisely!"

Andrew simply nodded and without a word leaning forward in his saddle touched his finger to the brim of his hat in acknowledgment, then turned to them and said quietly, "Just follow me please and do exactly what I do. Whatever else, don't make any sudden noise, is that clear? If in doubt just sit back and watch the boys, you'll get the drift."

As he spoke Dan and Everard appeared beside them with Jimbo Nichols and his two boys, then the rest of the men, and together they rode quietly all the way down to the big bottom paddock and talking quietly all the while started working their way around the cattle, slowly bringing the scattered lumbering beasts up off the ground where they had slept the night, to bunch them ever so carefully into one big coherent mob. Each time a beast made to protest or run the horse would simply block it, then turn it back once it had settled.

One after another after another the boys kept up their slow steady pressure and Ned marveled at their dogged persistence, and at the sensitivity and alertness of their mounts. Then he smiled inwardly realising that he had been right all along without fully realising it, and that this was simply putting the theory into practice.

Quickly he settled into the motion of the horse working its way in the half dark. As dawn approached and the sky brightened he felt his conscious mind slipping away until he sensed rather than saw the pattern of it falling into place; the native intelligence of the big mob as a whole against the dull foolish rush of one or two beasts cut off from the rest. It was like finding your wind on a long cross country run, and settling into the rhythm of it, and before long he felt himself left out on his own as Andrew kept Ian close at hand while he too got the idea.

Eventually he heard Don's soft voice close at hand encouraging him and he looked up to see that he was being watched. He turned to see Ian a little away off by himself now, and the mob itself lift off the ground and begin to move. It was exhilarating.

"Thank you, Mr MacFarlane," Don said clearly in the still air. "We can go now."

Near the gate some of the older riders strung out and quickly through into the next paddock formed long lines on either side of the track, and began slowly and steadily to walk up. Then the first of the lead steers broke through, and the mob itself began to move up behind them. As the last of them passed through the gate he noticed Don take a gold watch from his waistcoat, then with a quick glance put it back.

"What time do you make it, Don?"

"What?" He looked at him, then took the watch from his pocket again and shook it, then peered at the dial again. "Am I wrong, son? It's four o'clock, isn't it?"

At that he shook his head in frustration. "Never could get used to the bloody thing anyway. Moll and the girls gave it to me for Christmas one year, but if it's going to throw me out that's it." Then he threw the watch on the churned-up ground and rode away muttering to himself.

Ned got down off his horse and bent down to pick it up. When he looked at the dial it showed exactly twenty seconds past the hour and he stood ready to call Don back but he was gone. With a quick shake of his head and a wry grin he put it in his own pocket, and remounting went after him.

There was no let up once the mob was away, except that just on sunrise they passed the ringers waiting for them with fresh horses on the stock reserve, where Don stopped briefly to check that the wagons had passed by on schedule. Once they were clear they rode on hour after hour slowly walking the cattle along, every now and again as they came across some green pick slowing to let them graze.

While it was hot during the day there had been a reasonable amount of summer rain. With such cold nights out in this open country there was dew with quite a good deal of condensation on exposed surfaces. The bright sun each day brought a lot of young growth on the scrubby trees along the way, and on the grey-green saltbush understorey and green grassy flats in between.

Early after noon Dan and Bertram rode off toward the east following a brief parlay with Andrew. A while later he heard sporadic rifle shots, then soon after saw them away ahead in the distance catching up with the wagons. After another hour or so they came in sight of them waiting beside the road, and as they drew near they remounted and took their place outriding.

Just after three o'clock, a bit too early, they came up onto the wagons parked slightly away from one another with fires going, and Don rode on ahead to see what was up. He was met by their lead wagoneer standing out on the road waiting for him. Following a brief conversation he rode back all the way.

"Mr Collins, sir, if you don't mind," Don called out, and as Ned rode up he wheeled his horse and bade him follow.

When they got up close to the man they stopped, and were promptly introduced.

"Mr Thwaites, allow me to introduce you to Mr Edward Collins. He is the owner, traveling with us."

The man stepped out, ingratiating, and taking him by the hand started pumping it vigorously.

"If you don't mind, sir, I need more men up here."

Ned looked around and started counting, then back at the mob, then standing up in his stirrups at the ringers coming up far behind. He gazed around, scratching his head.

"What more men do we need? I thought we had it just about right, maybe a few over."

"What do you mean, sir?"

"What do I mean? I mean we have enough men. More than enough. It's a good team and I am very happy with it," he added for emphasis.

"No, I mean up here with the wagons," the other insisted.

Ned turned again and recounted.

"There are enough here. You have Ah Poy and Achmed, and Aloysius, and Kenny and Old Sam, and yourself with six women and those extra kids."

"But they are Boongs, and Chinee, and Sepoy, Mr Collins, sir. I need Englishmen with me. I ran supplies against the Boers, sir, and know my business. But I must have the men."

It took a few minutes to register what he was saying, but when it did Ned wheeled his horse and rode back to the mob. The ringers were starting to come up so he sent Everard back to talk to them and get them to slow, then went over to see Daniel.

"What's up, boss?"

"That Mr Thwaites, the front wagon bloke, he isn't too well. Can you or Thomas take him back into town in the sulky?"

Dan nodded that he would and Ned wheeled to go, then he stopped up short and turned back quickly.

"Who can drive the wagon?"

"Aloysius, good. He do all right."

"Goodo, you take that bloke in and we'll see you back tomorrow. Come with me."

They galloped back. As he drew closer to the wagons rather than come right in himself he sent Daniel along, then watched from the distance as he had Achmed and the old men unhook the sulky from the front wagon, then harness up one of Ah Poy's donkeys and load some supplies for the trip back.

Once they had gone he rode closer and called across, "Where are we supposed to be, Don?"

The other turned in his saddle to wave ahead, but turned back thinking a moment and nodded. "Here will do, no problem."

Andrew rode up then anxious at the delay, his head ringer on his tail, but Don intervened so Ned sat back listening to their exchange. In the event they took the mob up past the wagons to settle for the night, and as evening drew near hobbled the horses and let them graze out from where they were.

That night at the fire he sat back thinking over the day, then as he was about to turn in found Don's watch in his pocket and went over to hand it to him.

The other looked at him thoughtfully. "How far out was I, son?" he wanted to know.

"Well, from when I picked it up, about 20 seconds."

Don nodded, eyes distant, "You keep it in your pocket for me then, eh?"

CHAPTER TWENTY THREE

It took them several weeks to clear the great black soil plain, and skirting desert dunes over to the west begin to make their way north into the more broken country. As they rode along Ned found himself astonished at the complexity of the vast network of stock routes they traversed. Riding along day after day he listened intently to Don's stories about the old days; of how the government had set aside the wide interconnecting strips of crown land breaking up the various freehold and leasehold parcels to allow livestock to pass without hindrance, firstly beyond the old lines of settlement, then as the more remote outlying land was taken up to allow access to the big southern markets.

As a major engineering feat it was just marvelous; the survey absolutely precise with trigonometry stations set up for reference on high ground, which Don pointed out to him periodically as they passed by.

One evening as he was about to turn into his swag he felt a light touch on his shoulder and Everard said to him softly, "Boss, that old man want to talk you."

He got up and followed him over to their camp behind the Afghan wagon where he saw the old men and women sitting around their fire. Daniel stood to make a place for him, then Bertram and the other stockmen did likewise. He sat where they indicated, then all settled again he waited patiently for someone to speak.

Finally Dan leaned over and coughed slightly.

"Ned, that Uncle been telling you wrong story, all right? See this old man here, 'e boss for this country, from old time, eh? Long time before."

He indicated one of the old men sitting there, eyes piercing through him. He nodded politely.

"That one, Billy Nichols, all right. Old Billy, King Billy. He Bertram grandfather."

Then he indicated one of the women. "This lady, 'is sister, Edie Anderson. 'Nother boss for this country."

"Don talking you rubbich. He tell story wrong way, all right. All this road here old time blackfella road, long time before. Then whitefella came, follow old blackfella road belong this man now, belong 'is father, grandfather before that. Only later gov'mint man came up, measure everything up, write 'im book. Then more whitefella come along, push blackfella off."

He stopped and looked at him closely.

"No worry you, boss. We know you mob. Your mob been good to us blackfella. We live with you now, Wyandera, Eurongera, Dadjari, Chatham, right across. Like family. That Auntie Ellie our kids call her grandmother, that other one pinish, call 'im grandfather, like this mob 'ere now, but other side, you know. One road your way, one road our way, all right, no worry. Two road, we go two road, send 'im kids school, then bring 'im out teach 'im blackfella business. We teach you now, all right. Your turn now. You learn from us. This old man tell you a proper story right way, tell you properly, then you go two road like us."

He nodded at that and they smiled at him, their apprehension dissipating. Presently the old man coughed, then spat and cleared his throat, then taking a deep breath began to sing. Ned listened for a moment astonished, trying to pick up the words but they eluded him. He had heard them so many times before, whenever he was back on Wyandera, and so often night after night when he could not rightly tell whether they were in his dreams, or whether he was wide awake listening.

So he sat and listened the same way as he had become so accustomed to doing without ever really thinking about it. As the song went on and on he simply absorbed it. Finally it stopped abruptly and he looked up.

Everard was sitting there now where Daniel had been, and he tapped him on the knee and said in his soft quiet voice, "All right, finish now, we go to sleep. See you tomorrow, eh?"

He got up and left without a word, then right away rolled up in his swag and went straight off to sleep. Next morning he was woken as usual by the first stirring of the camp as Ah Poy bustled and clattered about making breakfast, and he got out and stretched then walked over into the bushes to relieve himself. Breakfast out of the way he quickly saddled up and rode out to take up his post as the night riders were being replaced, and one by one they started to come in for something to eat.

Over in the distance he could see the ringers, dark shadows against the soft glow of the dawn riding out back to where they came to bring in the horses, hobbled for the night so as not to wander too far, then he turned his attention to the mob.

As daylight broke the wagons moved off again and they waited for Don to give the signal. When it came they slowly lifted the herd up off the ground then allowing the old steers up front to take the lead got them all moving again. As he took up his position tailing them Ned felt rather than saw Everard just behind him on his left flank, and without a word they rode along quietly together.

Just as they passed the now vacant campsite Don called out to them, "There is one missing, Mr Collins, if you don't mind," then he wheeled his horse and rode on up to the lead.

He and Everard looked at each other and shrugged, then shaking their heads turned their horses and went back the way they had come. As the head ringer approached he simply grinned and tossed his head in the direction they should go, and after the string of horses passed they turned off into the bush where he had indicated.

They picked up the tracks quickly enough and followed them. Before long Everard stopped abruptly and pointed ahead. There were some crows flapping about in a tree and nearby they could see the cow mostly hidden in the undergrowth. As they rode up she came at them trying to protect her newborn calf there on the ground, and Everard deftly blocked her allowing Ned to get in close. He dismounted and the calf got up suddenly and started bawling, making Everard work with the mother to keep her steady, but Ned picked the calf up bodily and in one movement placed it across the saddle and quickly remounted.

All the way back the calf bawled loudly with the mother coming on behind making even more noise, so they set up a fast walk on past the ringers. Eventually they came up to the mob and Everard took his place there on the flank while Ned went on ahead to catch up with the wagons. Finally he came alongside Aloysius driving the lead wagon and leaning over passed the calf across to him, leaving him to worry about it, then dropped back and waited for the others to catch up.

As Don came by he pulled him up a moment.

"How did you know, Don?"

"What's that, son?"

"How did you know there was one missing? There are two and a half thousand head. I mean, I know you are good but you can't be that good."

The other looked at him oddly, then looked away scratching his head, and back at him again.

"Well, fact is I thought she was going to drop yesterday, so I was keeping an eye on her. When she wasn't there this morning I reckoned she'd gone off to have her calf. That's about the size of it."

Ned's jaw dropped and Don looked at him even more oddly, then spurred his horse and began to ride off. After a few yards he stopped and looking back over his shoulder said, "Sharpen up, there's a good lad," then rode off again shaking his head.

Ian and the others rode by all glancing his way, smiling to themselves, until he turned his horse and walked back to where he met up with Everard again and took his place. They rode along together for some time, until finally Everard picked up his mood and glanced over at him.

"Not your fault, boss. That lazy plurry Jimbo sleepin' on the job, that's all."

"All right, fair enough," he said after a moment. "How many more are there?"

"All that lot we brought in from Tom Rooney place, after that Ian start working with your father, when everyone waiting for you that time, exam time, eh?"

"It that right?" He looked at him, then turned his gaze up ahead to where he could just see Don through the slight morning haze.

He spurred his horse to a trot and caught up with him.

"How many more, Don?"

"Two hundred odd."

"We can't carry that many calves, can we? Surely not."

"We'll be right, son. Another day or two and we can stop."

"For how long?"

"Week or two, if need be, maybe longer."

"Really?" He looked confused at that. "Why didn't you say anything about it before, Don?"

The other stopped his horse at that, and sat gazing at him a moment.

"Nothing to talk about. That's the way it's going to be, so there's nothing to be said." Then he turned to look at him, thoughtfully now. "What is it you'd want me to be saying to you, son."

"I don't know," he shrugged. "Just tell me things."

He nodded. "Well, if I do that I end up using up a lot of them words, that you're most likely going to forget anyway, then I have to tell you all over again. No, better to just show you, and get you to do it, then you remember it the rest of your life. You never know what might come up, time to time, do you."

Then he leaned over close and said quietly, "Son, I never had much of a chance at that clever book larnin' of yours, so it's not my place to judge. Maybe you are right, maybe I'm wrong; like I say, I am in no position on that score. But I do know what I do know, and as you stick by me you'll see what I mean off your own bat."

Ned nodded, "That's fair enough, Don, no worries."

"Right then. In two days we will be up on the Bundingor Lakes and we can stop over there as long as we need. After that it is a fairly short hop, another week or two, and we'll be home."

It came as no surprise then that he was as true as his word. Late that afternoon they camped on top of a low range. While they made their way slowly among great weathered outcroppings of granite that made it difficult to keep the mob together in one bunch, there was nonetheless plenty of good grass and they took their time passing over. Just before noon the next day with the sun right up overhead they came out abruptly onto the edge of the escarpment and looked out over vast shimmering expanses of water patching the landscape far into the distance, and they all stopped to take in the panorama.

Then the camel wagon came up, and as soon as it broached the final outcrop into full view old Billy and Edie began singing again, wailing loudly this time, with the other women joining in chorus.

Ned turned to listen to it, then Everard leaned over quietly and said to him, "This their country properly now. That old man born there, same that old lady. Father, grandfather all buried down there; all that mob. They call out grandfather, tell 'im. Call out, coming down now. Tell 'im, it's us coming, no worry. All our mob coming down now." Then he nodded, smiling shyly.

The song went on all night. There were three more calves dropped during the night and early next morning they made space for them in the big lead wagon, then as the new day brightened enough to light their way began the long descent down onto the northern plain. Even then it was not until late that they arrived at their destination.

Later as Ned looked back on that day he thought it was really one of the strangest of his life, with the cattle picking up the smell of water and wanting to move up, and the old people singing all the way and calves bawling, and Don riding back and forth issuing sharp commands as they worked to keep the mob clear of boggy patches until they came finally onto clear hard ground sloping straight down into the water, and they let them drink.

After a brief consultation Daniel and Bertram took leave to follow the camel wagon on a good way further to set up a separate camp, and the next day they went on further again into the heart of their traditional country to make a more permanent stop.

CHAPTER TWENTY FOUR

Over the next week they had their hands busy with calving. Even then it took another five days before the last cow dropped, and another week again for the calves to grow strong enough to walk on with the mob. In the meantime some of the main herd wandered off, getting away through the sheer distraction as men worked day and night trying to keep them together.

Don did not appear to be so worried about it; mainly concerned with keeping the unbranded calves together. He could send some men back later for a pre-muster to round the rest up, or when the neighbouring station owners had finished mustering themselves come back and help draft them out. The only other problems they had were with dingoes coming in at night skulking about the camp; the boys earning extra cash taking scalps they could hand in later to collect the bounty, and with wild bulls trying to cull cows out into their own feral herds which they simply shot.

Game was plentiful, so they supplemented their diet of salt beef, boiled cabbage and damper with fresh kangaroo meat, and ducks and pigeons, and one day Thomas and Jimbo even brought in a large pig much to Ah Poy's pleasure. With it he cooked up an extra special banquet for them with cold cuts of pork all next day, and fried pork strips and eggs for breakfast the day after to finish it off.

Then something happened Ned did not expect. During a meeting with Don and Andrew one afternoon they decided to push on again the next day, so after they had finished he took his gear with him and went up along the lake shore to clean up and take a bath. It was nice in the cool water and after he had bathed stayed for a swim. Back on shore he took his old shirt and dried himself, then setting his shaving mirror on a bush lathered his face and began to shave. He became wholly engrossed in his task, until almost finished suddenly he heard his horse nicker and quickly he looked up startled to see Elizabeth there on her horse watching him.

"Elizabeth, what are you doing here?"

"You are late, so I came down to see how you were all going. When you weren't in the camp I came looking for you."

"What, all by yourself? We are a week away from Eurongera."

She nodded, distracted. She was gazing at him intently and he looked down to realise that he was standing there naked. He cocked his head at her, annoyed.

"So, how long have you been there?"

"Quite long enough."

"You shouldn't be looking at me like that."

"Well, Mr Prudery Collins, let me tell you, that being the way you feel perhaps you should be somewhat more decently attired."

He turned and looked directly at her, still not thinking to cover himself.

"The simple fact is, Miss McKenzie, that we are not married!" Then for some odd reason yet unknown to him added, muttering to himself, "Not yet, at any rate."

She glanced away, then back at him frowning, and blushed.

"Am I to accept your thoroughly rude remark as a proposal?"

He looked at her steadily for a moment, then shrugged and nodded.

"Yes, well, it is by the looks of things. Now kindly leave me be. I'll catch up with you, all right."

She turned her horse at that and rode off a short way, and Ned listened as she stopped just out of sight. She was not going to leave he knew. He felt himself stirring at the thought of her when suddenly he heard a child's giggling laughter and looked around to see Angus close by watching him. He was naked as well and much, much younger now than he ever remembered; barely six or seven as he thought back on it later, but before he could say anything the little boy dashed behind a tree and disappeared.

At that he quickly finished his shave and washed his face in the fresh lake water, then dressed in clean shirt and trousers sat on the log to pull on his boots. Packing up his things he mounted his horse and rode out to where Elizabeth waited. As he drew alongside she leaned across and kissed him full on the lips, and held him to her.

"I have missed you so terribly much, Ned Collins, ever since our picnic. I am so very sorry. I know mother is angry with me now, and so will father, but I simply could not wait any longer to see you again."

He held her away from him for a moment. She was trembling.

"This is not like you. What is it? What's going on?"

"I simply don't know, I don't know."

"All right. It's all right, Please don't be upset."

He held her again, then after a moment let her go and turned his horse. Together they rode on back toward camp. About a hundred yards out they were met by Cath with Ian close behind, both worried as if he had been lost and they were out looking for him. When they saw Elizabeth there with him they reined their horses and looked at each other, then sat silently until they came up.

"Elizabeth?"

"Hello Cath!" she smiled.

They looked at Ned, confused.

"What is going on?" Ian wanted to know, but Ned simply shrugged, shaking his head, then spurred his horse and rode on with Elizabeth close by his side.

When they rode into camp Don was standing there waiting. He took one sharp look at them, nodding knowingly to himself. As they dismounted he stood watch, but when Ned began to walk across to his swag Elizabeth broke away from him and ran over to her father. He held her close for a long moment, then at arm's length looking her in the eye.

"It's all right, lass," he said. "That's what has been ailing you all this time, isn't it."

She nodded, then started to cry softly and he took her in his arms again to comfort her. Ned stood back somewhat at a loss, Don eying him carefully over his sobbing daughter's shoulder.

"Haven't been doing anything you shouldn't, have you Ned?"

"What? What do you mean?" he stood there astonished.

Elizabeth pulled back from him, mouth agape. "Daddy, how can you think such a thing. No, of course not!" she cried.

He was about to say something but right then Cath and Ian rode in and dismounted. Don turned, and then taking off his hat stood scratching his head.

Finally he looked up and said, "Cath, take Thomas and Andrew with you and ride on home. Tell your mother Elizabeth is here with us safe and well. Let her know what has happened, all right?"

She nodded.

"When you have done that ride over to the mission at Dadjari and tell the preacher to come over." Then he turned to them collectively and said almost to himself, "No good dragging these things out. Let's get it over and done with, shall we?"

Then he turned to Elizabeth. "Put your swag over there please, daughter, behind the wagon. You will sleep there where I can keep an eye on you."

Glancing briefly at Ned he then swung on his heel and walked away.

That night Everard came over again to tap Ned gently on the shoulder to wake him, then stole silently away into the dark. He got up to follow and before they had gone too far they came upon a campfire off a little distance from the main camp. Old Peter was sitting there making a billy of tea, singing softly to himself. As he motioned them to sit near him Sandy came up from the side and Ned reached out to shake his hand before taking his seat, and the other pulled up a log and sat there opposite him, gazing intently and nodding quietly to himself.

Finally he said, "You're doing well, lad. Much better than we expected."

Ned shrugged at that, bemused, then cocked his head suddenly.

"You didn't come here to tell me that, surely not. What's going on, you old bastard? What are you doing with Elizabeth?"

Peter chuckled to himself, and Sandy looked away a moment then back at him again. He waved his hand dismissively and shrugged.

"Well, no problem. Angus jumped the gun a bit, that's all. We'll be right."

"What? What are you doing?"

"Don't be cranky, son. Everything is going along just fine. But we can't tell you any more else you'll bugger things up. And if we did you wouldn't believe it anyway."

He glared at them a moment, shaking his head, then sighed, "All right then. I won't ask. Just tell me what I need to know."

Sandy leaned forward. "After you are married take your family back down to Wyandera and stay there. Stay there with Ellie, all right, and make that your home base."

Then Peter said something to them in his language and Everard pricked his ears up at that, but Sandy simply nodded.

"That wagon driver bloke you sacked is causing us big trouble. He's been talking to the Welfare so we might have to bring the remaining families back up here out of harm's way. The missionaries over at Dadjari are good people. They will look after them."

"Ian and Cath are maybe going to live on the farm up in the Wellesley," Ned replied. "We might buy another place closer to Weethangara, or maybe between there and Mount Tambla on those good river flats. Maybe both."

"Is that right? When will that be, do you reckon?"

"Not for a bit, Sandy. We were not really planning on doing anything much for a while, apart from running cattle for the army and what have you." Then he glanced away thinking, "Well, we weren't going to, at any rate. What's on your mind?"

157

The old man sat back sucking his teeth thoughtfully for a moment, then spoke briefly with Peter in the language. When they had finished he nodded and said, "All right, that won't hurt."

"What about Sam Clancy and his boys?"

"Oh, well, don't worry about them. I know he's got your father on edge with all his bullshit, but I tell you what," he leaned over conspiratorially, "let him take Chatham off your hands. We can set it up, make him think he's won something over us, and he'll get real cocky after that. We can sort him out at this end."

Then Sandy stood suddenly to shake hands.

"You may not see us again, lad, but then again maybe you will. If anything comes up let Everard know, all right."

Everard took his arm then and led him away. After a few paces he turned to look back but they had already disappeared, campfire and everything, so he went straight back to his swag and rolled up in his blanket and went to sleep.

Next morning Don sent him back to take Cath's place ringing the spare horses while he kept Elizabeth close by his side the rest of the way home. They were a little short of men now but the new hands had learned their ropes so they needed little supervision, and this was the home run now anyway so rather than dawdle they kept the mob moving along at a steady pace.

Around noon the next day they came up on the camel wagon and after a brief parlay Achmed agreed to pack up and come with them the rest of the way home. There was a heated discussion among the old people about what to do but Everard sat quietly with them and in his soft gentle voice relayed the news about the Englishman Thwaites talking to Welfare, and the idea they tossing around about bringing all the families back up north with them on the next trip.

The current station owner did not like them being there anyway so they were all better off returning to Eurongera with them. If they liked they could go and live on the mission at Dadjari for a while, where there was a store and the children could go to school. In the end Everard agreed to stay with Bertram and when the chance came go with him to meet some of their own people still here on the big Bundingor Lakes run, and let them know what was happening.

Two days later they came up off the huge drainage basin forming the inland lake system and out again onto open red soil plain country where they followed the main wet season feeder channel right up into the southern boundary of Eurongera Station itself. Another two days after that they came in sight of the big old homestead way across on the horizon and Don sent Jimbo off to let Andrew and Thomas know they were coming in early tomorrow morning, and to have everything ready for the mob when it arrived.

CHAPTER TWENTY FIVE

Many, many years later Ned was to relate the story over and again about how he being the owner of Eurongera Station was refused permission to sleep in the main house, but was made to sleep in one of the staff cottages with an accountant. The way he told it never left the children guessing that the accountant was their great-uncle Ian, but as he became very old and finally incontinent he would shut up after that, and shake his head and look at them strangely, and not say another word.

In a way Mollie was relieved, and she respected his good manners and decorum after those years of living with a wayward daughter who she had thought was going to be the better of the two, and because of that in whom she had in her own way invested so much more, and kept her close. She shrugged and got on with it. She knew in her own heart there were few good men this far out away from the line of settlement, and as she thought about it more turned her head away from Elizabeth's adolescent tantrums toward the fine choice the girl had made in her own clear mind, and the reason for it so she thought, and as her wedding day approached she softened.

On the day itself there was little in the way of festivities. The minister arrived in his sulky finally and Ian led Ned up the steps onto the front verandah and handed him to his bride, waiting there to be given away by her father. The congregation at large comprised the station overseers and stockmen and their women, and beyond them rings of old people around their camp fires singing and clapping to their own tune. Ian for his part had cleaned their cottage out and scrubbed it spotless, then lacking traditional flowers had the place strewn with eucalyptus and grevillea he and Cath collected from the surrounding bush.

Once their vows were made there was nowhere to go. They had no rings to exchange so they used woven kangaroo hide strips in their place, until such time as they could visit a proper jeweler. Ah Poy and Mollie made them the best dinner they could have imagined, except that apart from family their only guests were the foremen and head ringers and their mixed broods. Children everywhere. When it was over Ian and Cath made a great show of taking them all the way around the homestead perimeter in a sulky decorated with ribbons and trailing empty soup tins, which made an awful clanging rattle on the stony ground, before depositing them regally at their cottage. Once safely at home they shut the door and left the world outside.

The two looked at each other awkwardly, shy now with the pressure suddenly off, then Elizabeth turned abruptly and went to their room and shut the door. Ned was left standing there somewhat aback, but after a moment he went to the stove and made a pot of tea.

Presently she came out having changed into a light summer frock, and stood there smoothing the creases.

"Do I look nice?"

He nodded, smiling.

She glanced away briefly and frowned slightly, then went to gaze out the window.

"Have we done the right thing, Ned? I mean, it feels so strange now. I really don't know what came over me."

He thought about that a moment but decided not to reply. He did not want to go down that track with her, but keep his own counsel.

"I have made a nice pot of tea," he said finally. "Would you like some?"

She nodded shyly and came over and sat down. He filled her cup then setting the pot down reached over to take her hand and squeeze it gently.

"Elizabeth, you are my wife, and nothing I can possibly imagine would want me to change that, ever." He paused, then shrugged, "I know we are young but we're old enough. We'll manage."

She put her cup down and with that hand reached over and cupped his cheek, stroking it gently with her thumb. He leaned his head into it and sat thoughtfully, lost in the caress. After a long moment he took her wrist and put her arm down on the table.

"Finish your tea before it gets cold. Then you can show me around the place."

She looked at him, and he paused and added, smiling, "We'll go out the back way. Don't worry, they'll leave us alone. We can go for a long walk, don't you think, just you and I."

While she drank he went to change back into his work clothes, out of the bad suit Don had sacrificed and Mollie spent hours trying to make fit. Presently he called out to her to come and help him out of it since the pins around the small of his back which held his pants together were hard to reach, and he pricked himself time and again trying to get them out.

When she came into their room and saw what he was trying to do she put her hand up to her mouth and giggled, then turned him around and had the job done in no time. Without thinking he bent down and stepped out of them and stood there in his underwear, and she sat on the bed blushing.

"Oh Ned," she looked up, "you must think me terribly forward."

"No, I don't think that."

He dressed then and took her hand. "Come on, show me around the place."

Out the back door they stepped down off the porch and along a rough path through a broken patch of garden some long gone overseer had planted, or his wife and family at least, then turned off toward the river.

As they strolled along hand in hand Elizabeth finally looked up at him and said, "You know, Ned, you and Ian are so very handsome, do you know that? Cath and I used to swoon over you. When mother allowed her to go and live on Wyandera with Ellie then kept me home with her, it was very hard to bear."

"Forgive me, I know jealousy is a curse," she went on, "but I couldn't help myself."

He squeezed her hand again then turned and looked at her, walking backward, and stopped, gazing directly into her eyes.

"Can I say something to you, Elizabeth?"

"Yes, of course."

"Ian thinks I am dumb. I know he doesn't quite mean it that way, not in some things, but he grew up with two older sisters and in my family there is only me. Some things I don't understand very well, or maybe too technical, or something anyway." He stopped at that and looked absently away. "Something happened, I don't know what it was, but after I was born mother couldn't have any more children. Like Ellie."

Then he shrugged, and turned and started walking again. "So here we are," he said finally.

By that time they had come onto a bend in the river, with its white sandy beach and broad sweep of water facing steep banks on the other side. Here the trees were tall and overhanging, making a shady private place; in the lowering afternoon sun surprising lovely off the vast stony plain they had crossed following the river up from the lakes.

"We used to spend all our time here, Cath and I, when we were little, and growing up."

She turned to him then. "When Cath went I sat here alone week after week, every time I was home, just thinking about you. The old people over there would be singing and singing and singing for hours, and it was all so very enchanting I honestly thought they were singing for me, singing for me to bring you here."

"What did you just say?"

"Singing to me, Ned. It was so very strange, so utterly beautiful, it stole my heart away."

He looked at her intently, probing, then walked over a way to the edge of the water and turned to look back at her once more. He looked away again and back, his eyes narrowed, pursing his lips, then abruptly turned on his heel and walked back across to the cottage.

Every day as they went out on their walks the camp was deserted and they said little to each other. Every night Ned lay awake tossing and turning while Elizabeth slept. It was not until a five days later that he finally dropped off to sleep. She worried over him, and cooked his meals and washed his clothes, glancing across at him occasionally, but left him be.

Sometimes he called out to Sandy, in the wee small hours, then mumbled about Angus and that soft-talking Everard, and Daniel, and Peter Old Bloody Foley you bastard, then burbled and went back to sleep. Early one morning she woke to find him in a fever, his limbs shaking and in a sweat, so she left him in bed and went to pour a hot bath. When she came back he was tangled in the sheets so she gently unwound him and stripped him of his pajamas, then standing him up walked him out to the bathroom and sat him in the warm soapy water.

She undressed herself then and stepped into the bath opposite him. Taking up the cloth she washed him all over. She stood and took a dipper and filled it with warm water from the tap, and sat again slowly pouring it over him, rinsing his body and talking to him quietly.

As she wiped his face his eyes focused finally and he looked at her.

"Elizabeth, what are you doing?"

"I am your wife, Ned, and I have had enough of this. That's enough, do you hear me?" Then she started to cry.

He reached up to wipe her tears but she pushed his hand away impatiently and went back to her task. That done she stood him up and stepped him out of the tub and dried him off, then drying herself walked him back to bed and tucked him in. She went out again to empty the bath and tidy up. Bone tired she went back to bed finally and tucked herself in next to him.

He slept, and slept and slept. Elizabeth woke occasionally to check on him, then went out for her ablutions and came back in to sleep once more.

Late next morning, almost noon, she woke to find him sitting there on the edge of the bed in a bathrobe, with a tray full of hot breakfast and a pot of tea. He held it while she sat up and pulled the sheet up to cover her breasts, but he reached for a knitted cardigan and put that on her instead.

When she had finished breakfast he took the tray out to the kitchen and left it on the bench, then came back in to sit with her. She watched him closely for a moment, her hands in her lap, but he leaned over and took them and placed them by her side. Then her held her forward and bared her shoulders, and taking the cardigan from her sat her back against the pillow.

"You think I am handsome, do you?" he wanted to know. She nodded.

"And that Ramsay fellow, that show pony, is it?" She nodded again.

"So you would rather him, a blackguard pirate, is that what you arc saying?"

She shook her head at that, giggling, then reached up and pulled him close and kissed him, caressing his cheek. "No, only you," she whispered softly into his ear

Then she held him to her and undid his bathrobe, and reached inside to touch and hold him. He let her, leaning in close to kiss her lips, then her neck and her breasts. Setting the sheets aside she drew him to her and they made love for the first time, then again and again all afternoon and into the small hours.

She was with child straight away, he knew it, that first day. Her egg was there already he thought, making her so very receptive, and when he asked her where she was in her cycle she simply told him.

There was no doubt in his mind after that, but he had accepted the way things were going to be. He knew then that they had fulfilled their part of the bargain, whatever it was; the family so desperate for another heir in case something happened to him was all he could think at that moment. He would have to trust they knew what they were doing.

CHAPTER TWENTY SIX

One morning near the end of the week they were having breakfast when there came a polite knock on the door. Elizabeth called out to wait a moment and they hurried to dress decently and make themselves presentable, then he went out to find Mollie on the front steps with a huge basket under her arm.

"I have brought you some things," she said brightly.

"Come in, come in," he said, and as she stepped back onto the verandah gave her a quick peck on the cheek.

She bustled into the kitchen and put the basket on the table, then turned to look her daughter up and down. With a quick glance at Ned she smiled softly to herself and began to unpack the basket.

"Mummy," Elizabeth said blankly, "Leave it. I will put it away later."

Mollie just looked at her, confused.

Ned quickly began to clean up their dishes and wiping the table down set out some clean cups, then went over to the stove and put on the kettle for a fresh pot of tea. Then he turned back to her and asked, "Where is everybody?"

"We have been here all the while, Ned."

"No, I mean, the place is so quiet. What is going on?"

She looked up at that. "They have taken the cattle up to Chatham and are bringing the rest of the horses back, that's all. The other boys have taken the old people and children over to Dadjari, to the mission, then they are riding across to Chatham to help with the horses."

"Really? When will they be back?"

"Our lot? Tomorrow some time, I expect. They will be here in time for Christmas."

Ned and Elizabeth glanced at one another, eyes widening.

"I bought some presents when we were in town," Mollie went on, "and some lovely paper and ribbon. I thought it would be nice if we had everything wrapped under the tree before they got back."

Then she reached into the basket and took out a small package wrapped in soft green velvet.

"Ned, I know you have Don's watch so I want you to have this as well."

He reached over and took it from her, and sat a moment unfolding it. It contained the original presentation case and gold chain that Don had never used, but left sitting on the mantle above the fire place in the main house.

Elizabeth looked stonily at her, then stared daggers at her husband.

"All right, Mummy, please, we will be over directly."

She stood ready to go, but Ned took her arm and nodded reassuringly. "Give us ten minutes or so. We'll love to help. And thank you for the things. We'll be over."

Then he escorted her to the door.

Back in the kitchen Elizabeth was furious. "Ned, you have no idea!"

He held his hand up, then put his finger to his lips, and as she went to speak reached over and did the same with her.

"Elizabeth, I don't want to know, all right."

She stamped her foot in frustration.

"No," he said. "Sit down a moment."

Then he held both her hands and looked at her very directly, waiting until she settled.

"Ned, you are my husband," she said softly to herself, almost inaudibly, and he nodded.

"Yes I am, and you are my wife. But I am also the owner of all this, the big decider. You are the wife of the big decider. I didn't ask for it and neither did you, and there is far too much we simply do not understand yet. I honestly don't know what is going on yet, all right? I need you with me more than you can imagine."

Then he leaned over and kissed her, adding, "And now we have a baby to look after."

After a moment he leaned back thoughtfully. "Your mother is just trying to be nice. She is losing a daughter, both daughters. Maybe she is as confused as we are."

She looked at him, then stood and went into the bathroom. After a while she came out with her face clean and hair neatly brushed, with a light rouge and new lipstick. She went into the bedroom and brought out her father's watch, and taking up the gold chain clipped it onto the top ring then standing him up slipped the watch into his fob pocket and set the cross piece into his fourth button hole. Then she changed it to his fifth, and back to the fourth again, and finally satisfied took her comb and tidied his hair.

"The main trouble with you, Mr Edward Arthur Collins, is that you are the maddest loosest most eminently sensible man any of us has ever met."

Then she took his hand and led him over to the big house where she made herself right at home, as she had from the time she was such a little girl, bossing her mother around mercilessly. In no time at all she had paper strewn all over the floor and presents wrapped, with Ned out the back looking for a nice athol or she-oak to serve as a Christmas tree. When he brought one in they set it in a tub of damp sand and decorated it with ribbons and tinsel, and dried figs and bags of raisins, and muscatels hung in bunches, and small paper wrappers of boiled lollies.

As they worked he looked around the big house, then presently took one of Don's guns down off the rack over the fireplace and filling his pockets with cartridges went back out again to bag a few ducks on the river. There were plenty of them, coming back in to graze on the water with the station so quiet now, and he filled his bag.

Walking back across the river flat a huge raucous flock of galahs swooped over suddenly and he took a quick shot bringing one down. With the one bird flapping around screeching helplessly on the ground the flock circled thickly overhead allowing him to bring down another dozen they were so thickly clustered, before the cloud of birds came to its senses and flew off out of range.

Ah Poy had heard the shots and was waiting for him at the back door.

"Ah, velly good Mister Ned. Good shot. Nice duck for Clissmass, I cook 'im up number one, orright?"

Then he looked in the bag and saw the galahs there as well.

"You like galah! I cook 'im galah pie, extra special. No worry, Mister Ned!"

Then he took the bag into the kitchen and emptied it straight onto the floor. Taking one of his sharp filleting knives he picked up a galah and without bothering to pluck it split the breast skin with his thumb and peeled it back over the wings to expose the breast fillets, which he deftly trimmed away with his knife. Then he threw the carcase down on the floor and bent to pick up the next, then the next one after the other. After he had finished the pile he reached for his chopper and diced the breast fillets into cubes, then placed them in a covered dish in the meat safe.

Ned watched him closely as he started on the ducks.

"You need any help, Ah Poy?"

"Mister Ned, you go now, orright. I fixee number one." Then he looked up at him. "You want do someting for me? Go shoot 'im goat, orright. Plenty there upriver. Two young nanny goat, bring 'im back, I fixee proper dinner. Make 'im happy Clissmass evlybody."

Leaving the gun there on the verandah he went inside again and looked over Don's rifles, including a fine Lee-Enfield .303 from the Great War, and an American 30-30 Winchester. Finally he picked up a small single shot .22 from the small arms factory in Lithgow, and with a handful of bullets went out again and made his way upstream in the general direction Ah Poy said there were goats.

Certainly there were plenty of tracks around, but the sun was high and it was still a bit hot so he settled there under a tree and waited. After an hour or so as the sun began to dip, in the lengthening shadows he heard their bleating as they began to come in to drink. As they came in sight he picked one off in the neck and dropped it, a young doe about half grown, and the rest scattered in fright back the way they had come.

Quietly reloading he waited another half an hour until the small herd came gingerly back in toward the river. He bade his time until the leaders passed, then another young doe the same as the first appeared and he took it too with a clear head shot.

This time he simply stood and went over and picked them up, and with their legs together threw them over his shoulder. Taking up the rifle he went straight back to the kitchen and deposited them on the verandah. Ah Poy wasn't there so he went inside. The house was empty as well.

Carefully cleaning and oiling the shotgun he had used earlier, then the small rifle, he put everything back in order before leaving by the front door. Mollie was in the garden pruning her roses and she stood and smiled at him as he went past. There was blood on his clothes so when he got home he stepped straight out of them and had his bath, then when he was clean put them in the tub to soak in the now-cold water.

Mid-morning next day they heard the welcome thunder of hooves, and drawing aside the curtain watched the horses come racing in across the bare flat with Cath at the lead taking them through into the yards.

Together he and Elizabeth went out and crossed over to see how they were going. As they came up everyone stopped to stare. Don trotted in through the dust behind them, leading a mare with a foal at foot. As he pulled up he dismounted, and turned and gave his daughter a peck on the cheek, then lifted her face to his and gazed steadily into her eyes.

She smiled at him shyly. Satisfied, he turned then and shook Ned by the hand, glancing as he did at the gold watch chain. Nodding to himself he led the mare and foal through the gate.

Inside the yard he called back over her shoulder, "Put the kettle on, son, we'll be there in a tick."

So they went back over to the cottage and made ready. Elizabeth had baked some scones with the flour and eggs Mollie brought over in the basket, and there was plum jam and fresh cream, and milk in the ice box from Ah Poy's house cow. She set the table with a nice checked cotton cloth and bustled about nervously while Ned looked on smiling inwardly to himself. Presently the horses were settled and the men let go, and their guests trooped noisily up the front steps, shaking the dust off on the verandah and leaving their hats and boots outside. Elizabeth went to let them in.

All seated politely at the table she passed around her scones and poured cups of tea, and they ate and drank. Nothing was said for a while until Ned finally coughed and they looked up at him.

"I didn't know you were going anywhere, Don," he said.

The other looked up at him dead-pan. "Why, was there something you needed a hand with?"

Ian guffawed and Cath reached over and slapped his shoulder, then glared daggers at her father. Andrew sat sipping his tea, nonplussed. Elizabeth looked across at Ned and blushed slightly, but he held her gaze steadily then returned to his conversation.

"I wasn't thinking about taking that mob on to Chatham straight away, that's all."

Don sat back in his chair, and taking his pipe out of his pocket filled it with tobacco and lit it. He took a few puffs, then gazed shrewdly through the smoke. "There is some good summer pasture up there, and we could use it."

"That's fair enough," Ned nodded. "How are we doing here, and Dadjari?"

"A bit bare, but with the rain this year come winter we'll recover."

Ned sat back thinking a moment, then leaned forward. "All right, this is what I want you to do. For now, run everything we have up onto Chatham and winter them over; everything you can muster. Come Spring cull everything we don't want, or might hold us back over the next five or six years; we'll come back up and help you if need be, then bring our best stock back down here. Only the very best. Leave the culls up there."

"Go on."

"By then we'll have a buyer for that place."

Don cocked his head. "You are talking about Chatham, are you not?"

"Yes, yes of course. Chatham. We'll get the place back after the war, they'll give it back. It will be flogged out by then and we can leave it lie fallow a few years, overall maybe six or eight years at most. We'll be right after that."

Ian was staring very directly at him by this. "What are you saying, Ned?"

"What I am saying is, Mr Ramsay, we are staying out of this one; keeping our distance. I know what that may mean to you, and I will respect your decision. I only need to know if you are with me or nor."

Ian looked at Cath, and Don and Elizabeth, and thought a moment, then nodded.

"Yes, we are with you," he said quietly.

"And you, Mr MacFarlane?"

"Yes, I am with you."

Don sat back, sucking on his pipe, nodding inwardly to himself.

CHAPTER TWENTY SEVEN

Two days after Christmas they rode out with the horses for Wyandera. Don's habit of not saying much just getting on with the job was starting to wear off on them, and the girls especially began to show their colours. Boxing Day was spent severely culling the horses amid heated argument over Ned's strict standards, and they left with only one third of those that had arrived from Chatham on Christmas Eve. When they left it was with a skeleton crew intent on making a fast run all the way, leaving behind the most number of hands he could afford to leave, opting instead to take Andrew with his years of experience along with them.

Three days out, a good way downstream along the river toward the lake system, Ned was tailing the mob when he heard riders coming up behind him at a fast trot. He turned to see who it might be. As his eyes adjusted he made out four horsemen approaching through the shimmer. When they came near he saw that it was Daniel and Everard, with Thomas and Bertram close behind. He pulled off the track slightly and waited, then when they came up he stepped out and they stopped.

"I told Don I didn't need any more men," he called as they came alongside.

They glanced at each other, confused, then rode in close looking at him.

He cocked his head. "Which way did you come?"

Bertram turned and waved his hand back toward the north-east rather than north. "Cut across Yammana, boss, no Eurongera. Close-up Dadjari this way. Eurongera long way."

He nodded at that, then turned and looked south awhile, thinking, and back at them.

"You're bringing the rest of the people back up, is that right?"

"Yes, boss. That Achmed come along shortly, bring 'im camel, wagon, supply, no worries. Take 'is time, that's all."

"So what are you doing coming up on us? Why don't you wait for Achmed, and ride with him?"

"Looking after country, boss," Daniel said, leaning forward in his saddle.

"All right," he said, turning to Everard. "So what is he doing here?"

"'E doctor now, properly, keep an eye on things."

"Witch bloody doctor, is it?"

"No, proper doctor, look after country, people, like old time. Look after baby now, properly, no worries."

"What? Baby?" Ned glanced up sharply. "What baby? What are you talking about?"

They all looked up the track toward the horses, which had slowed waiting for him. Elizabeth was just behind, there on the side of the track looking back at him, and Everard looked at her directly.

"That one, Ned." he said softly, earnestly, "That little boy, Angus, that one. That little boy your baby now. Everything all right now, keep an eye on 'im, all right. Look after 'im for you now, no more racing, bring 'im up properly this time."

Suddenly everything came in on him in a rush. Ned staggered back dazed. Without looking aside he crossed in front of them into the scrub a way and rode around a bit, then after a while came back onto the track and paused briefly beside them.

"If any one of you even thinks to mention a word of this to my wife, ever, I will kill you. I will hunt you down like a dog and I will shoot you myself. Do you understand that?"

They sat stony silent, gazing steadily at him, then he trotted right up to the head of the mob passing Elizabeth without a glance. After a brief discussion the three extra hands they had brought with them as ringers went over and got their gear off the sulky, then rode off north back toward Eurongera.

Then he called back loudly, "Bring your men up now, Mr Foley, if you please."

They started off again promptly, and Ned returned to his place tailing the mob.

Two days later they arrived back on the broad flat between the lakes where they had stopped to calve the previous month, and he decided to break there and wait for Achmed to come up with the camel wagon. He and Elizabeth set up their own camp away from the others, behind the sulky, and to keep order kept Ian and Andrew together with Cath by herself next to their cooking fire. The other men made their own camp away from them altogether.

Keeping themselves busy they built some temporary yards from cut saplings, and spent their days breaking in the horses one after the other and getting them working.

Eventually Achmed arrived and they packed everything onto the wagon and headed off straight away. The day after next they climbed slowly up the face of the tableland and settled at the top for the night, then early next morning continued on their way. At this much slower pace Ned changed his ideas, and with the extra supplies on the wagon to keep them going, rather than running along at a good pace decided instead to work the horses all the way. Twice a day he had them change their mounts, taking each horse through its paces then allowing it to spell before a new rider worked the animal again in their own way.

This was where Cath came into her own, he could see. She started watching them all with a critical eye, calling out with a hint or a tip, or a trick she had learned in competition. As luck would have it as they rode through the broken country on the southern slopes they came across a small mob of unbranded strays, so they took them along with them a good way to practice their drafting and cutting as they went along. At the end of that week they butchered a yearling cow for extra rations and let the rest go, then spent the rest of the day salting and drying as much meat as they could carry, and cut the rest into steaks.

By then they had come back into the northern stock routes where the district was more closely settled and the way defined by fences and bores to provide fresh water. That was where Elizabeth woke one morning vomiting and the news got out finally that she was pregnant. Cath came over and began to fuss over her until she got short shrift, while Ian simply stood back bemused, a new respect in his eye. Ned sent them to keep tabs on the horses, then called Andrew over to go fetch Everard which he did. Achmed was with him bringing a small box containing herbs, and bush medicine he explained; something like dried raspberries to settle her stomach.

While he was boiling some water and infusing them for her to drink Bertram came in with a bag full of freshly picked quandongs which he gave them, then turned his horse and went back to work.

The tea ready Everard let it cool then gave it to her to drink. She grimaced at the taste but soon had it all down, then he gave her some dry biscuits to nibble with instructions to do the same first thing every morning once she had brought up the bile from her stomach. Immediately after breakfast she harnessed the sulky, and placing her saddle and gear in the back put the picnic basket Achmed had made up on the seat beside her, full of cold cuts, fruit, damper and johnnie cakes, and sat impatiently for the rest of them to hurry up.

Over the next few weeks whenever she felt well enough she would ride, and improved quite a lot once she learned to eat small amounts frequently during the day and keep something at least in her stomach, rather than join the others in their three big meals. While mounted Cath would often drop back to ride with her and they spent a lot of their time just talking and being together. As Ned watched them like that he began to realise how little they had actually seen of each other these past few years, and let them be. Whenever they were near a town he sent Achmed in with Ian in the sulky to buy whatever fresh fruit they could get along with their other supplies, and that way by mid-February they were home.

CHAPTER TWENTY EIGHT

It was late in the day, so when they came up to the five-mile they left the horses and plant there on the reserve while Ned drove Elizabeth the rest of the way in the sulky. Ellie was out on the front verandah having heard the dogs bark as they came up the track, and when she saw it was them came down to the garden gate smiling happily. The moment she laid eyes on Elizabeth however she stopped, cocking her head thoughtfully, then when she stepped down off the sulky took both her hands and gazed steadily into her face, nodding quietly to herself.

As Ned came around from the driver's side and she let Elizabeth go, he leaned over and gave her a peck on the cheek. She glanced at him only quickly before turning to take them inside, but Ned took Elizabeth's trunk with the rest of their gear down off the sulky and leaving everything there next to the gate led the horse over to the stables where he unharnessed it and took it into a clean stall to brush it down. Only when he was done caring for the animal did he come back over to the house, and picking up the trunk took it inside before coming back for the rest of their gear which he left out on the verandah.

The two women were in the kitchen having a cup of tea. When he came in Ellie stood and led them both back across the passage to the main bedroom which she had made up awaiting their return.

"This is your place now," she said. "I had some builders in while you were away, and they made me a nice little flat at the back. I hope you won't mind, silly old me."

"I had a letter from Mollie," she went on, "sending me the good news. It arrived five weeks ago. I was so very pleased for you both so I had a bit of work done around the place, to make things comfortable for when you got back."

She took them both by the hand and stood back, looking up admiringly.

"Now here you are. Come along once you have cleaned up. I don't have much, a cold leg of lamb and vegetables, but there is some stewed fruit. We'll make do, I am certain."

Ellie turned at that and went out back up to the kitchen, then without saying anything Ned went back down the passage to the front door and brought up the trunk. He stood thinking to himself for a moment, then leaving Elizabeth to attend to her bath followed Ellie down to the kitchen. He stood in the doorway watching her at the stove, and she turned to gaze then directly at him. He held her eye for a long pause until finally she turned back with a sigh to her cooking.

"Come and sit with me Ned," she said quietly, then as he sat added almost to herself. "What's done is done, do you hear me?"

"Yes, I hear you," he replied, not angry with her simply tired and frustrated with the business, "but now I want you to hear me, all right."

She held her hand up at that to quiet him, then turned more fiercely determined to him. "No, I will not! There is nothing for you to say, young man. It's the way of things with us and there is not a skerrick any of us can say or do about it. I have nothing to say myself, Ned, and I will hear nothing from you either."

He was taken aback by that so she softened again, then sat and took his hand gazing directly into his eyes.

"My son Hamish is on a foreign field, in Belgium, and there is neither a scrap we can do about that. Thank God in Heaven we have Angus back with us, and when he arrives he can have his old room."

He looked at her again. "I told the boys I would kill them if Elizabeth ever found out."

"You do as you will, Ned, and you will destroy everything we have built up," her voice taut with dread. "We cannot force things, or interfere, none of us. You must not even think like that, not ever, or the darkness will engulf you."

Then she stopped and sighed, shaking her head sadly, and placing a bowl in front of him said simply, "Here, shell these peas for me, there's a pet."

Just after dawn broke early next morning they heard the horses come in so they rose from their beds and began preparing breakfast. Eventually they heard the loud braying snort of the camels complaining as they pulled in off the track, and not long after the thud of boots on the front verandah and up the passage. Cath and Ian burst in with Andrew close on their heels.

After lunch they were in the big yard with the horses when Arthur drove up in the car, so Ned gave his leave and went over to greet him. After a brief conversation he waved back to the others to keep going without him as they went up into the house and straight into the study. Elizabeth came down to see who it was and they took the chance to let Arthur know he was soon to be a grandfather. He smiled but didn't say much beyond cursory congratulations, and when Elizabeth went to make them some tea and scones he sat down on the big leather sofa and lit his pipe.

Ned sat at the desk looking across at him waiting for him to speak, and when he did not asked, "How did you know we'd be back, Dad?"

"We had a letter from Mollie about five weeks ago, son, said you were pushing along. I just took a punt you'd be here by now."

"So, what's happening?"

Arthur turned to look at him, barely disguising his annoyance. "That young Clancy is causing trouble for us, bad mouthing us around the public bars. Damned hooligan, I have a good mind to have him up on charges."

Ned looked at him, eyes wide, then quietly chuckled to himself.

"I fail to see the humour in it!"

Elizabeth came in with morning tea then left quietly while he gazed through the window into the far distance, thinking instead about Sandy and old Peter, and slowly nodded his head in recognition. Then he turned shrewdly to his father.

"We are not going to play their game anymore, Dad," he said. "We are a hell of a lot smarter than they are. How big a hole can we get him to dig for himself, do you think?"

The other gazed steadily at him through the smoke from his pipe, one eyebrow raised in askance.

Ned sat back in his seat, then picked up a pencil and toyed with it. "We might well be looking for a buyer to take Chatham off our hands, come spring."

"Those hooligans haven't got that sort of money, you know that as well as I do."

"Well, right now they don't, I'll grant you that. But maybe once the war starts they could be extended a bank overdraft, and a commercial line of credit, couldn't they, against the value of the place?"

"And against the strong price for cattle you suggest?"

He nodded, adding, "He will have signed contracts to supply the army."

"Why not simply do it ourselves?"

"Dad, you're not listening. To keep his contracts he will have to buy from us anyway because we own the surrounding country. We have good standing with our neighbours they will never have, never in a pink fit. All we have to do is maintain our breeding program on Eurongera and Dadjari, and work with Simon Wilson over on Yammana. And he will have to use our stockmen because his own boys are too bloody useless. Don and Andrew can handle things at that end. We'll be all right."

"He'll be in the pub all the time big-noting himself, you know that Dad," he went on, "making out he's in control of the whole shebang. He'll be the big boss running the show, that's what he wants, and Enid will be so proud of him. But his pasture will deteriorate and his stock will progressively lose condition while ours continue to improve. After the war we take the market back with our own product, then we foreclose."

"And we are to encourage him in his thinking, are we?"

A cheeky grin crept across Ned's face. "Only about being in control. Yes, why not? Of course we could. He is bad-mouthing us around the pubs, is that right? But in the public bar. You drink in the lounge, and in the dining room."

He thought for a moment. "What you could do, is one evening make out you had a bit too much to drink, maybe over a few ports with some of your associates. Start talking too loud, let's say about how that son of yours has turned into a spoiled brat; too long away at boarding school; got his cousin in the family way; making errors of judgment with the low price of horses; spending too much money."

Arthur gazed at him through his pipe smoke. "Go on."

"Later on one of the agents could let it drop that they have an old client facing financial difficulties, and has to let go some of his holdings. They could be buttering up Auntie Enid in the meantime and let her know quietly, on the side, that the client is young Ned Collins, and could she persuade Sam to help out a little, and take Chatham off his hands. She won't be able to resist."

"Mud sticks, son."

"Maybe, maybe not. I could grow a moustache and take on a raffish air, drive around in the Cabriolet whenever we are in town which will not be that often anyway; just enough to make that sort of impression and keep them grinning. Ian would be good at that. We could have a bit of fun,"

Arthur snorted and nodded quietly to himself. "Your Auntie Mollie is coming down, Ned. I don't think she knows about the baby yet, just doesn't want to be up there now by herself. She can stay with us if you wish."

Ned looked at him and shrugged. "It may be better to discuss that with Elizabeth, Dad. I don't think they get along terribly well. Anyway Cath has her heart set on Ian and I don't think it will be too long before they marry. We will have to organise a place for them to live, perhaps closer to town would be better."

"What do you have in mind?"

"I don't know, really. What she will need is somewhere to run horses; maybe set up a riding school I expect, something like that, but not too far out. Ian has to be able to get in to the office every day."

"Gordon Mackie at the store has a place only a mile out on the Old Murrool Road that belonged to his uncle. Would that do? It's a good forty acres with a permanent creek down the back, frontage both sides."

He thought for a moment. "I know that place. Out past the football club, isn't it, past the show grounds, with that old house on it? Yes, right, I guess they will want you to take them into town when you go. Maybe when you get a chance take them out to have a look, eh?"

He paused shrewdly. "Don't make it too obvious. I know Ian. He hasn't forgiven us for his scholarship yet, much less taking him on the way you did. When I started at Mount Tambla he helped me a lot and didn't even blink. He was just such a good mate to have around, and he still is. He helped Michael Donovan as well. I know what Cath sees in him. If we do any more for him he will start to resent it."

"Dad, listen, he is not just the handsome devil people see in him. He runs much, much deeper than that," he nodded to himself distracted. "Perhaps we can secure that Mackie block for them as a wedding present, then extend mortgage finance or something. Do it that way, better."

Arthur glanced cannily across at him. His boy had grown up and was speaking to him as an adult. He was about to say something, but just then the dinner gong sounded loudly on the back verandah and they went to the kitchen where lunch was waiting.

The land deal with Mr Mackie went through in good order. Ian perused the papers and accepting the subtlety of it as a compliment to himself signed off without comment.

Back on Wyandera Daniel with Everard constantly at his side shepherded their people away into the back paddocks, moving them around keeping them out of the houses and out of sight so the place looked deserted. Whenever welfare officers arrived they were faced with Achmed and his camels angrily wanting to know what on earth was upsetting them all the time, with all these strangers and coming and going. Finally early one morning they all slipped quietly away, and when the police arrived with their warrants a week late there was nothing more to be said.

From that point Ian began a formal courting of Catherine McKenzie. As the occasion arose they took the train across to Mount Tambla, then up to their place in the Wellesleys to meet his parents and sisters, and their respective suitors. While they were away Elizabeth would take Ned by the hand and they would go on their own long walks together.

At the start of winter Don arrived with Mollie in the big Chevrolet Six. She told Judith quietly that they had decided to dissolve their marriage and sue for divorce. Don said nothing about it since he did not actually own much anyway, apart from the car which he was happy to leave now the girls were off their hands, and his gold watch and chain that Ned now wore.

The only business he had to discuss concerned the restocking of Chatham Station in preparation for placing the property on the market. After only three days back, early one morning he got Andrew out of bed and taking a spare horse each to carry their pack saddles the two of them rode all the way back up to Eurongera alone.

It was during that visit that more of the pieces for Ned's post-war strategy fell into place and he went into town one day to obtain his driver's license. Leaving Don's Chevrolet for Arthur to use he then took Elizabeth with him in the Ford and began looking at properties on the rich river flats between Weethangara and Mount Tambla.

Eventually he found a place he liked with a neighbouring farm, and drove on across to Mount Tambla to discuss their purchase with his trustees. After long discussions over their concerns with the extent of his restructuring they sent for Arthur and Ian to come over as well, and bring everyone with them.

In the event they decided the best thing would be to form a holding company with Ned as majority shareholder, through his trustees wholly owning their new subsidiaries. The remaining shares were distributed among his parents Arthur and Judith Collins, Don and Mollie McKenzie, their two daughters Catherine and Elizabeth, and Ian Ramsay. Ellie wasn't fussed with it he knew, and all that settled instructed Mr Faulkner to proceed with the various company registrations.

As it happened Michael was due to arrive home from University two days later for his first mid-Semester break, so nothing further to be said Arthur took Judith straight home with him in the Ford, leaving the big Chev for the four of them to return when they were ready. They were having lunch in the dining room when he arrived from the train station, not at all expecting them to be there, and Patrick side-tracked him in the foyer to let him know he had visitors.

What followed was a completely madcap week. Some days they wished they had the Cabriolet to drive around with the dickie seat in the back, but finally it came to an end. With all promising to keep in touch the four drove back to Weethangara.

CHAPTER TWENTY NINE

The offer to purchase Chatham Station came through during the first week of August. Once that was settled Ned left Arthur and Ian to manage the Clancy account. He then quietly made his move to acquire the new property Belkoomie and its neighbouring farm. Working there in Sandy's study day after day he decided finally to follow his advice and base himself permanently at Wyandera. The homestead was very well established with a good feel to it; the country was first class, and as he left the option open to go into thoroughbreds and maybe retrievers later he realised that was the place for him to be.

With his coming and going, and heavier with child, Elizabeth began increasingly to stay home with Ellie. The moment the Belkoomie purchase was complete he made one last trip alone to Mount Tambla to consult with his old teachers and go over his plans with them. They took him out to the school farm and introduced him to a student in his final year at university by the name of Peter McCallum, who through his work had attracted the attention of the federal government's newly-formed Advisory Council for Scientific and Industrial Research.

After dinner at the hotel the two of them sat talking into the small hours, and sleeping on their discussions Ned asked him next morning whether he would like to help establish a prime Black Angus stud, and base himself on his new property at Belkoomie on salary rather than come up all the way from Melbourne every trip.

Before he left, over lunch on the farm next day he put another idea to his old teachers about making a joint facility available to their agriculture students if he were to construct new barracks out there with a shower block and associated mess, assuming that Peter McCallum were to find the project suited his research program. They all agreed to put the proposal favourably to the school board while Peter said he would discuss it with his colleagues in Melbourne. Then they arranged to keep in touch by letter so he shook hands all round and took his leave.

On the first day of September Germany invaded Poland. Two days later England declared war, bringing Australia into the conflict. Three weeks after that Angus came suddenly back into the world at five o'clock in the morning, leaving no time to drive Elizabeth into the hospital.

Ellie acted as midwife with Ned standing by to assist. The baby arrived quickly, only an hour after her water broke and the pains started. The moment he was clear Ellie quickly bound off his umbilicus and cut him free. Clearing his mouth with her finger she set him crying with a sharp slap on the bottom, then bundled him in a clean towel and handed him straight over to his father. A short while later the placenta was clear, and giving Elizabeth a wipe down with a warm damp cloth Ellie took the baby back and unwrapping the towel placed him naked at his mother's breast, then wrapped them both in a clean sheet and blanket to keep warm while she went to clean up.

Ned sat stunned, and for several hours they just looked at one another and at the baby while Ellie came and went fussing over them. Eventually she returned and sent him packing so the mother could get some sleep, and he went to the kitchen and made himself something to eat. After lunch he poked his head in the door to see how they were, then everything settled drove the car into town to let everyone know the good news.

For the next few months there was little to do apart from attending to the mares they had in foal, and milking the house cow and butchering the occasional sheep for the table, so Ned stayed happily at home with his new family. Often of an evening when it was quiet he would pick up the baby and sit with him in his lap on the verandah, talking softly to him like an old friend. Elizabeth sometimes came and watched them silently from the door, smiling to herself, then without a sound slipped back inside.

In mid-November the whole family was out for dinner and with their new house almost ready Ian and Cath took the opportunity to announce their plan to marry at the end of January, in the chapel at Mount Tambla Grammar. After some discussion they decided to have Angus christened there at the same time, saving a trip over. Mollie wrote to Don to come down, giving him two months without the car, and he arrived promptly on Christmas Eve leaving Andrew to manage while he was away. On that note Christmas came and went and the newly-weds planned a trip to

Sydney for their honeymoon, at Manly Beach for two weeks, before taking the train home.

The day before the wedding while they were all still together they christened the baby Angus Alexander Edward, and at lunch Mollie explained to everyone that she and Don were getting back together. They planned to live in the old Mackie house at Cath's new riding school, much to Elizabeth's relief.

Don typically said nothing, until later over a beer in the hotel lounge he had a quick yarn with Ned and Arthur about Sam Clancy. He had taken a disliking to the man but had conned him into a droving contract, and might spend the war years out droving on the stock routes, keeping Andrew on as permanent manager of Eurongera. He loved the solitude of the bush; it was in his blood he explained, and couldn't stand the idea of living in town or staying in the one place for too long at a stretch.

When Elizabeth came in with the baby, however, Ned couldn't help but notice how Don took him straight away into his lap and sat there with a tiny hand clasped tightly around his little finger while he quietly finished his beer.

After the wedding itself and the reception at Donovan's they stayed over for two more days to catch up with everybody. Patrick had enlisted in the army, along with Trevor Percival and a few of the others, and attended in his new lieutenant's uniform. Michael for his part had achieved a High Distinction in Chemistry and they were all very proud of him. The mood was no longer gay and hearty since the shadow of war hung over everybody, but they made the best of it and talked instead about family and business.

One thing that did interest Ned quite a lot was the news that command headquarters were stationed again at their old school, partly he knew for security as much as strategic reasons, but at the same time he began to worry that the farm would be neglected and they would have to reinvest entirely after the war ended.

The next day he drove out to the school with Arthur and Patrick in the big Chev, where they were met at the gate by sentries wanting to know their business. After a brief exchange one of them made a quick telephone call then stepped up and waved them through. A new headmaster, Mr Killen, was waiting for them in the quadrangle and he promptly invited them into his office.

After they stated the reason for their visit he reassured them that everything was in order and that the school board had already approved the scheme for co-locating their livestock husbandry program on Belkoomie. He apologised that they had not been notified but there was a letter ready to be sent which he promptly called his secretary to retrieve, and when she brought it in he handed it to them directly.

While they were passing it around he told them that the ACSIR had further provided Peter McCallum with the resources to complete his dissertation toward a doctoral thesis in veterinary science, on the assumption that he would assist in establishing a field station on the property. He leaned forward and explained that Peter's thesis was primarily concerned with disease control through genetic improvement and management of parasites in pasture, and they began a long involved conversation about that fitting well into their own program until the head glanced at his watch suddenly and begged to be excused. The project was important he assured them, and he would keep in touch personally.

On their way out past the guards Arthur suddenly asked, "Why don't you take your family home in the Ford, Ned, while us old people take the Chev?"

Dinner was subdued and thoughtful that evening. In the end, as they all packed to leave the next morning they rearranged things so Ellie and Mollie went back to Weethangara with Arthur and Judie in the Chev, while Don sat in the back seat of the Cabriolet with his daughter and his new grandson all the way home.

All the way Ned kept looking back at them in the rear-vision mirror, and it was through that mirror that it finally occurred to him that he was not in fact Old Don but Young Don; Sandy McKenzie's nephew by his older brother Donald McKenzie, and Elizabeth his great niece. They were both as much bound to the scheme of things as he was, in their taciturn, unknowing way. At that moment he realised that this new baby Angus was not only Don's grandson but his first cousin. He was also his own mother's cousin once removed, whom they had lost through sheer bloody misadventure when they had such grand plans for him in bringing their scattered establishment up to where they felt it was secure finally.

He shook his head and sighed, not wanting to explore the implications further, though neither angry nor frustrated; like Ellie becoming more accepting of the fact and getting on with the job knowing full well how important the land was to them all, and what they were up against.

Better for him to get on with improving their lives than fight, or worse hold everything up arguing the pitch and toss. It was not until then that the significance of Auntie Ellie's 'little chats', and his mother's quiet prudence and persistence finally came home to him.

All the way home Everard kept singing inside his head. That was the other thing. They were bound together just as Sandy and Old Peter were bound. It was not Angus it was him; Angus was out of the race because the kinship bonding with Daniel had failed, except that they needed him there in the next generation because he too was fey. With himself there now, at that point there was also Ian on the other side, in the real world, to make things work. The time had come.

When they got home Don went into town with Arthur leaving Ellie on Wyandera with them, and the next day moved into the old Mackie house where for the next week he busied himself painting and tidying up around the building site, and finishing off the rails on Cath's horse yards, while Mollie made them curtains on her new sewing machine from material they had selected months before.

The newly-weds duly arrived home from their honeymoon not by train but in a new Ford Deluxe Station Wagon, which was the latest thing sporting an improved engine over Arthur's Cabriolet. It had timber paneling along the sides, transverse leaf spring suspension and Lockheed hydraulic drum brakes. Don took one look at it, and a few days later had Arthur bring him back out to Wyandera where he slept the night with the baby tucked in beside him. Early next morning he took his horses and rode off alone all the way back up to Eurongera.

CHAPTER THIRTY

In early February Ned received two registered letters in the one mailbox delivery, one from Mr Killen giving him formal notification of his board's approval of the Belkoomie scheme, and another from Peter McCallum containing a long list of attachments for him to sign and return. Having done that he sat down to write to Mr Faulkner, asking him to contact a reputable building firm asking them to send a man out to Belkoomie and quote on the construction of a barracks and a shower block and mess, and to let him know when it had been received and he would come over.

After lunch he took Elizabeth and Ellie with the baby into town and leaving them with Judith dropped by to see Arthur in his office. Cattle prices were buoyant with Chatham Station buying well, but on hearing the news he had them send a telegram immediately to Andrew not to overstock Eurongera in anticipation, but to conserve pasture and maintain quality.

With nothing else to do he stood around all afternoon listening to the reports coming in, and as he listened a certain unease began to creep in that slowly began to unsettle him.

Just before they were due to close for the day he had them send off another telegram to Andrew to report on the season up there, and send his rainfall figures for the summer. Straight away he sent another saying if need be shed stock east onto Yammana and south into Bundingor for agistment, and keep Eurongera and Dadjari in good condition.

As he paced around worrying, at the last minute he also had a message sent out to the mission at Dadjari asking them to go find Everard and tell him Ned wants to know how the summer had been. Ian was watching him closely by this time and as he caught his eye raised an eyebrow, causing him to stop and frown.

He cocked his head. "Mate, I've had my head down too far worrying about blood stock and pasture improvement, and not thinking about the weather. But these summer patterns are off." He shrugged and gazed out the window. "Maybe I am wrong, maybe, maybe, I don't know. I want to run through the figures, can we do that?"

"The Meteorological Office in Melbourne may be able to help, if that's what is worrying you. I can contact them and have them send regular weather reports."

"Can you do that?"

"Of course. Preoccupation of the navy, don't you know. The Fleet Air Arm and the RAAF are very concerned with the weather right now as well, as are the civil aviation people."

"Can we set up our own weather stations ourselves, and be sending data back to them do you think, fair exchange?"

Ian nodded.

"Dad?" he turned to Arthur who sat there tapping a pencil on his desk, watching him closely.

"You are talking to an accountant, Ned."

"All right, yes." Then he paced around, glancing back and forth between them. "There is a big drought coming. I can smell it. How close is it going to be if worse comes to the worst?"

"If you are right, we can lose the lot if we are not careful."

He looked at him, "Apart from that, I mean. What is our fall-back position, ultimately?"

Arthur sucked his teeth. "Putting it that way, we don't really know do we?"

"How can we know? How can we work toward predicting how things might be in, say, five years?"

"The war will be over Ned," Ian chipped in. "It all depends on who wins, won't it?"

"We'll win. I'm not worried about that. Let's say we do. What then?"

"The bottom line, Ned," Arthur said seriously, "is there is nothing going to affect us that will not affect everybody else. We are positioned well. If we go there will be a lot ahead of us."

He looked up at him then, adding. "We came through the Crash in 1929 pretty well unscathed. It was the cities who suffered most, quite badly in fact; as bad as Germany from what I gather. What I don't understand from you yet is what this has to do with the weather? This season has been very, very good, excellent. A dry summer or two won't make any difference."

The premonition hit him then, and he stared out the window for some time before turning back to his father. "It has been too good by far, that's the problem. This amount of rain out of season is just not right. How long before we get a reply to our telegrams?"

"Three or four days, usually, time it takes for the postie to ride from Kanyina and do his rounds, then back again. The mission has a radio for the Flying Doctor. Their sked is 1530 hours, so we might have a reply back from them late tomorrow or early Wednesday, if Everard hasn't gone walkabout."

Next day when the reply finally did come it was from Daniel on the radio, telling him that Everard was away up country but that old man Billy Nichols said there was a proper big dry coming.

Three days later a long telegram arrived from Andrew with detailed information from each of the outstations confirming that the country right across was too good, with far too many wildflowers out and trees bearing too much new seed, so he sent a reply back to await Don's arrival and confer with him then get back to them straight away.

All that morning he paced anxiously back and forth, then just before lunch called everyone in to Arthur's office and shut the door.

"How is the Clancy account coming along?" he wanted to know first.

"Steady," Arthur said. "Better than we expected, perhaps, but steady."

"All right, thanks for that. Leave him be for a while, eh? What we are going to do ourselves is move out altogether. We keep all our stations, and when Sam runs out of cattle to sell and runs out of credit we will take

Chatham back as well, maybe three years at most. In the meantime I want them all destocked."

"Are you serious?"

"Yes, very serious." Then he leaned forward. "Don't worry about the war. Our real problem right now is that we are headed for one hell of a drought. I am prepared to wager that when Don gets back up to Eurongera he will say the same."

They all sat up at that, alert now and listening intently.

"Dad, I want you to engage another droving plant, but on the quiet. Nobody local. Bring them up from South Australia if you have to. They are to bring all our prime breeding stock back down here to Wyandera. We will split them up here and send some over to Belkoomie perhaps, and the stockmen can return home from there. Then find me a station manager for Belkoomie, whoever you think is the best and offer him a good package."

He sat and thought a little longer, tapping his pencil. "Do you remember that Mr Tanner, Dad, who Sandy had working for him a while back, when he was mucking around with the rice? Can you get the word around, and find him? We need a farm manager over there as well, who knows something about fodder crops and the rest of it."

"What you are saying," Ian wanted to know, "is that prices are going to start going up because of this drought, and the war; because supply will be short?"

Rather than answer him Ned glanced across at Arthur who sat nodding quietly to himself before replying in his stead. "Assuming Ned to be correct, and worse does come to the worst, about two years I would anticipate. By then we will be supplying yearling beef, am I right?"

"Well, yes, that's about the strength of it."

"Collins," Ian exclaimed, "you have the damned hide to call me a pirate. But what you are yourself is a flamin' bushranger. That's the whole truth of it!"

Ned picked up a paper clip from the desk and threw it at him, then grinning from ear to ear got up from his chair and went outside. He turned as they followed him out and shook hands all round, then went to pick up Ellie and his family for the trip home.

CHAPTER THIRTY ONE

Angus was rolling around vigorously by this stage and full of mischief. Every time they bathed or changed him they had to keep hold to stop him from falling off the table, and even then he would squirm and catch their eye. He had a peculiar way of holding his head as he did so, causing Ned to check him over and over for malformity but found none, and eventually tried instead to simply put it out of his mind.

At dinner each night he took to having him sit in his lap while he ate his food, like he did on the verandah, holding him with one arm around him while he ate from a fork in his other hand. The baby's eyes would follow the food, so one night he slipped a morsel of cold lamb into his mouth and watched while he chewed and sucked on it with his gums.

After that there was no stopping him. When he finished breast feeding he would want more and more solids all the time so Ellie started making him stewed meat with vegetables, and fresh apples and pears cut into chunks. Soon he was pushing himself around the floor, then rolling onto his back awhile then back onto his stomach again, and he would glance across at them burbling happily to himself.

By eight months he began to sit up and scoot around on his bottom, and before they could blink one day he was near the sofa in the office and simply leaned forward and grasping the leather upholstery pulled himself up on his feet. He wavered there for a moment then sat straight back down, but liking the idea pulled himself up again, then looked around at them smiling happily. That was how he started getting around exploring the house.

One day a truck pulled up across from the house, at the end of the track there. Ned leaned back in his chair and pulled the curtain back to see who it was. Rollie Tanner got out and looked around, then walked across. He was not much older at all, quite as he remembered him, and he jumped up out of his chair and went out down the garden path to greet him. As it was he towered over him now by a good four inches and the other looked up at him smiling broadly as they shook hands.

Formalities over he took him by the elbow and led him into the office, then called out to Ellie to come look who's here.

Elizabeth showed up first with Angus on her hip. The moment he saw who it was he smiled and chuckled, and leaned over to be held by him so she passed him across. Ellie followed close behind, and wiping her hands on her apron came into the room then leaned in close for a peck on the cheek. Taking him by his free hand she shook it vigorously with both hers, her eyes smiling and sparkling with pleasure. Elizabeth left the baby and slipped back to the kitchen where she was heard making tea, and a little later as the men settled down to discuss their business she came in with a tray of fresh pikelets with strawberry jam and cream.

Ned bade her stay when she had finished serving, and the five of them sat for the next hour pouring over his plans for Belkoomie and its associated farm enterprise. He discussed the project in detail, emphasizing what standard was expected and the reason for it, then when he finished asked Rollie fairly bluntly whether he was up to it.

The other simply nodded, typically a man of few words. "Sure, start tomorrow. We can head straight across now if you like."

"We? Is the family with you?"

"The missus and kids. They are in the truck, waiting."

"Is that right? Why didn't you bring them in? How have they been?"

"Not too good, to be honest." the other replied. Then he paused, and with a frown said, "Most places want a single man; don't want a wife and kids running around."

The others looked stunned, then turned to each other shaking their heads.

"How many children do you have now, Mr Tanner?" Ellie wanted to know.

"Seven."

She glanced at Ned, then said deliberately, "Well, you had better bring them in."

He looked at her, then went out and down through the gate across the yard where he stopped at the truck. Immediately from the back canopy there disgorged a tribe of grubby, unruly children, and from the front cabin a thin gaunt woman in a loose frock stepped down carrying a toddler on her hip. They all followed him back across to the house.

Ellie watched from the window, her face hard, then as they came up the path went out onto the verandah to meet them. Rollie stood back embarrassed, but she reached up looking into his eyes and gently stroked his cheek, then turned to his wife and taking her by the hand led her inside and straight down to the kitchen. Sitting her down at the table she came back out into the passage and herded the children in as well, and calling Elizabeth up to help promptly set the fire going in the stove and began cooking.

Presently she came out into the passage and called down to the office. "Ned, take Mr Tanner and kill one of those wethers in the front paddock for me, there's a pet. They can have the front house for the time being."

Rollie stood at that, embarrassed again. "Beg pardon, Mr Collins, we didn't mean to intrude like this."

Ned looked at him curiously, distantly, then shook his head. "You are the last person who has to apologise to anyone, Mr Tanner. A few people might well be apologising to you in my book. No, you are very welcome here."

Then he pursed his lips. "It just doesn't look like you'll be starting tomorrow, that's all, not if Ellie has her way. No matter, you can help me here until you are on your feet then I'll take you over myself and show you around."

CHAPTER THIRTY TWO

During first semester Ned found himself busy with a great deal of correspondence and a lot of working through finely detailed submissions from his old school, and from Peter McCallum's veterinary department.

In many respects he was fortunate Rollie Tanner had showed up when he did because he was now able to leave the day-to-day work around the station to him, and had time to think. For the first time he began seriously to appreciate Sandy's legacy, in the way things were ordered and no less in his Aboriginal teachings, and especially the reason for going droving with Don when he did and having a serious look at the country, listening to their stories on the way.

Aside from his walks with Elizabeth and Angus, who he was now carrying around on his shoulders, often during the day he would go for great long walks by himself, or saddle up and ride all the way around the station boundaries looking at the history of the place; in old fence lines, and banks and bays, and cut channels and places where exotic plants and weeds had displaced the native.

One big patch in particular worried him because it was bare and salt-scald when he could not understand why it would be like that. He asked Ellie, and as she thought more about it came back and told him there used to be a big reed bed there at the top of the swamp they had banked off for pasture. The next day he rode out with a shovel and started to undo all the work that had been done; letting things return slowly and gradually to nature, and see what happens.

At night he sat in his study writing up his reports, and writing letters, and Elizabeth would come in and sit with him while Angus slept, then when he was done take him by the hand and pour a hot bath, and they would love one another before falling asleep tangled together.

As the mid-year break approached he decided that rather than try to organise too much more in writing he might be better to focus his efforts on the practicality. His next round of letters expressed frustration that despite everyone's best intention the project was not progressing the way he thought it should, and perhaps they should come out during the mid-year break and he would show them what he meant to convey. Nobody had any problem with that being so busy with their own duties so a general meeting at Belkoomie was arranged for late June.

Ellie had the extra children in her little classroom every day, keeping their mother quite as busy assisting with their lessons and showing her how to continue helping them all with their reading and writing, and doing their sums. Plenty of food in the house and her toddler weaned off her finally, with enough rest Anne Tanner lost her gaunt, wasted look and soon took to the task with enthusiasm.

By the middle of June they were ready to leave. As things had turned out the family move coincided with Ned's plan to be over on Belkoomie a week ahead and see that everything was in order before his guests arrived, so one morning they set off in Don's old Chevrolet with Rollie's truck following close behind. The older Tanner boys wanted to ride in the Chev with Angus since he had taken to them so, and after some discussion Ellie came with him in the front seat while Elizabeth was quite as happy to sit in the back seat with the three boys.

She had grown up traveling back and forth in this old car, cutting across from Eurongera through Dadjari east to the highway, then the long run south taking two whole days getting to school, and two days back each holiday with no chance of going anywhere during the short breaks except sleep in the big empty dormitory, or like Ned stay over with friends when she had the chance. This was the first time Ned noticed her coming back into herself, overcoming her shyness to point out sights and tell stories all the way keeping the children entertained.

It was early evening when they arrived and the workmen had knocked off for the day. After a brief discussion they turned around and went over to the farm, where pulling up at the house they all spilled out and began unloading the truck. That done Ned took the Chev back across to the main homestead where they lugged their own things inside and both families settled in for a fairly spartan night.

He was up again at first light and before breakfast went across to the building site to look around. The work was coming along very well and he was pleased with the result so he went for a walk around the property, down along the broad river flats and back up again to get the place into perspective in his mind.

As he strolled back up along the track a truck drove in through the front gate and stopped at the new barracks where several workmen got out. He lengthened his pace and shortly came up and introduced himself to the builder, a Mr Bradford. Following a brief discussion the man set his men to work then followed Ned up to the house where he called out to Ellie and Elizabeth.

Over cups of tea and more rifling through plans and paperwork he had brought across with him they agreed to have one of the workmen stay on and help renovate the homestead once the barracks and mess and had been completed, being the main house and manager's house on Belkoomie, and the farmhouse on the neighbouring property.

With no manager in sight for the duration of the war, once he discovered the man was married with a young family and needed steady work to keep them going, they went out again and called him over, inviting him to live there in the manager's house with his family while he finished renovating rather than travel back and forth every day.

Ben Cooper it turned out later was Mr Bradford's son-in-law. He was a good carpenter with neat habits and a clean tidy finish to his work. Within the week the mess and shower block were completed and with the building team gone he came out over that weekend with his wife and two children, and they moved into the house. Promptly on Monday morning he knocked on their door to report for work, and Ned brought him inside and handed him over to Ellie to show him what she wanted done.

The main Belkoomie house was of the same vintage as Wyandera and Eurongera; built during the late Victorian heyday a whole generation after old Alexander McKenzie's original Weethangara homestead. She wanted the place kept in that style. The work she wanted done duly organised she took him over to the new barracks where she had him mount a blackboard which she painted herself, then sending him back across to the house to start work she went and rounded up all the children they could find on the place.

Ellie had Elizabeth and Ann Tanner looking after the littlies as she had for so very many years the native women at Wyandera, while she set the older children to their reading and writing, and doing their figuring as she still called the arithmetic.

CHAPTER THIRTY THREE

Later the following day Peter arrived on Belkoomie with his academic supervisor, Professor Ken Basford from Melbourne, with Mr Kroonenberg the new agriculture master at Mount Tambla accompanying them. As the cooees echoed across the station calling him up to the house, Ned left off repairing a fence and fording the river rode in on his horse to introduce himself. For the rest of the afternoon and next morning he showed them the adjoining properties while they took samples and made measurements, and tossed a few ideas around.

Just before lunch as they were coming back up to the house Michael Donovan arrived unexpectedly, having borrowed his father's old car for the drive out. He roared in helplessly through the front gate and drove round and around trying to find somewhere to park, until they stopped him there on the track and he got out. After introducing him to the others Ned walked with him up to the house. He told Ned then that Trevor Percival had been killed in action, and that Patrick was listed as missing, presumably taken prisoner since there was no trace of him when there reasonably might have been, so they lived in hope.

That done he declared his reason for driving all the way out, which was to glean their opinion on some new veterinary pharmaceuticals his own department were developing, so they invited him to sit in on their discussions. After lunch they adjourned to the front room of the house, which Ned had set up for himself during the week to roughly duplicate Sandy's old study at Wyandera.

The agreement they hammered out finally was primarily concerned with commercial viability since at the end of the day Ned had to pay dividends to his shareholders, where they for their part had to prove their research in the field. Ned reckoned that the best way that could be achieved without having to explain the science to men who often could not even read, would be to use this knowledge to improve their livestock and have the market decide how that was to be valued by the industry.

Perhaps in the meantime they should establish a subsidiary company partly owned by his own holding company, and partly by what commercial wing ACSIR might wish to establish at their end, with Mount Tambla Grammar free to use the new facility as adjunct to the school in perpetuity.

Before the lawyers and accountants started work on the detail Ned mentioned that they could well start on improving the shorthorns due to arrive on Wyandera from up north any day now, and which he could have across here within a month or so.

It was at that point Michael spoke up, expressing his excitement at the new intestinal worm treatment discovered last year at the Melbourne laboratory, and perhaps they could assist in trialling that also while they had the chance. If things went well the Donovan family would be inclined to invest in the new drug, he said, and they all turned to look at him in surprise.

Peter McCallum turned to Ned gravely shaking his head, "First this place must be quarantined, Ned, let's be clear about that. No offense to Michael, I agree with him, but it should not be done here, no, your other property perhaps, but not here. One of the reasons Belkoomie is so valuable to us is because it has lain fallow for so long and the ground is clean. We are far better to keep it that way."

Ned glanced back and forward between the two and nodded, leaning over to jot a note in his diary, then sat back looking out the window tapping his forehead thoughtfully with the pen.

"If I follow you, we should drive back over to Wyandera and intercept the drovers," he said finally.

He started to say something else but tensed suddenly as dark hit him with a great rush, and he reeled back almost collapsing into his chair. Recovering a little he gazed about him, confused. Something dire was afoot. and he slowly went pale with dread. Beads of cold sweat broke out on his forehead. Taking his handkerchief he mopped his brow trying to shake it off. Abruptly he stood to go, nauseous, then stopped and taking a deep breath apologised and made his leave.

"Please excuse me will you," he said weakly, "I have to go check on something. If you can spare a week perhaps we should go check that mob coming across. Michael will return you to Melbourne when he goes. I think Ken and Hans have to be getting back straight away. Thank you all, gentlemen, I am sorry I have to go now, good afternoon."

He shook hands quickly all round, his face wrought with anguish, then dashed out to find Elizabeth.

Straight away he bumped into her in the passage and she looked up, startled, then took his hand and hurried back with him to their room where Ellie sat on the bed rocking back and forth holding Angus in her lap, his small body pale and limp. He lifted his eyelids and checked his pulse. He was alive but breathing weakly.

"Enid," Ellie croaked almost inaudibly. "Enid has him."

"What? What are you talking about."

"My sister, Ned. She has hold of Angus. She wants him."

Ned took Angus's hand and immediately felt the other dark, insistent, presence. He turned to Elizabeth. "Go now please, Elizabeth, and shut the door. Take our guests outside and show them around the school, something, anywhere, just out of the house. Please, hurry, it's all right."

The moment she left and they were alone he quickly took Ellie's hand in his right, then had her hold Angus's left hand so the three of them formed a closed loop. He shut his eyes then and slipped into that dark space to stand there facing the haggard, faded crone, staring her directly in the eye.

"Enid," he said to her, "Let him go."

"Bastard!" she screeched, spittle running from her mouth, then reached over with her free hand trying to claw at him with her fingers.

He backed away, avoiding her, and they stood there a long moment staring each other down.

Finally he shrugged, shaking his head, denying her, "I have had enough of this, you horrid bitter twisted old hag. All my life I have had to put up with your ways and I am tired of it. We are all tired of it."

"He's mine," she cackled at him. "He's mine! I took him the first time, put the rabbit hole there I did, had that horse goin' like the b'jaisus I did, but for that interferin' black bastard, and now it's you agin me, you rotten little shit. Wretch! Spailpeen! Insolent upstart bastard! You want to take me on is it? Mine for yours, is it? Give him to me!"

Ned went numb with shock, and his gorge rose. "You! Rotten bitch! It was you all along was it? You made Ellie barren, then you killed Angus! Then you hurt my mother! You made her barren too. But you didn't count on me, did you! I am the one big mistake you made! Damn you to hell!" He began to reel again but recovered and turning on her in a fury went to strike her down.

A voice rang out from somewhere right behind him, "Don't do that, Ned! Don't even think of it, or she will have you too. She will suck you dry. She is setting you up. That's what she wants."

He felt his arm being grasped. Sandy had hold of him, then pushed him aside to tackle the dread apparition by himself. He felt more hands reach out to grab him and Peter and Everard were there as well, both holding him away. Sandy had a firm grip on Enid and she spat and clawed and scratched at him, but he ignored her and turned to Ned telling him to get the hell out of there, and take Angus as quickly as he could and leave. Take him outside the house, as far away as he could.

Ned came back into his senses and saw that Ellie was dead so he let her hand go then prising the other from Angus laid her down gently on the bed. Picking up the baby he took him straight up the passage past the kitchen and out the back door. The moment they were outside he felt him stir, and open his eyes and smile weakly, and Ned held him close then going around the side of the house crossed over to the barracks where they all clustered around him.

"Ned, Ned, what happened," Elizabeth wanted to know, but he shook his head.

Finally he said quietly too her, "Ellie had a heart attack. She was holding him too tight, that's all. He will be all right."

He held them both in his arms for a moment, then presently noticed people standing there so he turned and said to them, "I am sorry,

205

everyone, please excuse us. My aunt has just passed away. She had a heart attack I think. She was holding the baby and squeezed him a bit too tight."

They all glanced at one another shaking their heads in disbelief, while Ann Tanner turned away sobbing quietly and some of the children began to cry. Elizabeth looked at them, then taking the baby on her hip let Ned go.

"No," she said, "oh no, please don't cry. Ellie wouldn't have wanted that. No, she was good. She lived such a good life and she went the way she wanted. We should be happy for her."

Ned turned to Michael and Peter and the others. "Come and help me, please. She is lying awkwardly on the bed. She needs to be laid out properly. Mr Kroonenberg, if you don't mind, send out a doctor, and notify the police, and Professor Basford, is that all right with you? I am terribly sorry about all this."

He turned away, then back again. "I am very happy with our discussions," he finished. "You have both helped enormously, I want you to know that. Keep in touch will you?"

Back inside the house Ellie was lying there on her side. She looked as if she were sleeping peacefully, her face calm like a small child but her body like a rag doll scattered and crooked on the bed, with one hand under her face and the other holding her chin as if she were thinking about something interesting that had caught her attention.

Ned picked her up and carried her out to her own room where Peter spread a fresh sheet on the bed and they laid her out straight with her hands clasped, and he took another sheet and spread it over her. It was mid-winter and cold so they left her there not thinking to intervene further until the doctor arrived, but as they went outside again he broke away and walked off by himself toward the river. Michael held Peter back so as to let him go, and very quickly Ned found himself dashing through the trees wondering whether he had lost his mind altogether.

Eventually Elizabeth found him sitting on a log overlooking the river. She came up and held him to her from behind, grasping his shoulders and nursing his head against her breast.

Eventually she leaned down and whispered in his ear, "Dear Ned, we have another baby. Let's think about that. Ellie was so happy when I told her."

"Yes," he nodded quietly, almost to himself. "It's Hamish."

"What did you say?"

"Hamish," he repeated softly. "Old Hamish, Sandy's father. It's him. Their Hamish, Ellie and Sandy's Hamish, is in Belgium and can't get back, so the old fellow has taken his place. The clan is gathering. Things are happening. Maybe that's what had Enid so stirred up, or something else is going on, I don't know."

"Ned, what on earth are you rambling about?"

He sighed, looking away into the distance for a long moment, then leaned back against her and reached up to take her hand.

"Nothing," he said finally. "It doesn't matter, it's done. Now it's our turn."

Then he reached up again and took her other hand, and wrapped her arms around him.

"When did you know, Elizabeth?"

"Only this morning, just now as a matter of fact. You were there in your meeting and I simply had to tell somebody. Ellie was so immensely happy, do you know that, then all of a sudden she went all queer. She had a tight hold of Angus and wouldn't let him go, sitting there staring stoned face at me like that. I had to came to find you."

He nodded again quietly, and letting one hand go unwrapped himself then stood and turned to her, taking her in his own arms to hold her close. Then he stepped over the log and taking her hand began walking back with her to the homestead. As they came out onto the green pasture he stopped and looked around him.

"Do you know what Ellie told me once?" he said. "She told me her parents came out here from the famine in Ireland. When they got here all the land had been taken up. It was very hard for them, you know. That is what tormented her sister Enid; what made her so bitter, having to look after everyone the way she did. When their father died their mother went to pieces, and she had to raise of the children all by herself. She blamed Ellie for everything, then when Ellie took Sandy away it was the last straw. She went raving mad after that."

"Old Tom Clancy was alcoholic like their father, and she pulled him out of a pub one day and married him just to spite everyone. After they had a brood of kids he was killed. He was rotten drunk one day and fell under a wagon, and she had to start all over again. That's when the trouble started."

Elizabeth let go of him and stepped away, and stood there one arm across her breasts and holding her head with her free hand, then wiping a loose strand of hair away turned to him shaking her head wearily.

"Husband, I cannot pretend to understand your business. I just don't have that sort of brain, or inclination I must tell you. What I need to know is whether there is any more trouble in it. I need to know what risk there is for my children. I don't care what names you give them, or who you imagine they are or where they are from. I am their mother. They are not something else or somebody else, they are my children, from my own body. That is what they are, and who they are, and you their father. They come from our loving one another, nothing else."

"Elizabeth . . ." he began, but she cut him off short.

"Don't you come near me, Ned Collins! Sometimes you frighten me so, even on our honeymoon, our most precious time together, and I have had enough of it. I want to know now. I want to know do you want to be my husband, and our children's father, and enough of this nonsense!"

He turned and walked back away a little as she had done, then waited and waited for her until she softened.

"There is a madness in the family, Elizabeth. I don't fully understand it myself. Sandy called it a curse, but Ellie thought it was a gift you know. I think she understood the thing better than anyone. What I know myself is that Angus is the same, and you need to know that too. I don't know about Hamish, not yet at any rate."

"Go on," she said.

"Normally everything is all right, you know that yourself. It is only times like these it comes out when, I don't know rightly, fundamental things happen in the family. I simply don't know more than that. Nobody has explained it to me better than that, except we are not to be angry or afraid or upset because that is what the dark side of it feeds on."

He looked at her intently then.

"Elizabeth, you must understand that's the reason I am heir to all this. It doesn't make rational sense, I know; it never did to me anyway. You are just not to be afraid of anything, all right."

Then he turned away, frustrated himself, and took a deep breath before continuing. "I'm not to be afraid either, or angry or frustrated with any more of this when things don't turn out right. We are on our own now Ellie's gone. She kept an eye on me, but now it's us and we aren't even of age yet. You are the mother now. Yes, I am the father. That's it. We agree. But there has to be a rule, and that's what it is, all right?"

He turned his head sharply, eyes bright and ears pricked like a warrigul up toward the track leading from the front gate, then glanced back at her.

"The doctor is here."

He inclined his head and she did the same, and without saying anything further stepped up and took his hand.

CHAPTER THIRTY FOUR

Elizabeth sat in the back with Angus playing on the seat next to her all the way home, while Michael and Peter followed the hearse in Stan Donovan's old car. It was very late in the day when they arrived, almost dark, and driving up the track they saw all the house lights on with the big old generator thumping, and Ian's and Arthur's cars both parked outside.

As they came across their headlights were picked up glancing through the front window, and Ian appeared on the verandah then quickly went inside again to let everyone know they had arrived. Arthur and Don followed him out down the path and through the gate to meet them as they parked the cars along the garden fence. Ned got out and opened the back door of the Chev to let Elizabeth step down, then reached inside to pick up the now sleeping boy off the seat.

By then Judith and Mollie were there so he left Elizabeth to go with them and went over to the hearse where the men were already drawing out the coffin. It had no weight and did not need the seven of them to carry it, so while Ian took the foot Don picked up the head of it and started up along the path and onto the verandah.

"In the kitchen, Don," Ned called over to them. "Put her on the table, all right."

"Oh dear, wait a minute." Mollie brushed past then hurried along the passage to the kitchen where she began to clear the table, putting everything holas-bolas onto the bench near the stove. The men waited outside in the passage until she finished, then went in and placed the wooden coffin squarely and reverently on the table. That done they stood back and looked at one another, then Ned following them through the door with Angus in his arms frowned suddenly and cocked his head.

"I didn't think you were going to be here, Don. I thought you'd be away."

The other stood there a moment, but Judith intervened and came over from the stove and said quietly, "Why don't you men leave us a while. Let us get things organised."

She pushed them all toward the door just as Arthur came in. She caught his eye and he nodded, and taking his son by the arm led him back out and down the passage with Don close at heel. Back in his study Ned broke loose and straightening his shirt sleeve went over to the front window to stand staring out through the glass. Then he turned abruptly to see them all there in a circle watching him.

"All right," he said. "Tell me what."

"Don't you want to sit down, son," Arthur offered.

"No, Dad. Just give it to me please."

"Ned," Ian broke in, "the Police Stock Squad arrested Sam Clancy over a week ago on the South Australian border, with a big lot of our cattle off Dadjari."

He nodded. "What are our losses?"

"Negligible."

"He didn't get his hands on the mob for Belkoomie, by chance? Will they be here?"

"Two days, maybe three at the outside," Don replied.

"Good, no problem then. Anything else? Where are they, does anyone know?"

"They were released on bail, but we don't know where they are."

"All right. Who went surety, do you know? And what is Enid doing? I need to track her down in a hurry."

Nobody said anything, just glanced at each other and shrugged, and he looked around then down at his desk. He sighed to himself and turned back to the window to lean his shoulder against the frame.

Judith and Mollie came in with food and Arthur went to get some beer from the ice box. As he did so Ned glanced suddenly at his mother and crossed from the window to help her with the dishes.

Standing beside her he leaned in close and murmured, "Mum, I need to know where Auntie Enid might be right now."

"She is in hospital, Ned. They brought her in yesterday morning."

"What happened?"

"She had a stroke, and they have her in a coma for the time being."

"Will she live, do you think?"

She sighed and shook her head, then looked up at him. "Knowing that woman she will outlive all of us, she is that stubborn. Now don't ask me any more please, son, and button your lip or you will get me into trouble."

"All right, thank you," he said, but she took hold of his arm, unsteady suddenly.

"Ned, don't."

"Leave it, mother, you know the harm she caused. Anyway it's too late."

She took her hand off him and looked away, then nodding to herself began serving the food. He felt a nudge from behind and there was Arthur passing him a glass of beer.

"You do the honours, son, I think that's appropriate."

The room hushed and he found everyone waiting on him suddenly.

"There is nothing much I can say," he said after a pause. "I don't really think there is anything anyone can say. Ellie was a Malonie, and married a Scotsman as you know. But all those old Wyandera and Eurongera people up there called her grandmother, did you know that? To me she was a fairy godmother. Not only me, but a lot of people. I honestly don't know any of this would have been possible without her. Now she is taken from us when we least expected; things happen like that. I suppose we just have to take up what she left us and move on, which is what she would want. Sandy too I should say, don't forget."

Then he raised his glass. "Let's just keep them both in our hearts."

"Aye," they echoed softly, then after a moment the room broke into hubbub again.

He took a few sips of beer, then feeling the room a bit close went out onto the front verandah for some fresh air. Standing there at the rail a small pebble rattled across the boards and he went down to the end to look out into the darkness. Everard came up where he could just see him in the dim light spilling from the house. He was naked but for a string belt and pubic tassel. His entire upper body was painted in intricate designs, with his face almost solid white ochre except for his eyeballs seemingly on fire.

"What's up?" Ned whispered to him.

"Can't find 'er boss, no good puckim witch. She gone, disappear."

"In hospital. The medicine is making her sleep. You'll have to wait while she wakes up."

The door opened and more light spilled out from the passage so Everard slipped back into the darkness. Ned turned to see Don come out onto the verandah, like him feeling it too close inside, or perhaps he missed him and came out to see where he was.

"Here, Don," he called softly.

He had a fresh bottle of beer in his hand and as he came near topped up his glass then poured himself another. He put the bottle on the top rail close within reach, and stopped to tamp a wad of tobacco into his pipe and lit it.

"Don't you want to tell me what happened?"

"Nope."

"Why not, Don."

"Management prerogative. Anytime you don't want me on the job just say so."

"I didn't mean it like that."

"That's a fact." Then he paused, drawing on his pipe thoughtfully. "Andrew and those South Australian boys of yours will be here in a day or two. Nice mob they are bringing down, our best breeders."

Ned glanced aside trying to glimpse Everard but he was gone, so he turned his attention back to Don.

"The reason I brought Peter McCallum over is to help set up this place as a quarantine station for Belkoomie. And Michael is completely new as well. Maybe you are the better man than me to work with them and get them doing the job properly."

"All right. What's on your mind?"

"Well, everyone on the place has to be useful. Everyone has to be able to get in and have a go, and be ready to fill in anytime. You be my coach and trainer. Start with them. We need a good manager in the big house over on Belkoomie as well, and maybe you're the man for the job. You happy with that?"

Don cocked his head at that, glancing sideways at him. "Righto, we can do that all right. But you won't get station hands doin' any of that book larnin' of yours. You realise that, don't you."

Ned sighed, "Well, yes and no. They need to come up a bit still, a lot of those blokes. Ellie already had things kicked off on that score. Elizabeth and Cath, both your daughters you know, they'll keep it going. But that's not what I mean. What you can do is help the others down out of their ivory tower a bit, and teach them the practical side of things like you did for us."

He turned to face him squarely then. "I mean, these are powerfully bright boys, among the best in the country in their fields of study, but there is no point in them trying to tell everyone else how to do things; they have to be able to show them. To win respect they must have the same working skill as the men. They must have the same skill the men have and better, and work alongside them. Then we'll start getting somewhere instead of pulling apart all the time. That's the killer, Don. That is what's been going wrong in this country, right from the start, if you know what I mean."

The other nodded, then leaned back off the rail and standing up straight, tapped his pipe out on his boot. "I get what you're drivin' at young Ned. I like what you say, and I'd have to tell you you're a hell of a bright lad yourself workin' it out like that in your own head. All right, let's see how we manage."

Then he cocked his head dismissively.

"Ah, bugger it anyway. We're here for a bloody wake not a board meetin'. Right now that bottle looks a mite lonely, wouldn't you say? And it looks like it's goin' to be one hell of a long night. Stay there son, and I'll go line a few up."

He proved to be right. Nobody apart from Angus got much in the way of sleep until early morning, then they were up again at first light to dig Ellie's grave with picks and shovels there in the hard clay next to Sandy, on the other side from old Peter and right across from her little schoolhouse where she would have wanted to be. Then they washed and tidied up before lifting her coffin from the kitchen table to carry it reverently down the garden path and out the gate, then slowly in procession along the front fence until they had everything set up over the hole they'd dug.

There they said their prayers for her. There was nothing much anyone could add and nobody wanted to say much anyway, so when they were done they simply lowered her into the ground and covered her with flowers from her own garden, and gum leaves and twigs of ti-tree and grevillea from the bush around, then left for the men to fill it in.

Everybody made their various ways to bed after that. The house the Tanner family had most recently occupied was neat and tidy and it was no trouble to make up the spare beds. When Don and Ned both crashed there Ian and Michael joined them and the spillover from the big house was accommodated without fuss.

It was thus late afternoon before Cath brought over a fresh pot of tea and some cups, then went around shaking them awake until they all tumbled out and came to sit at the table in the kitchen. When Ned took up his cup and went outside onto the porch with it nobody noticed much, until Elizabeth came over with Angus on her hip wanting to know why he was out there by himself. He simply turned to her and shrugged, smiling, but before he could answer Don came to the door. The moment the baby saw him he reached over to be taken from his mother, and Don instinctively took him. Cath was right behind, and from over her father's shoulder she reached around and tickled the tot on the neck causing him to squirm and giggle.

Ned pricked up, staring at her suddenly. "How long, Cath?"

She looked at him oddly, frowning. "How could you know, Ned? Did Ian tell you?"

"No, you look stunning right now that's all. Glowing, like Elizabeth."

The two sisters stared at each other wide-eyed. Don poked his head in the door. "Better get yourself out here, Ian," he said.

"What's up?" Ian came out, still bleary-eyed from the night before.

"Goin' to be a dad, are you?"

"What? No, we don't know, it's a bit early yet."

"Nah, it'll be on. You'll be right. Just so you know, you're goin' to be an uncle again while you're at it."

Ian looked at him, nodding. "Is that right? Yes, well, no doubt about you is there Don McKenzie. Prime Eurongera heifers, the whole country knows about them."

"Ian!" Cath reached over and cuffed him but he ducked back inside chuckling merrily.

Presently Peter and Michael followed him out with some cold bottles and poured beer all round.

CHAPTER THIRTY FIVE

Their contentment was short-lived. Just as they were about to settle down again for another session they heard hoof beats cantering up the track from the main gate, and as they came into sight slow to a walk. The group on the porch glanced at one another not expecting cattle for another day or so, but it was Sam Clancy in the lead with Seamus Malonie just back of him, and Pete and Tommy Clancy coming up behind. They rode on past to the main house where they stopped.

Ned stepped down from the porch and started walking across. "Are you looking for something, Mr Clancy?" he called over to them.

They turned to see him there. "Yes we are, matter of fact. You. We're looking for you, mate. You're a fuckin' shit!" Sam wheeled at that and spurred his horse right onto him.

Ned glanced swiftly out of his way then as he drew alongside reached up and grabbed him by the shirt, taking him down as the horse thudded past then pushed him brusquely away. Sam dusted himself off, then fists raised came at him again but Ned danced away, pushing him aside once more.

It happened again and again, until Ian called from the porch, "Hit him, Ned!"

"I don't want to bloody-well hit him. This is bullshit."

"Bullshit is it?" Sam snarled, then moving in low came up suddenly and took a real swing at him catching him just below the eye. Ned went down as Sam came in pummeling at him on the ground. Suddenly Ned was right there again on the half back flank down hard from a high mark, holding the ball under his left shoulder while they kicked at him with their boots and tormented him and hurt him. He lost it then. In a blind rage he to his feet and grabbing Sam by the shirt collar drove his right fist right into his face, dropping him like a bag of chaff.

Seamus was off his horse coming at him, but without waiting Ned drove straight into him and taking him by the shoulders head-butted him in the face as well. Blood spattered as someone's nose went to pulp, but Ned just stood there butting him again and again and again until he too dropped senseless to the ground. Next thing he knew he had Pete's horse by the reins and whipping its head up he pushed sharply bringing horse and rider down sideways together. Before Pete could recover Ned stepped over the horse and walloped him mightily right in the side of the head and he went straight out cold.

Then he looked around for Tommy. Tommy. Sniveling runty bastard. Finally he saw him there still mounted, backing slowly away from him as he approached, then he wheeled his horse back down the track toward the gate and gallop off.

Ned turned to survey the mess, then called across to Ian to hold the horses for him as bodily he picked up one after the other and threw them across their saddles. Finally mounting Sam's horse he shoved him forward over the pommel and turned to go. Then he stopped and looked around, shaking his head wearily, and dismounting again passed the reins back to Ian. Waving his arm in the general direction of the gate, without a word he went inside to the bathroom.

Elizabeth followed him in but gently he turned her out and shut the door. At the basin he ran the tap and cupping his hands under it dashed the cold water onto his face, then again, and a third and fourth time. Finally he straightened up and taking a towel dried himself, looking in the mirror to see only a small bruise under his left cheekbone, and a bump right there in the middle of his forehead.

Outside he went back across to the main house and spent the next half hour looking around for Sandy's collection of Highland single malt whisky he knew to be hidden around the place somewhere, finally locating a good dozen bottles behind a panel on the bookcase in the study. Victory won he reckoned this must be the reason for keeping them there so long. Then he went and found Arthur and dragged him back over to the other house with him.

That night none of them ever forgot. Ned had always considered Don taciturn, never realising how funny he could be once he found his stride. He had neither realised how young he was when his father Old Don died, and as he listened and laughed uproariously along with the rest of them he came to see just how much the loss still pained him after all those years. Cath and Elizabeth both called in but left early seeing it was becoming a men's night, and Arthur staggered across some time after the wee small hours leaving the others to lose track of time entirely.

Finally somebody happened to mention that it was getting light outside.

Mollie appeared on the doorstep then with a big jug of tomato juice into which she had mixed a few of her 'ingredients', and made them all take a deep draught before turning in. After she had gone they lined up along the porch for one last long pee then went inside and washed their faces to freshen up, then tucked themselves under whatever blankets they could find and went straight off to sleep.

Just after noon Andrew MacFarlane rode in. Don went out to explain the situation to him and asked could he hold the mob over on the reserve if he wouldn't mind, and bring them in first light in the morning. He turned and pointing across to the top paddock let him know where he wanted them, then back inside the house curled up under his blankets and went back to sleep.

Later in the day when they eventually made their way across to the house it quickly became clear that the women had had a session of their own, with empty beer and gin bottles and half a whisky bottle still there on the table, although there was plenty of food cooked. Ned picked the whisky up and looked at it, then took it back down to the study where he restored it to the cranny behind the bookshelf. Back in the kitchen he sat at the table and looked around at everyone.

"Sandy would have enjoyed that too, you know," he said quietly, almost to himself. "He didn't have a proper wake, did he."

"Isn't that a fact," Don agreed. "We did them both good, I reckon. Auntie Ellie would have been right happy with a send-off like that, and I'll bet she is. Now, let's see what we have for chow."

"There is a some nice stew there, Don. Just what you boys need right now," Judith said. "And Ned, there is some fresh bread there in the oven which I think will be done nicely, if you would like to slice enough for everyone."

With the aroma of fresh baking filling the kitchen everyone's spirits rose, and with new bread sliced thickly and smothered with hot stew and vegetables the transformation was remarkable. After an early dinner they all helped with the washing up then went about cleaning both houses, with empty beer bottles going into crates and the rare whisky bottles wiped clean and lined up as trophies along the top shelf of Sandy's old book case.

While they were there Ned took down the gun case and took out the hand-made Greener to inspect and clean it, which started a whole new conversation about the man who made it and how it had come into Sandy's possession all those years ago. For the rest of the evening they went around the old study picking up bits and pieces and talking things over.

Eventually Ned opened the panel in the bookcase and took out the half-empty bottle, and they finished that off and prepared to settle again for another night until Michael yawned and got up and stretched, announcing that he was done in. That set everyone else off, and after he went for a hot bath and turned in they all followed suit.

CHAPTER THIRTY SIX

The old familiar crack of stock whips and the soft lowing thunder of cattle on the move had them straight out of bed just after sunrise next morning. Don was already up with fresh tea on the make but the boys quickly pulled on their trousers and boots, and tucking their shirts in hurried out to greet the drovers as they made their way past.

"Let them do their job, boys," Don called them back. "Sit down and have your cup of tea."

By then Ned was out crossing over from the main house just as the mob passed, coming through the dust and noise in their wake, and stepped up onto the porch. Seeing tea there on the kitchen table he sat down and helped himself, then on second thought got up and began to make toast. He was hungry so when they came back in he sent Peter across to the main house for bacon and eggs, and presently he returned with the big pot of cold stew as well so they put that on the stove to warm it up.

Andrew rode across finally, having got the mob settled where Don wanted and his men out riding with them while they became used to the place. Dismounting he tied his horse to the rail and politely knocked on the door.

They bade him enter, then introducing him all round Ned went back to cooking their breakfast, listening carefully while Don heard his report and as they spoke drew Peter McCallum unobtrusively into the discussion, then Michael, and Ian finally. He marveled at Don's skill with them; his patient foresight and grasp of the essential nature of things, and from that point began making his final decisions.

By time he had finished serving breakfast, and they sat around enjoying their cup of tea wholly engrossed by then in the condition of the mob, not thinking he began clearing the table and set his hand to washing up.

Elizabeth arrived then with Angus and without a blink passed him straight over to his grandfather, who took him from her likewise, and picking up a towel began drying the dishes. The sink cleared and drained Ned leaned over and asked her quietly to go and get her sister, and bring Arthur across too. As she did so the sound of their boots on the back porch caused the others to turn around enough to interrupt their conversation, and taking the opportunity Don stood and suggested they might go and look at the mob itself.

Andrew stayed behind to finish his breakfast while they went to saddle up, and after he was done Ned took his plate to finish the washing up. As he stacked the last of the dishes he turned to him, a thought striking him.

"Andrew," he wanted to know, "is there anything I need to know about Sam Clancy's arrest? Anything you can tell me?"

The other looked at him, then looked away thoughtfully. "No, I don't think so. He knew what he was doing. He knew he had the wrong mob taking them in the wrong direction, and that's the end of it."

"Fair enough. What do you think about that, yourself?"

"Well, you want me to be honest with you?"

"Yes, of course."

"For the life of me I don't know what you thought you were doing letting him have Chatham to start with."

Ned cocked his head and sighed, and glanced out the window. "For family reasons, basically," he said finally. "He is Ellie's great nephew, you know, like me but on her sister's side. We wanted to try him out, see how he'd go."

"Well, you found out quick, that's a fact. If you don't mind me being forward with you."

"It's all right. Don't worry about it." Ned turned to him again. "So, what are your plans, Andrew?"

"I'd like to stay on at Eurongera, in my present position if you don't mind." He paused, and looked at his new boss directly. "I have plans to marry Evie Foley and settle there."

"Is that right?" he looked at him steadily. "How does everyone feel about that?"

"Good, yes, no problems. Daniel is going to be my best man."

"When is this going to be?"

"Spring, maybe. Before Christmas anyway."

"All right, you need time off? Anything else we can do?"

"No, thank you anyway. We'll be right. Dadjari needs some help though, they get a bit short with so many people living there now."

Ned thought for a minute. "Let them have as many killers as they need, start with your culls then work up. Clear the country while this drought is on, then we'll see how we go."

He was about to continue but the horses were outside so he simply said, "Anything else, let me know directly."

"Right you are."

"Well, all right, let's have a look at this mob you brought down for us."

CHAPTER THIRTY SEVEN

Angus was lying on his side on the front veranda, head resting on one outstretched arm peering intently at something. With his free hand he reached over occasionally, toying with the thing, and as it tried to move away dreamily kept it turning back around in a circle with his chubby finger. Elizabeth was there with him, sitting in the swing seat darning socks. When Ned came out he gave them both only a passing glance until the sunlight glinting iridescent gave him pause, and a shock of premonition. He bent down to look closely.

"What have you there, Angus?" he asked softly.

"Cissmus beedal, Daddy."

"What did he say?" he asked, turning to Elizabeth, puzzled.

"It is a Christmas Beetle. You know, Ned, a Christmas Beetle. Of course you know."

"Well, I never thought, after all these years. They had a different meaning for me. I always looked at them as drunken beetles." He stood staring out over the horse paddock for a moment, then turned to Angus. "Let it go, son. Let it fly away, there's a good lad."

Angus rolled over on his tummy, then his hands and knees, and stood up. He bent down and picked up the beetle, and cupping it in both hands toddled over to the top of the steps and flung his arms high in the air. With a loud humming buzz it took wing, turning quickly in its wobbling flight back over the veranda roof and high into the trees beside the house.

As they watched it go Andrew came up the track on his horse and waited patiently there in front of the house until he had their attention.

"Those boys are camping up at the five mile, Mr Collins. Shall I have them moved along?"

Ned looked at him, "It's a public reserve, Andrew. There is nothing we can do to stop them being there."

The other looked away a moment, then shifted in his saddle to face him more directly.

"With respect, sir, the mob for Belkoomie is about ready. It can be inconvenient for us."

"In what way, do you suggest?"

"They can harry us. The stock squad may still take a while to track them back down this way, and they can do us harm in the meantime. If that's what they are thinking, hanging around here. I can't think why they have stayed on, otherwise. You'd reckon they'd be miles away by now."

Ned looked sharply at him. "What made you say that?"

The other simply shrugged, tipping his hat back to scratch his head. Ned felt Angus at his trouser leg, pulling himself up to stand there beside him watching, and then Don called across from the horse yards to see what was up so he waved him over. As the situation was explained to him he listened carefully, then with an odd glance in Ned's direction turned to Andrew's mount, took hold of the reins and walked back with it over to the yards, shaking his head side to side. There he spoke briefly to Andrew, who rode off along the track back toward the swamp.

Elizabeth was no help either. She sat quietly, concentrating on her darning, until Ned felt Angus tugging at his trouser leg and she looked up. She stared at Angus a moment, then up at her husband, and then put her work down to look away quietly into the sky above the treetops.

Eventually Ned simply sighed to himself. Bending down he lifted Angus into his arms and went down the steps. Crossing over to the yards he walked passed Don without saying anything, beyond handing Angus over while he caught and saddled his big bay gelding. Climbing into the saddle he walked it out through the gate, then leaning over to take Angus he sat him comfortably in his lap before taking off abruptly at a canter onto the main track where Andrew had just come.

Out on the road he could feel the little boy's body meld into his, settling into the rhythm of the big horse's long loping stride as if he were part of it. He gave the big bay its head and let it run on into a full gallop, while the faster they rode Angus just seemed to breath it all in. He could feel him lean forward taking control of the animal, his arms too short to hold the reins but guiding his own big hands to his will, until Ned pulled him up finally and brought the pace back to a steady canter. Angus tried to urge him on again but he held the horse back firmly, talking quietly into the boy's ear to settle him and the horse.

The distraction ate up the miles. Without noticing it they came right onto the reserve almost past the camp before realising where they were. The men stood as they went by, watching intently until they reined in all of a sudden and turned back to where they were. Ned pulled up to stand away from them a little distance, not wanting to go in too close, and they stared at each other for a long moment before Pete stepped forward as if to take the reins.

"As you were, Mr Clancy!" Ned barked, and the other froze. He looked them over.

"I know your troubles, can't say I don't," he called across, "but we've had our own fill of it you have to acknowledge yourselves. It's not your fault, the way the cards fall, but it's not my fault either. It's just the way things are."

They stood listening.

"Here's the transaction," Ned continued. "Until we are shot of your evil hooligan ways you are getting the same chance as the late Mr Buckley. This afternoon you will move your gear off the reserve. For the time being you can have the back house, across from Mr Foley's former residence. Mr MacFarlane will get you settled. Tomorrow you will report, Sam Clancy, you and your brother Tommy to Mr MacKenzie, Pete Clancy and Seamus Maloney to Mr MacFarlane. It's that, or you go work it off in gaol."

He swung his horse to go, but turned back.

"And another thing. I will not have my men dressed like outlaws. When you get to Mount Tambla, Sam Clancy, you will take your brother into town with you and get yourselves new outfits on our account. Mr McKenzie will give you a list of what you need. You other two, Mr MacFarlane will get you fitted out on the way back up to Eurongera. That's it."

226

Without waiting for a reply he brusquely wheeled again and set straight off back the way he had come. Angus was only a little subdued on the way home, wanting to settle into a steady pace that ate up the miles without lathering the horse, and taking control of the reins again as if it was he riding and not his father, who let him go, preoccupied with his own thoughts.

CHAPTER THIRTY EIGHT

Two days later Ned was in Arthur's office in Weethangara. He had driven into town in the big old Chevrolet, not wanting to run into the Clancy boys with old wounds reopened and hurting; not until they had cleared off back north to Chatham with Andrew at least, and with Don over to Belkoomie and he could breathe easily. He simply had to trust his own judgement, and trust his managers, and not worry too much over their day-to-day operations.

Maybe he should take a run back up to Eurongera with Andrew, then across to Dadjari to spend some time with Everard finally. He started to day-dream, when presently Ian knocked lightly on the door to tell him there were two policemen wanting to see him.

"What do they want?" he asked, suddenly alert.

"They have seven hundred odd head off Chatham impounded up on the border, over west of Yammana on the other side of the lakes there; that mob Sam and his boys were taking across to South Australia."

"Is that so?" Ned looked at him, a dawn of recollection glimmering in his eyes. "Damn me, I'd forgotten all about them."

"Tell them," he said after a pause, "tell them thank you, we will go and get them. Have the paperwork in order, Ian. Have it done tomorrow, will you."

"Is that it? Don't you want to see them?"

"No. No need. No, you can handle it. Tell them you will attend to it personally. Then send Dadjari a telegram saying we want Daniel and Everard to meet us there in four weeks. Tell them to bring some of the men with them, with Ah Poy and Achmed set up for a long trip, for a run down to Adelaide. And get your gear ready, we are shorted-handed. You can come with us. Make yourself useful."

Ian stared at him intently, but Ned simply returned his stare, eyebrows raised in askance, until the other broke off with a sigh and shaking his head went about his business.

On his way out the back door, Ned called after him, "Make that three weeks, Ian! Tell them three weeks. Go see the sheriff now, straight away, don't leave it until tomorrow, and be out home later, all right, as soon as you get sorted. We'll get away from there first thing in the morning."

As it was, late afternoon Cath showed up as well. The moment he saw her in the car with Ian he knew there was no point arguing, she had that look about her. In his heart he was glad to see her along, but at the same time an unease set in that started to prickle at him. After dinner they settled down for an early night, or tried to; nothing was coming together right in his mind. He was still fidgety. When Angus continued climbing into his lap wanting his attention he put him down abruptly and went outside.

There was a nickering and movement at the horse yards, and soft voices carrying across the moonlit yard, so he went over to see Don and Andrew working quietly there together with just one lantern to see up close. He stood leaning on the rail quietly watching them, not saying anything, until they finished and standing up noticed him there.

"Ready to roll?" he wanted to know.

"About as ready as we're going to be," Don replied, then after a moment added, "What are you up to, Ned?"

"That Chatham mob, I thought we'd take them on to Adelaide and get what we can for them. All reports are they're in good nick." He paused. "I thought we'd have a look at the country while we're there."

"Fair enough. You'd better take that cousin of yours to show you the way, but. I can't use him."

"Really? What about Tommy?"

"Yeah, he'll be right. I'll get him settled." Don replied.

"What about you, Andrew?"

Andrew continued tidying his tools and gear before saying anything, and even then came out through the gate, holding it open for Don then closing it securely, before finally clearing his throat.

"Well, for what it's worth, you ought to take Seamus with you as well. He'll be right, bit subdued now with that pug nose you gave him, and he'll keep Sam sorted. He's a damned fine stockman, too. The pair of them are, as a matter of fact. The pity of it is they didn't get your upbringing, if you don't mind me saying so."

Ned stared at him a moment, and turned to Don. "Why can't you keep Sam then, Don?"

"Like the man said, no upbringing. He's a flamin' warrigal, Ned. Not what you want on Belkoomie. Maybe better to keep him with you here when you get back, on Wyandera, where you can keep an eye on him . . . supposing you want to keep him on the payroll. If you send him back up north he'll only cause more trouble. You're stuck with him, I'd say." Don paused for emphasis, "You'll have to learn to get along, won't you?"

He knew they had him over a barrel. Rather than contest the matter he simply sighed to himself, shaking his head in resignation, then looked up and said, "All right. Let them know the arrangements. In the morning we'll help you get away, then once you're clear we'll take off. Good night, then."

He turned to go but stumbled over something. Angus was there, right behind. He must have toddled across from the house, seeing them there at the yards, and he tripped over him. The little boy didn't say anything, just a loud ooph! as he sat abruptly on his bottom. As he found his feet again Ned bent down and picked him up.

"Oops, sorry, mate," Ned said softly, brushing the dirt from his pajamas. "Are you all right?"

"Bad, Daddy," Angus said, his face serious.

"Bad? Daddy bad? Sorry, I didn't mean to trip over you. I didn't see you there. I'm not bad, I didn't mean it, I'm a good Dad."

"Not bad Daddy. Bull. Bad bull."

"Bull? A bad bull? Where is the bad bull?"

Angus turned in his arms, pointing away over toward the northwest.

Ned turned to the others. "Do you know what he is talking about? We are not having any trouble with the bulls, are we?"

"No, no trouble. He's a funny little fella," Andrew ventured, "he often comes out with things like that, and they turn out to be right." His eyes widened momentarily and he shook himself, as if to shake something off. He turned and walked quickly away into the night.

"What do you think, Don?"

"It's best not to think about it, lad," Don said after a moment, as they strolled back to the house. "Maybe he is onto something, maybe not. Keep your eyes peeled."

But he did not. Back inside Angus was already asleep in his arms so he put him straight to bed, there in his old room, before coming back down the passage to find Elizabeth in bed asleep herself. By the time he bathed and snuggled in next to her, next morning he had forgotten all about it.

CHAPTER THIRTY NINE

The land further to the west of their usual track north along the established stock route was much less developed, with narrow unmade roads wending a slower, wearier way across vast riverine saltbush plains entangled with innumerable landlocked billabongs and dry stream beds made to stand out from the plain by long lines of river redgum, and grey and yellow box off into the far horizon. Ned wondered that they hadn't simply gone north, but Sam had taken the early lead saying he knew the shorter route that would save them days. As they rode along it soon became clear he and Seamus knew the country, and had obviously spent a lot of time out here, so making good progress as they were he let them have their way.

About a week out they began moving away from the long rippling sequences of tree lines interspersed with river flats into much lower stretches dominated by mile after mile of tall bulrush clumps, in places high over the horses' heads. The reeds were yellow, dry and rustling, but as Ned looked around he realised that when the rains came this place would be green, and they would be up to their girth straps in water. At night pigs rooted around in the dense undergrowth, though only occasionally during the day did he sight them since they took flight squealing and grunting at their approach. It was losing his horizon after being used to the open country that made him nervous, but the two ahead rode on quietly and confidently, day after day, only setting their own camp a little away from theirs of an evening and pretty much keeping to themselves.

Early one morning he lost sight of them completely. They had got away early, while Cath, Ian and he were tidying up their breakfast things and preparing for the day's ride. Initially they had appeared to him just a little too far ahead, but when he looked up again from wiping his plate they had disappeared from view. An impish half-chuckle suddenly in the back of his mind made him look up. Without saying anything to the others he quietly went back to readying his gear. He could hear the two hooligans thinking, in his own way, nothing especially malicious but impertinent, careless, disrespectful; going away off into the distance playing their own game and leaving them to play theirs.

Once they had saddled up and on their way again he rode over next to Ian.

"You remember that book in the library at Grammar everyone used to read, with all those grubby thumbed pages?" he wanted to know.

"You mean Chaucer?" Ian grinned, raised eyebrows at the question.

"No, not Chaucer. They only read some of Chaucer, not all of it, only the dirty bits. No, there was another one, an American. Not Mark Twain either, another one, Thoreau, I think, something about living in the woods."

"Walden. Life in the Woods."

"Yes, Walden. That's the one. Do you remember what he wrote about some poor boggy Irishman; something about fishing?"

"Poor John Field."

"Yes, Poor John Field. That's it. What did he say about him?"

"Poor John Field!" Ian thought a moment while he collected his memory. "*Poor John Field!*" he recited finally, "*I trust he does not read this, unless he will improve by it - . . . *"

Ned interrupted, "No, not that bit. Start from the beginning, where he goes fishing. The bit about luck."

Ian looked across at him, then away again trying to think.

"*Before I had reached the pond some fresh impulse had brought out John Field,*" he went on eventually, "*with altered mind, letting go "bogging" ere this sunset. But he, poor man, disturbed only a couple of fins while I was catching a fair string, and he said it was his luck; but when we changed seats in the boat luck changed seats too. Poor John Field! – I trust he does not read this, unless he will improve by it – thinking to live by some derivative old-country mode in this primitive new country – to catch perch with shiners. It is good bait sometimes, I allow. With his horizon all his own, yet he a poor man, born to be poor, with his inherited Irish poverty or poor life, his Adam's grandmother and boggy ways, not to rise in this world, he nor his posterity, till their wading webbed bog-trotting feet get talaria to their heels."*

"That's it exactly," Ned exclaimed. "You're a bloody good man, Ramsay, the best. Best investment I ever made!"

"Why do you want to know that?" Ian glared at him scornfully.

"What does 'talaria' mean? That's what I could never figure out."

"Talaria? Like little wings. You know, the Greek God Mercury, the Messenger. He had those little wings on his heels that gave him speed."

"Is that right? Well, I'll be damned. Those couple of hooligans playing their little game up ahead there, that's what they are themselves, aren't they, with their Adam's grandmother and their boggy ways, not to rise in this world. Now I understand something else about them. What do you think they are up to?"

Ian looked across at him, a frown sharply creasing his brow.

"What? Did I say something? Tell me," Ned came back at him, only half-grinning and eyes sharp.

Cath on his offside had been listening in, and she reached over to pat his shoulder, shaking her head, "Ned, as much as we love you, and you know we love you very dearly, sometimes you're just so slow on the uptake."

"By which you mean?"

"I don't know, Ned," she replied thoughtfully. "People are the way they are. Sometimes I think you expect far too much, and are disappointed when they don't deliver, when they are already doing the best they can. I see it in your face a lot, you know, not just sometimes."

"Maybe I am right about all that," he brindled. "Maybe I do expect a lot, but we must. We all must. I forget things, I know, and dream a lot, but that's why this job was given to me. I brought myself up to the task and you with me, both of you. I earned it all fair and square, everything. They all knew . . . . ," he pulled himself up at that and rode on ahead, without speaking further.

He called back after a while, "Anyway, be that as it may, kin or no kin, that's really no excuse for these bloody hooligans to be buggerising us around the way they do. There's no reason for it. All right then, if that's the way they want it, if that's the way this trip is going to be, all right, let's see who's the better at it, them or us."

He stood up in his stirrups and gazed around awhile, getting his bearings, then without a word abruptly turned his horse back northeasterly and rode off at a fast trot leaving the others to catch up as they could.

It took until noon the next day before he was confident he had made the right decision. As they rode he caste about, stopping occasionally to reorient himself, then once clear of the tall rushes limiting his view and back up into the river country they made their steady way upstream. Ian and Cath followed along without comment. Nobody spoke. Eventually in late afternoon they came onto a track running roughly north-south that had seen better days, but which looked as if it was in fairly regular use. While the others waited Ned rode south along it a way and came back.

"Yes, this is it. I was right. There may be a ford up there ahead, and if there is we will cross over and camp there. The others will be along directly."

The river crossing turned out to be only about half a mile away. The water was still deep enough and they had to take their boots off or get them wet, but once across they rode on a short way until they found a clearing that looked like a usual stop and made their camp.

Close to dusk Ned held up his hand for silence, and shortly they could hear amid the splash of someone else crossing the river a low murmur of voices interspersed with rough laughter. It went on briefly as they waited, then stopped abruptly ahead of a tense stillness as Sam and Seamus quietly walked their horses past.

"You're good, Collins, I'll give you that," Sam growled.

"And you will keep that in mind, Mr Clancy," Ned curtly replied. He turned indicating a clear patch close by. "Camp there if you will, where I can keep an eye on you."

"How on earth did you manage that?" Ian leaned in close wanting to know, as the two men rode on a little before dismounting.

"Don't ask, Ian. You don't want to know." Ned answered thoughtfully. "Talaria perhaps, for want of anything better. Maybe call it talaria, yes, that'll do, why not?" Straightening up to turn his gaze far to the north a moment, he spun abruptly on his heel to face Ian directly.

"When you get back," he said, "once we get Chatham back on our books, go up to the Lands Office will you, and have the name changed to Talaria Station. That will be good, it will bring us luck. When this drought breaks finally that country through there will get the first lot of rain, so keep the stock numbers down until then."

"Why not just leave things be, Ned? It's not so easy to get names changed like that," Ian wanted to argue.

"No, that's all right. Do it," the other insisted. "I never did like Chatham. Don't like the name. It's the name they gave Prime Minister Pitt when they made him a lord. But he lost the Americas, he and Lord North."

"That's got nothing to bloody-well do with anything!"

But he was no longer listening. Instead he was off at a brisk pace back down the track toward the river where he stripped off his dirty riding britches and waded into the clear still water for a bath and a swim. Ian stood there a moment longer until Cath brushed past him toward the river as well, so shaking his head he followed suit.

CHAPTER FORTY

The next day saw them re-establish their order of travel, with Sam and Seamus taking an early lead and the others trailing along at a comfortable distance.

Ten uneventful days later they came down off the western end of the escarpment out onto the vast Bundingor Lake system stretching away off north-easterly into the distant haze. This side of the lakes had a different aspect to it, running on eventually into the arid, semi-desert country across the border to the west whereas the rainfall during good years filled the system from far to the east, from where the Great Dividing Range made heavy grey clouds spill their load before allowing them to pass out to sea. The lake water had receded markedly from their last visit, the bed cracked and dry with dead dry scrub on the margins not a lot different from the huge tracts of desiccated cumbungi swamp to the south, in which they had almost lost their way the week before.

As they rode in over the still broken landscape toward the lake proper a rider appeared on their right. He must have been waiting up on top, keeping an eye out for their arrival, and when they appeared he followed them down. It was Daniel. Rather than coming in close he simply waved them on then led the way down further through the dry scrub until they came out farther on again to their wagons and a fairly large camp. As they rode up he called out loudly in language and presently a number of men came out to greet them, and taking their horses and gear led them away to be watered and brushed down.

Ned stood looking around for a moment until Daniel indicated a patch of low trees away from the main camp, from where Everard was making his way toward him. It was the same Everard, but he looked completely different now from what he remembered, as if he had wizened and aged in the meantime, aging years instead of the months since he had last seen him. Daniel deferred to him reverently, then turned away to attend the new arrivals, leaving the two there to make their new acquaintance.

For the rest of the day they sat there under the shade talking quietly. As it came on dusk one of the boys brought Ned's gear over, and some food for the both of them. Far into the night they sat in deep conversation, stopping occasionally while Everard stoked his little fire to boil his billy and make tea, and it was not until early next morning that they stopped finally to nap. At first light as the main camp stirred Ned got up and came over to see Ian.

"Ian, wake up," he nudged him gently with his boot, then as he stretched and sat up yawning sat down next to him on his swag.

"The mob is fairly scattered," he went on the moment he had his attention, "but not too badly. Lucky we have this dry spell so they have stayed in close to the water, otherwise they would have been all over the place by now. It will still take a day or two to get them mustered. Rest here today while the boys scout around, then tomorrow we can get them all round them up in one hit so you can get away fairly quickly."

"Me? Aren't you coming with us? This was your trip, Ned."

"Ah, change of plans. I am going bush with Everard for a while, maybe a few months or more. You may be back from Adelaide before I get home, so you will be running things for a while. Elizabeth will be all right. I let on before we left that I might be away a while. I promised I'd be home in time for the baby, but that's seven-odd months away. That gives me the winter up here. I'll start back when I am done with this business."

"All right, boss. Do what you want. Now let me get some more kip. Ah Poy promised not to wake me too early, so you can bugger off too." Ian turned over and tucked himself back in under his blanket.

Ned reluctantly did has he was bidden. His mind was aflame, but gazing around at the still-quiet camp he shrugged and after a moment wandered over to Everard's camp where he rolled out his own swag and lay down. Presently he too nodded off to sleep.

Close to mid-morning some of the boys started coming back in for smoko. Ian and Cath were nowhere to be seen, so after a brief conversation Ned saddled his horse and rode out looking for them. The track led a long way north, far up toward the northernmost tip of this first big lake in the system, and the sun was just starting to dip toward the west before he came upon any activity. Men were pushing small mobs of cattle together, steadily forming them into a bigger and tighter mass slowly moving south as it went along.

Coming in close to the tree line along the dry edge of the lake he noticed a bull in there among the trees, so diverting from his way a little he rode over to move it up into the mob with the others. It kept avoiding him, however, so he rode on deeper into the trees trying to get behind it. As he did so a voice came into his mind, like a child singing a song, but from a far, far place. The bull was huge. He hadn't seen anything like it before. It stopped there, paying no attention to him, so he sat watching it awhile.

It was a big old wild bull, he could see, a mickie bull, watching the men on horseback making off with his cows. It pawed huffing at the ground occasionally, raising dust and snorting, still out of sight there among the trees, and shaking its great head in annoyance.

The singing child cried louder and louder in his thoughts. It was Angus. Angus was calling out to him. Ned reined in his horse, shocked. Tiny hairs prickled at the back of his neck, and he looked around to see where any immediate danger lay. The men were all on horseback, going about their job oblivious to the bull's presence. Cath! It was Cath. Cath was off her horse, bent over checking its front offside hoof.

Ned spurred his horse straight into a gallop, calling out to her, "Cath! Cath! Get on your horse!" but she went on unheeding of the noise of cattle around her.

He spurred the big horse into a rush toward her, yelling and screaming, just as the bull started its charge. She paid him no attention, intent on caring for her own horse, the sound lost anyway in the cracking of whips and bellowing and general melee, until the mob itself started to spook and some of the men looked around to see what was happening.

The bull thundered toward her, like a freight train picking up speed, and all Ned could think to do was get his horse somehow between it and Cath. At breakneck speed he nudged his mount closer and closer, until Cath's horse shied knocking her sprawling. The bull was almost on her when suddenly with a wild banshee howl Sam appeared from the midst of the milling cattle and leapt straight from his saddle onto the massive head coming at him. Ned heard a loud OOF! as his breath was punched from his body, but Sam hung on there between the giant horns, arms wrapped around them like a wrestler with his legs dangling helplessly from its great snout. The animal was blinded and pulled up short, disoriented suddenly, trying to dislodge the nuisance.

Cath scrambled up out of the way while Ned rode in using his horse to shield her. Sam was being tossed around mercilessly like a rag doll savaged by a pup. The bull threw him bodily into the air, and from side to side trying to make him let go, then finally head down butted him straight into the ground. A loud shot rang out, then another, and with a moan the bull went down mortally wounded. A third shot came as it lay there in its side legs flailing, until abruptly it went completely still.

Ned dismounted and went over to Sam, who finally let go and rolled slowly, painfully, onto his back with one arm still jammed under the bull's head. When he saw Ned bending over him, with his free hand Sam pushed him away, and kicked at him with one leg.

"Piss off, you fuckin' shit!" he snarled.

Ned stood back, stunned.

"Stand away, Collins, or I'll bloody well shoot you too," Seamus called from somewhere close by, then after a pause, "Y'all right, mate?"

"Nah, bastard's got me, done me in, busted me bloody guts. I'm a dead man. Ah, bugger it," he chuckled then winced at the sharp pain. "Anyway, we got the bastard. Tell the boys we got that fuckin' great mickie, eh? We got the bastard, didn't we? You and me, mate, not this cunt, not this Collins fuckin' prick, eh?"

"Yeah, we did all right, that's a fact. Shut up now, eh?"

By this time the rest of the men had gathered around, and lifting the great horned head eased Sam's arm out from underneath and set him straight.

"Fuckin' thirsty. Gimme a drink, ya cunt," he slurred at Seamus, who took a flask down from his saddle and removing the cork put it to his lips.

The whisky burned his mouth and Sam gagged on it, then he coughed once and fell back.

Seamus knelt silently watching him as Sam's eyes glazed and his face faded to a grey mask of what it had been, then looked around bewildered before taking an anxious swig from the whisky. He shrugged then and set the flask back in his saddle bag.

"Good bloody riddance, crazy bastard," he mumbled softly almost to himself, then half-turning to flash at Ned a moment he remounted and started to ride away south toward the camp. He stopped a little way off and turned back, calling out, "Bury the bastard there, eh? He'll go off before we get him anywhere. Nobody's gonna fuckin' miss him. Stupid bastard he is."

Nobody moved. They stood watching him carefully as Seamus sat there on horseback gazing around, riding back and forth into the distance awhile and back again, endeavouring to collect his scattered thoughts. Shaking his head finally he simply shrugged, then rode back and dismounted.

"No, I know what to do. Burn the silly prick," he declared. "We can't fuckin' bury him or every time there's a full fuckin' moon he'll be out there riding that fuckin' great bull all night scarin' the shit outa the blackfellas. Burn the prick, better, him and the bull both together, or we'll be in strife still. Better this way. He'll think he's a fuckin' Viking chief, goin' off to fuckin' Valhalla. That'd be him all right, off into the sunset whoopin' and hollerin', and there'll be no holding him back. That's the only way we'll get rid of him, eh? We'll tell the boys we sent him off proper, no worries, but that'll sort out all the bullshit finally; him and fuckin' Grandma. We just won't tell the boys that, eh? Fuck them too."

He burst out suddenly, defiant, angry, the grog taking hold, "Fuckin' witch! Ugly fuckin' old witch! Fuck 'em! Fuck yez all! Fuck everybody!" then stood there gesticulating, waving his arms about staggering only slightly, holding his ground as the hurt and pain of lost childhood and all the years wasted boiled up inside him, glaring at Ned with tears streaming down his battered face, defying him too. "Fuckin' crazy bastards. The lot of yer. You too Collins, you're no bloody different, yer all the same, the entire fuckin' stupid clan, eh? Fuck it! I've had enough!"

He reached up and took the whisky flask back down from his saddle, and raising it to his mouth drank down a single great draught, spilling it down his chin before passing it over to Ned.

"Right! Do it or be damned. Let's see the bastard off proper. Sit him up on the fuckin' bull, eh. Gimme a hand with it," he slurred, then yelled red-faced angrily at them, "give me a fuckin' hand will ya!"

Ned stood there, dumbfounded. Then something clicked in his brain, and he nodded to himself and chuckled, then raised the whisky to his own lips and drank. He drank deeply, and passed the flask back to Seamus who drained the last of it and threw it away.

"Get some wood, a lot of it," he said to the men. "Build it up high, a real bonfire. We'll do it right this time, eh? Wanted to be a hero, we'll make him a hero. We'll give him a send-off nobody will ever forget, and that will be the end of it."

He staggered slightly, bumping into Cath who took his arm holding him, steadying him, then seeing the look in his eyes reached up and with her fingertips gently touched his cheek before turning to mount her horse. Without a word she reached over and taking Ian's horse by the rein rode with him quietly back to working the cattle.

THE END

ABOUT THE AUTHOR

As an anthropologist, novelist and writer Gil Hardwick is a gifted and imaginative author. Over many years working as a field ethnographer in the vast Australian inland he has met real characters and had real-life adventures, bringing his personalities and his plots to vibrant life. Writing from life, he neither shies away from real social issues and at times confronting dilemmas.

Well worth reading.

www.ingramcontent.com/pod-product-compliance
Lightning Source LLC
Chambersburg PA
CBHW071143260626
47162CB00003B/899